David A. Wells, Making of America Project

The Relation of the Government to the Telegraph

A Review of the Two Propositions now Pending before Congress for changing the

telegraphic service of the Country

David A. Wells, Making of America Project

The Relation of the Government to the Telegraph
A Review of the Two Propositions now Pending before Congress for changing the telegraphic service of the Country

ISBN/EAN: 9783337226985

Printed in Europe, USA, Canada, Australia, Japan

Cover: Foto ©Andreas Hilbeck / pixelio.de

More available books at **www.hansebooks.com**

REPORT OF THE COMMITTEE

OF THE

Chamber of Commerce of the State of New-York,

ON

PACIFIC OCEAN TELEGRAPHS,

IN CONNECTION WITH

THE COMMERCE OF THE WORLD.

PRESENTED TO THE CHAMBER, MARCH 2, 1871,

BY MR. SAMUEL B. RUGGLES,

CHAIRMAN OF THE COMMITTEE.

New-York:

PRESS OF THE CHAMBER OF COMMERCE.

1871.

PACIFIC OCEAN TELEGRAPHS.

To the Chamber of Commerce of the State of New-York:

THE Committee charged with the subject of Telegraphs and Postal Affairs, respectfully

REPORT:

That the subject of a submarine cable across the Pacific was first brought to the notice of the Chamber by a resolution introduced on the 5th of May, 1870, and duly referred to the Committee for consideration.

That resolution was in the following terms:

Resolved, That the Chamber of Commerce of the State of New-York approve of the system of oceanic telegraphic communication, and respectfully ask that Congress may pass, at an early day, such laws as will facilitate the manufacturing and laying of a submarine cable across the Pacific, from the western coast of America to the eastern coast of Asia, thereby completing, with lines now in operation and with those soon to be laid, telegraphic communication around the world.

The Committee having bestowed upon the resolution the careful attention due to the importance of the subject, on the 20th of December, 1870, reported it back to the Chamber, modified and amended as follows:

Resolved, That the Chamber of Commerce of the State of New-York regard a well-regulated system of telegraphs, by sea and by land, as a matter of primary importance to the interests of this country and of the world; and respectfully ask that Congress may pass, at an early day, such laws as will, without creating any monopoly, facilitate the laying of a submarine cable across the Pacific

Ocean, from the western coast of America to the eastern coast of Asia, thereby completing, with the lines now in operation, and with those soon to be laid, telegraphic communication around the world.

The resolution in this form having been unanimously adopted by the Chamber, authenticated copies were transmitted by their order to the Senate and House of Representatives of the United States.

In presenting this resolution to the Chamber, the Committee were prevented by want of time from fully stating the facts and considerations which, in their opinion, would justify its passage; in view of which, the Chamber, on the 2d of February, 1871, directed the Committee to embody and to report in writing to the Chamber those facts and considerations, with any further or supplemental information which might be useful.

In the present report the Committee have examined more in detail:

I. The locality and length of the telegraphic lines already established, and of those which are still needed to complete a communication around the globe:

II. The influence of the work, when completed, upon the commerce of the world, and especially the commerce on the Pacific and the Indian Oceans.

The telegraph line when completed will necessarily embrace the 360° of longitude encompassing the globe. This great circle is divided in two segments, unequal in length, but each containing a continent and an ocean. The Western embraces the Western Continent and the Atlantic Ocean, extending from San Francisco, in California, to Valentia, in Ireland, over 112° of longitude; while the Eastern embraces the Eastern Continent and the Pacific Ocean, extending from Valentia to Shanghai, in China, over 132° of longitude, and thence across the Pacific Ocean over the remaining 116°, thus completing the entire circle of 360°. Of these two segments of this great terraqueous line, the Western, from San Francisco to Valentia, has been finished largely, if not mainly, by the energies of the citizens of the United States. Of the Eastern segment, the portion crossing the Eastern Continent is now nearly completed. Two continuous lines extend eastwardly from Valentia, one inclining to the north through the United Kingdom, Germany, European and Asiatic Russia, to the present temporary terminus at Kiachta, an important Russian entrepot in Eastern Siberia, near the Chinese frontier, in north latitude 51°; while the other pursues a southeasterly course through France, Austria, Turkey, Persia, and other Asiatic countries, to Bombay, in Hindustan, and thence by way of Ceylon to Singapore, only 1° 30' north of the Equator. Kiachta is 116°, and Singapore 113° east from Valentia. The land line through Turkey and Persia being liable to occasional interruption in regions only partially civilized, a submarine line has also been laid from Italy through the Mediterranean Sea, the Red Sea, and the Arabian Sea, to Bombay.

By the lines above described commercial and other messages are now regularly telegraphed, without interruption, from London to Kiachta and Singapore. The charge from London to Singapore for twenty words and less, is $33.25 in gold; from New-York to Singapore, $48.25 in gold, and $1.50 for each additional word over 10 words. Even at this costly rate, messages are now constantly sent from New-York to Liverpool; four, during the day preceding the date of this report.

Singapore is an important focal point in the commerce of the East. It was established by the British Government, in 1824, and now enjoys a yearly commerce of nearly $50,000,000. It has lines of steamers running to Hong Kong, (near Canton,) in six days, and also to Batavia, Manilla and other important ports in the East. Through the commercial house of Messrs. A. A. Low & Brothers, of New-York, largely engaged in the trade of China and Japan, the Committee have ascertained that the extension of the submarine cable from Singapore to Hong Kong, about 1,400 miles, and thence to Shanghai, about 1,000 miles, is in active progress. By a letter recently received by Mr. Cyrus W. Field, and exhibited to the Committee, they are informed that the line from Singapore to Hong Kong will be laid by the 1st of May, and be in actual operation by the 1st of June next. It further appears by *The Overland Mail*, a newspaper published at Hong Kong, that the wire for the line from Hong Kong to Shanghai has all arrived, practically securing its completion within the present year. Induced by political or religious scruples, the Chinese Government has hitherto prevented the laying any telegraphic line on their territory, so that the terminus of the world-encircling line on the Eastern Continent will probably be established for a time in the light-ship at Shanghai, in the estuary of the Yang-Tse-Kiang, the great river of Eastern Asia. At this important point, the junction between the northern and southern lines will be made, through the enterprise of a Danish company, at Hong Kong, now actively constructing a line on land from Kiachta, about 1,400 miles, to the Sea of Japan, to be extended by a line under its waters, about 1,000 miles, to Shanghai.

The completion of these lines on the Eastern Continent, in connection with the lines now established in the Atlantic and upon the Western Continent, will afford to the merchants of the United States, without any line across the Pacific, the means of telegraphic communication, not requiring more than three days at the utmost, with every important commercial port in the civilized world north of the equator. Similar facilities will soon be extended to the Southern Hemisphere by the Australian branch, leading southeastwardly from Singapore, across Sumatra, Java and other islands of the great Eastern Archipelago, or along their coasts, into Australia, as far as Melbourne, in 37° south latitude, with a total length exceeding 3,000 miles. The Committee are informed by Mr. MILLER, of the Royal Mint of Australia, and now in the United States, that this Australian line will be completed to Singapore within the present year.

It must, nevertheless, be evident that the very circuitous communication from New-York, and still more from San Francisco to Eastern Asia, by way of the Western Continent, the Atlantic Ocean and the Eastern Continent, with its necessary stoppages under the best administration, must always be far more costly and dilatory than a communication by a single independent line leading directly across the Pacific, saving in distance at least ten thousand miles, and transmitting a message from San Francisco to Shanghai in ten minutes. Its peculiar value in war, as an organ of the Government, in properly directing naval operations in those distant waters, can hardly be over-estimated. We should also bear in mind, that with telegraphic lines under both the Atlantic and the Pacific Oceans, each will connect the two continents, so that any interruption in one of the oceans may be remedied by the working of the line in the other.

A far higher public necessity for a line directly across the Pacific is found in the fact, that the whole of the American Continent, over which it would be extended to the Atlantic and thence to Europe, is subject to the sole political rule of the United States, or of the adjacent maritime Provinces of British America. The populations of these English-speaking portions of the world would be fully able, if consolidated by political union or allied by proper treaties, to protect the line, whether on the land or in either of the oceans, from any hostile interference; while, on the other hand, the line laid on the Eastern Continent, occupying the territory of numerous nations of Europe and Asia, widely differing in language, civilization and forms of government, will be necessarily exposed to capricious and arbitrary interruption, if not to violent aggression.

Two telegraphic lines under the Pacific have been suggested to the Committee, one commencing at San Francisco, in latitude 37°, and deflecting southwardly to the Sandwich Islands, in latitude 20°, and thence inclining northwardly, by way of the Midway Island, in latitude 27° north, to Yokohama, in Japan, in latitude 35° north, and thence southeasterly to Shanghai, in latitude 32°. Its length will be 5,480 nautical miles from San Francisco to Yokohama, and from Yokahama to Shanghai 1,035 miles, in all 6,515 nautical miles. The other and more northern line will extend from San Francisco along the coasts of British Columbia, Alaska and the Aleutian Islands to the eastern coast of Japan, and thence to Shanghai.

At the request of the Committee, the Professor of Mathematics and Astronomy in Columbia College, Mr. WILLIAM G. PECK, has accurately measured on the globe the linear extent of the "great circle" passing through San Francisco and Yokohama. His letter, appended to this report, states it to be 4,450 nautical miles. The circle passes within 200 miles southward of the Aleutian Islands, now belonging to the United States; on one of which, lying nearly midway on the route, the cable, if necessary, might be landed, without increasing the total distance more than 50 miles. The link in the chain from Yokohama to Shanghai, 1,035 miles in length, is common to both the northern and the southern routes.

It is not the province nor the wish of the Committee, nor would they recommend to the Chamber, to pass any judgment on the comparative merits of these rival lines proposed for the Pacific cable, nor to anticipate any question in respect to its construction, whether directly by the Government or indirectly through subsidies to incorporated companies. They would only insist on the vital importance of keeping any and every telegraphic line, under the Pacific or any other ocean or sea, as far as possible, free from any exclusive privilege or monopoly. The oceans and seas were created for the common use of man, and should not be exclusively appropriated by any individual, or any particular nation or race.

It is within the last sixty years, that the genius of FULTON, in ascending the Hudson River with a steamboat in 1807, was rewarded, however inadequately, by a grant from the State of the monopoly of the waters of that important channel of navigation, which obstructed its commerce until the year 1824, when the unlawful impediment was swept away by the supreme judicial power of the American Union. It would be strange indeed, if the Union should

8

now so far forget its own international moral duty as a member of the common family of nations, as to monopolize in any manner, or to any extent, the common oceanic highway between America and Asia.

THE INFLUENCE OF A PACIFIC OCEAN CABLE ON THE FOREIGN COMMERCE OF THE WORLD.

The peculiar value and efficiency of a world-encircling telegraph in developing and regulating the commerce of the globe become still more evident, in view of the immense and constantly increasing amount of that commerce; and especially when we consider the intimate relation of the commerce of every portion of the world to the commerce of the whole.

It will be the exalted office of such a telegraph to diffuse through all the markets of the world daily, and if need be, hourly information of the current prices of all commercial commodities, with the amount and condition of products and cargoes. This annihilation of commercial distance will render the trader practically omnipresent. With the constant stream of telegraphic information, pointing out from day to day the exact degrees of demand and supply—the vital elements of price—commerce, no longer consisting of the "adventures" inscribed on the merchant's ledger, will become an exact science, precisely determining every commercial movement containing the elements of profit.

Nay, more. Such a telegraph will cement still more firmly that all-pervading unity of commerce known in modern phraseology as its "solidarity." Differing only in degree from "internationality," which regards nations as forming one "common society," the term "solidarity," as applied to their commerce, denotes the absolute unity resulting from the community of interest where the commerce of each, forms a part " *in solido*" of the commerce of the whole.

This solidarity brings with it correlative rights and duties, with their consequences. Every facility afforded to any portion of the world of commerce enures to the benefit of the whole, while every impediment in any portion, whether interposed by nature or unwise legislation, injures the whole. Cheap and rapid transportation, which has already increased so largely the wealth of modern nations, is now the common *desideratum* of the commercial world. Every day and every penny saved in transporting a chest of tea through the Indian or the Pacific Oceans, is felt in its diminished price in the markets of Chicago, Hamburgh or St. Petersburgh. Every day and every cent saved in transporting a barrel of flour over any canal or railway in the United States, facilitates its sale in Havana, Liverpool or Canton. Like the life-blood in the human frame, ever ministering to the needs of all the members, the genial and vital stream of commerce, unchecked by needless obstruction, circulates through the globe, animating and strengthening all the nations, while the telegraph, the very brain of the commercial system, supplies the nervous energy which directs and guides the whole.

This universality or "catholicity" of commerce, so to speak, is no new idea in the New-York Chamber of Commerce. On the contrary, it has been the polar star guiding the institution from the very moment of its corporate existence. It shines out clear and bright, in the emphatic language of the Royal Charter granted during the Colonial era, in 1770, and fully confirmed by the State Government in 1784, proclaiming that "numberless inestimable "blessings had accrued to *mankind* from commerce," and investing the Chamber with full power "to encourage and promote, by just "and lawful ways and means, such measures as will tend to promote "and extend just and lawful commerce."

So far from breathing any local spirit which would confine the field of inquiry or action of the Chamber to the mere island of Manhattan, or within any narrow provincial limits, the charter broadly avows the comprehensive and wise design of the British Crown, "to give stability to an institution from whence great advantages "may arise, not only to our said Province, but as well to our Kingdom "of Great Britain," that Imperial Dominion, which even then had encompassed with its widespread dependencies the whole world of commerce. Under such instruction the Chamber has ever been impressed, and now more than ever, with the fundamental and pregnant truth, that the foreign commerce of the port of New-York is not local, but cosmopolitan, constituting no isolated independent unit, but an inseparable integral portion of the vast foreign commerce of the globe, morally united by one common bond of interest.

The practical importance of this view is obvious, when we find that the whole yearly commerce of the United States (being $849,793,476 in 1868, of which the port of New-York had $498,623,192) now constitutes hardly one-tenth of the foreign commerce of the world.

AMOUNT OF FOREIGN COMMERCE AND ITS PROGRESS IN THIRTY YEARS.

In collecting the facts needed for showing the total foreign commerce of the civilized nations, the Committee have endeavored also to ascertain, as far as practicable, its progress during the thirty years ending with 1868, that being the latest year for which official tables were accessible.

The period thus selected is one of pre-eminent importance, embracing the truly golden age of commerce, in which steam more fully enlisted in the service of man, won its greatest victories over the land and the sea, vastly augmenting the commercial dynamics of the globe, not only in accelerating and cheapening the transportation of the products of interior regions to the seaboard, but in practically bridging the oceans themselves and conjoining the continents.

It was not until the autumn of the year 1838, that the first ocean steamer found its solitary way across the Atlantic. At the close of 1868, large fleets of steamers, much exceeding in capacity the sailing vessels of the mercantile marine, and swiftly impelled by this superadded power, covered all the seas and oceans.

Up to the year 1838, only 1,497 miles of railway had been constructed in North America, and furnished only with feeble engines drawing slender loads. At the close of 1868 there were in operation, with engines doubled in speed and quadrupled in power, 44,802 miles in North America, 56,660 miles in Europe, 4,474 in Asia, (principally in British India,) 1,424 in South America, 789 in Australia, and 583 in Egypt and other parts of Africa, exhibiting a total development in the civilized world of 109,177 miles, of which at least 100,000 were brought into use since 1838, with their enormous apparatus of steam locomotive engines counted by tens of thousands, untiringly laboring by day and by night in transporting and exchanging the vast and varied products of the globe.

It was on the 27th day of February, in the year 1844, that MORSE sent his first telegraphic message by electricity, 41 miles, from Washington to Baltimore, uttering with characteristic and solemn emphasis his grateful ejaculation, " What hath GOD wrought !" At the close of 1868, as stated to the Committee by Mr. GEORGE B. PRESCOTT, the electrician of the Western Union Telegraph, there were 130,698 miles of electrical telegraphic line in operation in the United States, 90,000 miles in Great Britain, and 405,151 miles in Continental Europe, with 27,402 miles of submarine cable in the various seas and oceans, having a total linear extent of 572,183 miles, exceeding more than twenty fold the circumference of the earth.

It was not until 1866 that the noble perseverance of FIELD and his associates, after arduous and repeated efforts, practically established for commercial purposes their cable in the bed of the Atlantic.

These splendid triumphs over the obstacles of nature within the brief period of thirty years under review, superadding to the pre-existing forces in use by man a power, equivalent to that of twenties, if not fifties, of millions of human laborers, have necessarily caused an immense expansion in the commerce of the globe. They afford the only adequate ·explanation of the enormous, and almost incredible realities disclosed by the official statistics, exhibiting an increase in the foreign trade of the three leading commercial nations exceeding more than tenfold their increase in population within the same period; and a rate of increase more than half as large in the foreign commerce of the remaining nations.

Summed up in brief, the population and foreign commerce of the United Kingdom of Great Britain and Ireland, of France, and of the United States of America, respectively increased as follows:

POPULATION.

	In 1838.		In 1858.	In 1868.
The United Kingdom, ..	25,903,697	..	28,389,770	30,380,757
France,................	33,738,188	..	36,236,322	*38,342,818
The United States,......	16,025,761	..	29,568,110	36,500,000
	75,667,646	..	94,194,202	105,223,575

Increase in 30 years, 29,555,950, being 39 per cent.

FOREIGN COMMERCE.
[Computing £1 at $5, and $1 at five francs.]

	In 1838.		In 1858.		In 1868.
The United Kingdom, ..	$541,605,515	..	$1,521,833,055	..	$2,616,570,415
France,..............	378,895,720	..	†945,080,000	..	‡1,595,820,000
The United States,.....	222,504,020	..	607,257,571	..	849,793,476
	$1,143,005,255	..	$3,074,170,626	..	$5,062,183,891

Increase in 30 years, $3,919,178,636, or 443 per cent.

It will be seen that the rate of this immense increase was highest in the two first decades, from 1838 to 1858, commencing with the earliest developments of this superadded steam power on the land and the sea, during which the amount was carried up, in round numbers, from $1,143,000,000 to $3,074,000,000, being nearly 270 per cent., or 9 per cent. yearly for the twenty years. In the last decade, from 1858 to 1868, when the new impulse had partially spent its power, the rate of increase so far slackened, that the total of 1858, $3,074,000,000, rose only to $5,062,000,000 in 1868, not quite 60 per cent., or 6 per cent. yearly.

---

* Including 744,249, annexed in Nice and Savoy.
† By sea, $678,000,000; by land, $266,000,000.
‡ By sea, $1,070,000,000; by land, $525,000,000.

This diminution of rate in the last decade shows the necessity of caution in any prospective estimate of the increase in the future. While, on the one hand, a still further development of the powers of steam and electricity may stimulate still more actively the production and transportation of the world, we are compelled by recent experience in both hemispheres to take into account the possibility, to say the least, of exceptional interruptions and retardations by war, and the supreme national necessities which it may involve. In view of those contingencies, it would hardly be safe to assume that the rate of six per cent. yearly increase exhibited by the last decade will continue undiminished throughout the remaining thirty years of the present century, carrying up the existing amount, as it would at 180 per cent. in the three nations, to $14,170,000,000. A more cautious estimate, at 3 per cent. yearly, would carry the amount only to $9,112,000,000.

The Committee make no predictions in respect to the future, but merely state the preceding sums as the arithmetical results of the two different rates of increase. They rest content with the $5,062,183,891 actually existing in 1868, and with the increase in the foreign commerce of the United States to $991,896,889 in 1870, from $849,793,476 in 1868, as sufficing to show the transcendent importance of establishing and maintaining between these three maritime nations a wise and thorough concord, which shall at least secure the telegraphic cables in the oceans from any hostile aggression.

It may also be reasonably expected, that the large and steadily increasing foreign commerce of the remaining and more interior nations of Europe, the major portion of which is on the sea, will lead their enlightened rulers to similar views of the necessity of peace, as affording to maritime commerce its only effectual security.

The Committee have used their best efforts without success, to obtain official tables showing the commerce of these remaining nations and its progress in tabulated form, with the precision which has been attained with respect to the three maritime nations. Some of the Continental countries make no official returns of their exports, while the estimates of some of the others are in a measure conjectural.

During the last twenty years repeated efforts have been made by the public authorities and writers in France and elsewhere to tabulate the foreign commerce of the world, the general results of which have not differed very widely. After carefully comparing the varying estimates by the British Board of Trade, the United States Bureau of Statistics, the " *Dictionnaire du Commerce*," and other statistical works in France, aided by the results annually condensed from official tables in the "*Almanac de Gotha*," the Committee submit the following summary to the Chamber as an approximate for the years 1860 and 1868, sufficiently accurate for the present purpose. Disregarding fractions of a million, the foreign commerce of those nations was as follows:

	Population.	Foreign Commerce.	
	In 1868.	In 1860.	In 1868.
Germany,......................	38,768,000	$550,000,000	$756,000,000
Netherlands,.................	3,616,000	360,000,000	377,000,000
Belgium,......................	4,901,000	210,000,000	304,000,000
Denmark, Sweden and Norway,.	7,779,000	125,000,000	138,000,000
Russia,.......................	69,884,000	252,000,000	337,000,000
Austria, ...	35,449,000	187,000,000	340,000,000
Italy, ...	25,585,000	250,000,000	316,000,000
European Turkey, Roumania and			
Serbia, ...	16,828,000	130,000,000	140,000,000
Greece,......................	1,375,000	16,000,000	16,000,000
Spain and Portugal,...........	20,884,000	140,000,000	187,000,000
Switzerland,.......	2,517,000	120,000,000	130,000,000
	227,086,000	$2,340,000,000	$3,091,000,000

Increase, 32 per cent. in 8 years, or 4 per cent. yearly.

In any estimate of the future growth of the foreign commerce of these Continental nations, now amounting to $3,091,000,000, it should be remembered that the superaddition of steam transportation, in fostering the growth of their commerce in the past, was, in proportion, far less than in France and the United Kingdom. With an aggregate population of 227,000,000, occupying a territorial area more than tenfold that of France and the United Kingdom, they had, up to 1869, only 37,000 miles of railway; while France and the United Kingdom, with a population of only 69,000,000, had in operation more than 24,000 miles, nearly completing all the important portions of their railway systems. The continental nations still have left large interior regions, affording very extensive fields for future development, especially in connection with the inland seas giving them access to the Atlantic. They are, moreover, using active efforts to increase their maritime commerce and naval force, as fundamental elements of their political strength.

It certainly is not impossible that, under these influences, the rate of increase in their foreign commerce may, for some time to come, fully keep pace with that of France or the United Kingdom. At the yearly rate of only 2½ per cent., the existing amount would increase to $5,322,000,000 in the thirty years ending with 1898.

In respect to the countries, other than the United States, in North and South America, including the West Indies, the Committee have been able to obtain reliable statistics only from a portion of their number. Some of them keep no accurate tables of exports, while the commerce of others is stated in quantities and not in values. The aggregate of the commerce of the West Indies, a subject of direct and constantly increasing interest to the United States, can only be ascertained with accuracy from the official tables kept by the various nations trading with the islands. As the amount thereby deduced ($282,897,306) falls very considerably short of the amount ($420,580,919) estimated in the official report published in 1866, at Ottawa, by the Commissioners from British America for ascertaining the trade of the West Indies, some further examination may be proper. The Committee, therefore, ask leave hereafter to submit to the Chamber any supplemental statement which may be needed, for correcting any material error which may be discovered.

Subject to this reservation, the Committee believe that the following summary will not vary materially from the actual amounts:

1868.		Exports and Imports.
" Dominion of Canada," (not including Newfoundland or Prince Edward's Island,)...		$129,533,194
Mexico, only partial returns, (estimated,)		27,000,000
Central America,...		11,292,000
New-Grenada or Colombia, ...		11,018,000
Venezuela, no returns, (estimated,)		10,000,000
Brazil, ...		160,133,721
Argentine Republic, ...		63,650,000
Chili, ...		55,500,000
Uraguay, Peru, Bolivia and Ecuador, only partial returns, (estimated,)...		40,000,000
West Indies.—Cuba and Porto Rico,................	$174,050,279	
British West Indies,.................	60,756,022	
Haytl and San Domingo,............	22.691,005	
Other West India Islands,......... .	25,000,000	
		282,497,306
		$790,624,221

The statistics of many of these nations and countries, owing mainly to the frequent and violent changes in their political condition, are too fragmentary to furnish the means of showing, with any approach to accuracy, the increase of their commerce in the past.

The singular mutations of commerce, under political changes, are strikingly manifest in a portion of the West Indies. The "Tableau" of Commerce, of the year III. of the first French Republic, states that, in or shortly before the year 1792, the commerce of France with San Domingo amounted to *two hundred and seventy-one* millions of *livres*, $54,200,000; and that its commerce with the United States amounted in that year only to *thirty-one* millions of *livres*, $6,200,000.

The "Exposé Comparatif" of France shows that in 1867 its commerce with Hayti was only $6,420,000, while its commerce with the United States was $70,200,000.

GENERAL RESULT.

It results from the preceding examination that the total foreign commerce of the European and American nations, in which is included all their commerce with the Asiatic countries, consists as follows:

Commerce of the European nations, ...	$7,203,390,415
" " American "	1,640,822,697
	$8,844,213,112

Of this total, a little more than one-tenth consists of commerce with countries and localities more or less civilized, in Asia, Africa and Oceanica, which have no commercial tables, or none which are accessible, and consequently are not included in the statement of nations exporting and importing. That portion is stated from the returns of the nations trading with those countries, and represents an actual movement of commodities of like value. Of the remainder, assumed to be nine-tenths, the value of the commodities actually moved is only one-half; for the reason that the commodities tabulated as "Exports," in the tables of any nation exporting, re-appear as "Imports" in the tables of the nation or nations to which the commodities are exported, whereby the values are duplicated. This being the case, the aggregate value of the commodities actually moved is,

One tenth of the $8,844,213,112, or	$884,421,311
And one-half of the residue, $7,959,791,801, being	3,979,805,901
	$4,864,317,212

Although the Committee have confined their examination to foreign commerce, it should be borne in mind that the proposed Pacific Ocean Telegraph will also exert a beneficial influence on the coasting trade of many of the nations. This is specially true in respect to the United States, with its long lines of coast on the

Atlantic, the Gulf of Mexico and the Pacific, requiring in the coasting trade with the Pacific, the circumnavigation of the continent of South America, passing for more than ten thousand miles along the coasts of foreign nations.

It is much to be regretted that no official account has yet been kept by the United States, nor by any other maritime nation, (as the Committee believe,) of the values of the property moved in their coasting trade. Its amount in the United States undoubtedly far exceeds, and in the United Kingdom probably approaches, if it does not exceed, the total values actually carried in their foreign commerce.

COMMERCE OF THE PACIFIC AND INDIAN OCEANS.

The Committee have deemed it necessary to ascertain and to state somewhat more in detail, the amount of the commerce of the European and American nations on the Pacific and Indian Oceans. Forming a part of the total above exhibited, it has a peculiar interest, not only in being primarily and directly connected with the proposed Pacific Telegraph, but in being closely interwoven with the commerce of every other portion of the civilized world, and the daily necessities of all its varied population.

These great oceans have played and will continue to play a very important part in the great drama of commercial progress, emphatically the epic of the modern ages. The history of Eastern Asia, covering an epoch of nearly four centuries since VASCO DE GAMA doubled the Cape of Good Hope, is filled with the lights and shadows of one long struggle of the maritime nations of Europe to secure, and as far as possible to monopolize, the trade of that fertile and fragrant portion of the globe. The rich products of the Spice Islands under the burning sun of the equator, repeatedly became the scene of cruel war between cold-blooded trading nations on the Northern Ocean; while the field of bloody struggle in Hindustan extended from the groves of Ceylon to the frozen summits of the Himalayas. The long-continued conflicts in these remote regions of the earth were not solely for commerce, but often for empire, intermingling with the broader struggles at home for the mastery of Europe. Within the present century, we have seen the navy of England, in defending and preserving not only her national existence but the liberties of the world from the tyranny of the first NAPOLEON, sweeping the commerce of his empire from every ocean of the globe to the utmost bounds of these distant waters, so that in 1807, in the vivid language of a writer of the day, "not a single merchant ship bearing a hostile flag could be seen traversing the Atlantic or crossing the equator." As late as 1811, at the height of the fearful struggle on the land, the magnificent island of Java, the Cuba of the East, which had shared the fate of Holland, was wrested by England from the grasp of France. Restored on the pacification of Europe to its former owner, it still remains a precious remnant of the maritime and commercial power enjoyed in the palmy days of the Dutch Republic.

The struggle of centuries for the possession of Continental India, between Portugal, Spain, Holland, France and England successively contending for the prize, has practically closed with the lion's share falling to our ancestral England, apparently to be held, with the English-speaking continent of Australia and the outlying islands of New-Zealand, with their rapidly increasing commerce, only for a future and friendly competition, on a far broader scale, with the inheritors of her blood in the United States. It surely is not the least among the wonder-working effects of steam in navigating the land with a speed far surpassing that on the sea, that the railway now spanning our continent, with its electrical auxiliary in the Pacific, will bring the American Union into the close proximity needed for such a competition.*

The statistics of the commerce of the nations of Europe and America on the Pacific and the Indian Oceans, and its distribution among those nations, will fully appear, with some particulars of its past progress, in the table appended to this report. Summed up in brief, the commerce on those waters of the

United Kingdom, in 1868, was............................	$565,106,665	
France, "	59,840,000	
The United States, "	47,056,885	
Netherlands, "	51,500,000	
Hamburgh and Bremen, "	9,828,000	
Spain, "	1,750,000	
Sweden and Norway, "	460,000	

$735,141,550

The overland "Transbaïkal" commerce of Russia with China, in 1867, was 11,300,000 roubles, or.................... 9,040,000

$744,181,550

---

* Of the Anglo-Indian Empire, the islands of New-Zealand lie 1,400 miles east of Australia, and so much the nearer to the coast of the United States. They had 1,611 miles of telegraphic line in 1869, which must ere long be connected with Australia.

2

In addition to the interchanges effected by the preceding commerce between the European and American nations and the countries of Asia, there is now a large coasting commerce in the Indo-Chinese Basin. Of this " home trade," so to speak, a small portion employs the vessels of the Asiatic countries, while the residue is enjoyed by European vessels, principally from the Hanseatic Cities, interchanging the products of Japan and China with those of British India and the Australasian Archipelago. Like the coasting trade of the Atlantic nations, it serves to swell the total commerce interested in the completion of the Pacific cable.

From the detailed statements in the table, the following general facts will appear:

1. Of the commerce of Europe and America with Asia, on the Pacific and Indian Oceans, being in 1868, $735,141,550 the three maritime powers, the United Kingdom, France and the United States, had. 672,103,550

2. Their commerce on those oceans in 1854 was. . . . 330,079,742

    showing an increase in the 14 years of . . . . $342,023,808 being 103 per cent., or 7.35 per cent. yearly.

3. From the proportion of exports to imports shown by the tables of the three nations, we may safely estimate, that of the total commerce of $735,141,550, the exports to the Asiatic countries did not exceed $300,000,000, so that the imports from these countries were at least $435,141,550.

4. Of the last named amount, Australia and New-Zealand furnished $62,942,240, and the more tropical countries of Asia the remaining $372,199,310.

It is this latter portion which imparts to the commerce on the Pacific and Indian Oceans its peculiar interest, embracing the tea, the coffee, the sugar, the spices, the silk, the drugs, and the various other products of the tropics, which, in the progress of civilization, ceasing to be luxuries, have become necessities for the three hundred and twenty millions of Christian people, now occupying the temperate zone of Europe and North America. Intended for the consumption of such a multitude, these tropical products are concentrated, in large masses, in the capacious docks or warehouses of London and Liverpool and Havre and Antwerp and the Hanseatic Cities, to be thence distributed through the world by the united machinery of its common commerce, permeating and interpenetrating every artery and vein of human society.

It surely requires no great stretch of imagination or credulity to believe that a commerce so beneficent and civilizing, in a world like ours filling up with people so rapidly, is destined to large and speedy increase, especially if wisely aided by our national government. It is not for the clear-headed, far-sighted merchants of the United States to close their eyes upon the fact that, in the providential march of events, a field so vast is just opening to their well-directed energy. Still less will they fail to bear in mind, that "cheapness, the sovereign law of commerce, overcoming national "prejudices and national habits," will inexorably compel the products of every portion of the globe, and especially of its remoter regions, to take the shortest and cheapest way to market; that the distance, by sea and land, from the coast of China to the Mississippi River, by way of the Pacific Ocean, is less than one-third of the distance by way of the Atlantic; and that, as a necessary result, San Francisco, our own Pacific emporium, with her spacious warehouses soon to cluster around the "Golden Gate," will become the mart for largely supplying, at least a portion of our widespread interior, with the products of Eastern Asia. The commercial tables show the breadstuffs of California actively entering on their great predestined duty of supplying the daily necessities of China, Japan, Australia and New-Zealand; laying the foundation of a commerce of the highest importance to both the continents. The diplomatic wisdom of our timely treaty with Japan is now plainly evident, not only in the steadily increasing commerce between the two countries, but in the cordial diplomatic relations now fully established with the government of that intelligent and active nation.

It is for the statesman rather than the merchant to look out afar upon the coming ages, and discern the immense eventualities of these great tropical waters, once so remote, but now coming so plainly within the legitimate field of action of our young and growing Republic. The Committee will not attempt to lift the veil of the majestic future, nor seek in any way to measure or estimate the enormous stream of commerce and intercourse which must flow from intimate and friendly relations with the vast populations now accumulated in Eastern Asia. They will venture to hope that the existing commerce of the world, exhibited as one undivided whole, will be sufficient, in the eyes of the Chamber, to justify an earnest recommendation to the Government of the United States, to adopt vigorous measures, without delay, for connecting the continents of America and Asia by a submarine electric Telegraph, to be laid in such portion of the Pacific as may complete a line encircling the globe, and best subserve the interests of our country and the world.

The American Union, in its gradual but steady aggregation of empire, already possesses a water front on the Pacific, in two disconnected portions, embracing, taken together, twenty-eight degrees of latitude, and separated only by that portion still belonging to British America, extending from latitude 49° to latitude 54° 40', a parallel not wholly unknown in our political history.

On the opposite shore of the Pacific, the British Empire has acquired, by treaty or otherwise, territorial rights to some extent in or near some of the maritime cities of China, which may greatly facilitate the connection of the Pacific cable with the segment of the world-encircling line laid upon the Eastern Continent or under its adjacent waters. It will be providential, indeed, if the facilities thus enjoyed by the two nations, with their widespread territories on this broad ocean, shall lead them, at a moment like the present, when lasting concord is the prayer of every patriotic heart, to unite in completing the great achievement of our age, to be consecrated to Peace forever.

SAMUEL B. RUGGLES,
Chairman of the Committee.

CHAMBER OF COMMERCE,
New-York, March 2d, 1871.

———

At the regular monthly meeting of the Chamber of Commerce of the State of New-York, on the 2d of March, 1871, the following resolution, offered by Mr. SAMUEL B. RUGGLES, Chairman of the Committee on Telegraphs and Postal Affairs, was unanimously adopted :

Resolved, That Canals, Railways and Telegraphs form part of one common system of commercial machinery for facilitating and cheapening the commerce, interchanging, between nations, the varied products of the globe, in which any facility afforded to any part benefits the whole ; and that any needless imposition of tolls, expenses or other charges on any part of that system, is the fruit of a policy unfit for the present enlightened age, and injurious to the general welfare and advancing civilization of the human race.

APPENDIX No. 1.

LETTER FROM MR. WILLIAM G. PECK, PROFESSOR OF MATHEMATICS, &C., REFERRED TO IN THE PRECEDING REPORT.

COLUMBIA COLLEGE,
New-York, January 21, 1871.

DEAR SIR:

I have examined the globe, and find that the "great circle," through San Francisco and Yokohama, passes considerably less than 200 miles to the southward of the Aleutian Islands. This makes the route by these islands but little longer than by the great circle. I find on my globe, an island marked Belschevinskoi, that is almost equi-distant from San Francisco and Yokohama. This island is in latitude 52° and longitude 170° W. By measurement on my three foot globe, I find the following distances, which are not very far from true:

    1st. San Francisco to Yokohama, great circle, 4,450 nautical miles.
    2d. San Francisco to Belschevinskoi,   "   2,235   "   "
    3d. Belschevinskoi to Yokohama, \   "   2,265   "   "

            Total,..................   "   4,500   "   "

This gives but 50 nautical miles difference by the two routes.

I am, sir, yours very truly,

WM. G. PECK.

Hon. S. B. RUGGLES,
    Chairman of Committee of Chamber of Commerce, N. Y.

APPENDIX No. 2,

REFERRED TO IN THE PRECEDING REPORT.

COMMERCE OF EUROPEAN NATIONS AND OF THE UNITED STATES ON THE PACIFIC AND INDIAN OCEANS.

I. THE UNITED KINGDOM OF GREAT BRITAIN AND IRELAND.

COUNTRIES.	In 1854.		In 1868.	
	Exports to.	Imports from.	Exports.	Imports.
Mauritius, ...	£401,146	£1,677,533	£391,106	£1,061,999
British India, ...	9,620,710	10,672,862	22,253,231	30,071,866
Ceylon,.............	413,504	1,506,646	869,257	3,671,484
Singapore and Straits' Settlements,........	590,418	794,105	1,571,660	2,050,163
Hong Kong,.........	478,293	(Inc. with China.)	2,274,024	235,804
Java and Sumatra, ...	641,912	214,384	871,460	75,200
China, ...	548,823	9,125,040	6,426,010	11,481,565
Japan, ...	....	....	1,254,483	181,222
Philippine Islands, ...	354,972	652,158	994,199	1,824,795
Australia and New-Zealand,*	13,405,986	4,301,868	12,815,375	12,571,423
French Possessions, ..	....	56,082	2,074	72,593
	£26,455,764	£29,001,578	£49,723,079	£63,298,254
Exports,....		29,001,578	....	49,723,079
Exports and imports,.......	£55,457,342		....	£113,021,333
" " "	$277,286,710		....	$565,106,665

* The official " Statistics of New-Zealand," just received at the Chamber of Commerce, New-York, state its total

Imports in 1869 at.............................	£4,976,126	
Exports, "	4,224,860	
		$46,904,835
Imports from United States,....................	$345,545	
Exports to "	63,995	
		$409,540

II. FRANCE.

COUNTRIES.	In 1853.		In 1867.	
	Exports to.	Imports from.	Exports.	Imports.
Madagascar,.........	$180,000	$40,000	$120,000	$240,000
Ile de la Réunion, (formerly Bourbon,)....	3,500,000	4,340,000	2,400,000	5,000,000
British East Indies,...	1,200,000	8,240,000	3,060,000	19,180,000
Dutch " ...	260,000	1,860,000	500,000	480,000
Philippine Islands, ...	60,000	380,000	....	160,000
French " établissemens" in India, ...	120,000	3,420,000	260,000	1,720,000
China, Cochin China, Japan and Oceanica,	1,000,000	340,000	5,420,000	20,800,000
	$6,380,000	$18,620,000	$11,760,000	$47,580,000
Exports,.....................		6,380,000	....	11,760,000
Exports and imports,.......	$25,000,000		....	$59,340,000

III. The United States of America.

Countries.	In 1853.		In 1868.	
	Imports to.	Exports from.	Exports.	Imports.
British East Indies,...	$556,209	$3,581,726	$647,440	$7,476,294
Dutch " ...	383,706	384,583	144,263	1,903,875
Philippine Islands,....	65,375	2,465,083	56,202	3,963,684
China, ...	3,736,992	10,573,770	11,691,490	11,395,024
Australia, ...	4,287,002	....	4,848,984	85,125
Japan, ...	....	....	780,168	2,429,182
Hawaian Islands,.....	....	....	846,673	1,189,400
South Sea Islands and Pacific generally,...	737,877	17,371	100,536	39,972
Asiatic Russia,.......	....	....	52,724	15,849
Mauritius,...........	3,338	....	....	....
	$9,770,499	$17,022,533	$19,168,480	$28,488,405
Exports,....................		9,770,499	....	19,168,480
Exports and imports,.......		$26,793,032	....	$47,656,885

Aggregate Exports and Imports of the Three preceding Nations.

In 1853-4.		In 1867-8.	
Exports,.... $161,158,389		Exports,.... $279,548,875	
Imports,.... 168,921,353	$330,079,742	Imports,.... 392,559,075	$672,103,650

In 1867-8.

IV. NETHERLANDS.............Exports and imports, ...		$51,500,550
V. HAMBURGH AND BREMEN,.. " " "		9,328,000
VI. SPAIN, ... " " "		1,750,000
VII. SWEDEN AND NORWAY,..... " " "		460,060
		$735,141,550

Note.—There may also have been a comparatively unimportant amount of commerce on the Pacific and Indian Oceans, to and from Italy, Austria and Russia, not yet ascertainable.

THE RELATION

OF THE GOVERNMENT

TO

THE TELEGRAPH;

OR,

A Review of the Two Propositions now Pending before Congress for Changing the Telegraphic Service of the Country.

BY

DAVID A. WELLS,

Late U. S. Special Commissioner of the Revenue, Chairman of the Tax Commission of the State of New York.

———

WITH APPENDICES.

———

NEW YORK.

———

1873.

EXECUTIVE OFFICE,

Western Union Telegraph Company,

NEW YORK, *September*, 1872.

Hon. DAVID A. WELLS.

Sir : The relation—present and prospective—of the existing telegraphic system of the United States to the Federal
Government, is a subject which is certain, in the future, to be
earnestly pressed upon the attention of both Congress and the
country; and, in view thereof, it seems eminently desirable
that there should be presented to the public a clear and
impartial statement of all the more important involved facts
and circumstances.

The Western Union Telegraph Company, fully recognizing
your experience in investigating matters pertaining to the trade,
commerce and industry of the country, and your method in the
presentation of results, would, therefore, request of you the
preparation of such a statement; and, also, as the result of
careful investigation, the expression of an opinion respecting the
expediency of the two propositions, looking to a change in the
character of the telegraphic service of the country, now pending
before Congress.

In furtherance of such investigation, all information in
possession of the Western Union Company will be placed
without reserve at your disposal; but, in so doing, the Company
would disclaim in advance any intention or desire to anticipate
or influence conclusions. They ask nothing but what is right;
they trust that they shall not be obliged, through the exercise
of superior power in the hands of the Federal Government, to
submit to anything which is wrong.

I am, very respectfully, etc., etc.,

WILLIAM ORTON, *President.*

December, 1872.

To Hon. WILLIAM ORTON,
    President Western Union Telegraph Co.
Sir : In accordance with your request, I have made the

subject of the proposed relation of the telegraphic system of the United States to the Federal Government a matter of careful investigation, and herewith submit a statement of the essential facts pertaining thereto, with such conclusions as in my judgment seem warranted by the combined facts and circumstances:

PRESENT CONDITION OF THE TELEGRAPH SYSTEM OF THE UNITED STATES.

The telegraph service of the United States is at present performed by an association known as the "Western Union Telegraph Company"—the result, as the name indicates, of the consolidation of most of the telegraph interest of the country existing prior to 1866—and some *ten* other and rival companies, of much smaller capital and area of geographical operation.

The more exact relations of the "Western Union" to the other Telegraphic Companies of the United States may be thus indicated:

On the 1st day of July, 1872, the Western Union Company controlled and operated 62,032 miles of line; 137,190 miles of wire, and 5,237 officers or stations. Of this aggregate 1,212 miles of line and 2,742 miles of wire were in New Brunswick and Nova Scotia, and 512 miles of line, bearing one wire, in British Columbia; leaving 60,308 miles of line, and 133,936 miles of wire in the United States. The nominal capital of the Western Union is $41,000,000, and its gross receipts for the year ending June 30, 1872, were $8,457,095.77, derived from the following sources:

From the transmission of messages,.......·.....$7,040,803.53
"   "   press reports,......... 979,083.71
"   "   market " 107,579.72
"   "   weather " 137,522.88
All other sources,*........................ 192,105.93
                                          _____
     Total,.............................$8,457,095.77

The statistics of all other and rival Telegraph Companies in the United States were, for the year 1871, estimated as fol-

* Premium on gold from tolls, accruing from cable business, commissions on money transfers, etc.

lows: 11,785 miles of line; 24,340 miles of wire; 773 stations; nominal capital (estimated) $16,000,000. Since this date, however, there has been an increase in all of these lines, but to what extent cannot be definitely stated.*

Aggregate.—For the 1st of January, 1873, the telegraphic system of the United States may be thus approximately estimated :

Aggregate nominal capital, $60,000,000; length of lines, 80,000 miles; length of wire, 180,000 miles; number of stations, 6,300.

During the year ending June 30th, 1872, there were sent over the wires of the Western Union Telegraph Company, exclusive of messages sent by and for railroad companies, between stations on the line of the roads, and service messages of the Telegraph Company, 10,271,935 full paid messages; 660,203 partially paid and free messages; and 1,512,861 press messages ;† making a total of 12,444,449.

RECENT INCREASE AND DEVELOPMENT OF THE TELEGRAPHIC
SERVICE OF THE UNITED STATES.

The recent increase and development of the telegraph service of the United States, as performed by the Western Union Telegraph Company, is shown by the following statistics:

* Of the companies competing with the Western Union the following are the most important:

First. The "Pacific and Atlantic," which had in operation, in 1871, 4,155 miles of line; 8,280 miles of wire, extending from New York to St. Paul and St. Louis by Chicago, and to New Orleans by Cincinnati and Memphis.

Second. The "Atlantic and Pacific," operating in 1871, in connection with the telegraph of the Union Pacific Railroad, 4,155 miles of line, and 8,220 miles of wire.

Third. The "Southern and Atlantic," extending from Washington, along the line of the coast, to Montgomery, Alabama.

Fourth. The "Franklin," extending from Washington to Boston, 800 miles of line; 2,780 miles of wire.

Fifth. The "Great Western," with headquarters at Chicago.

Sixth. The "Philadelphia, Reading and Pottsville," owned and operated by the Philadelphia and Reading Railroad.

† The number of press messages given is an estimate obtained by dividing the whole number of words sent for the press by thirty, that number being assumed to be the average number of words embraced by ordinary commercial and social messages.

In 1866, subsequent to the consolidation of the majority of the preëxisting Companies, the Western Union Company owned and operated 75,686 miles of wire; in 1867 the aggregate was 85,291; in 1868, 97,594; in 1869, 104,584; in 1870, 112,- 191; in 1871, 121,151; in 1872, 137,191, thus showing an increase in six years of nearly 79 per cent.

The gross receipts of the Western Union Company from the transaction of business were, for the fiscal year ending June 30th, 1867, $6,568,925; 1868, $7,004,560; 1869, $7,816,918; 1870, $7,138,737; 1871, $7,687,448; 1872, $8,457,095.

The net receipts for the same period, after paying operating expenses, but including no expenditure for construction, or for any other purpose than the maintenance and operation of lines, were, for 1867, $2,624,919; 1868, $2,641,710; 1869, $2,748,801; 1870, $2,227,965; 1871, $2,532,661; 1872, $2,790,282.

The increase of telegraphic business on the lines of the Western Union Company since 1867 is also worthy of particular attention, as affording to some extent a gauge or standard for estimating the contemporaneous commercial and industrial activity of the country. Thus, from 1867 to 1868, the increase, measured in per cents., was 8·9 per cent.; from 1868 to 1869, 23·8 per cent.; 1869 to 1870, 15·4 per cent.; 1870 to 1871, 16·2 per cent.; 1871 to 1872, 16$\frac{4}{10}$ per cent.

Such being in brief the actual condition of the telegraphic system of the country, two propositions, each looking to a radical change in the character of its service, are now being pressed upon the attention of Congress and the public, and their acceptance eagerly sought for by their respective advocates.

THE GOVERNMENT PROPOSITION.

The first of these, originally brought forward by Hon. C. C. Washburn, of Wisconsin, in 1869, presented to Congress, in the form of a bill, in 1870, and subsequently endorsed by the Postmaster-General and the President of the United States in his annual Message, December, 1871, proposes that the Federal Government shall take possession and own the entire telegraph system of this country, incorporate it with or make it an adjunct of the existing postal system, and place the whole business of transmitting and delivering messages, and of constructing and operating lines, exclusively under the control of the Post-office

Department. The right to enter into such possession, apart from the right of "eminent domain," unquestionably vests in the United States, in virtue of an Act of Congress passed in 1866, and subsequently accepted by the Western Union and other Telegraph Companies, which provides that all Telegraphic Companies then in existence, or which shall be thereafter incorporated under State laws, may have the privilege of constructing and maintaining lines over the public domain, over and along any military or post roads, and across navigable streams or waters, with the right to take from the public lands all necessary building materials, and to preëmpt and use such portions of the unoccupied public lands, not exceeding forty acres to every fifteen miles of line, subject to the following conditions: 1st. Priority in respect to the use of the lines by the Government and its agents, at rates of compensation to be determined by the Postmaster-General. 2d. That the United States may, at any time after the expiration of *five* years from the passage of the Act, purchase all the lines, property and effects of the several companies at appraisement. 3d. That no company shall avail themselves of the privileges conferred by the Act until after a written acceptation of its obligations and restrictions.

The bill reported to Congress in 1870 by Hon. C. C. Washburn, the Chairman of a Select Committee of the House on the telegraph, and which (with one exception, to be hereafter noted) is understood to represent the present proposed scheme of Government absorption of the telegraph, provides essentially as follows :

First. That on and after a time specified the business of transmitting telegraph messages in the United States shall vest exclusively in the Government, and that any person or company who shall *transmit or receive* any telegraphic message, device, or information, except as authorized and permitted by the Post-master-General, shall be liable for each such offence to a penalty not exceeding *one hundred dollars.*

Second. That the United States shall purchase by appraisement the telegraph lines, property and effects of all existing Companies.

Third. The tariff on all messages shall be fixed at a uniform rate, irrespective of distance, of twenty-five cents for each twenty-five words, including date, address and signature, and of one cent for each additional word ; the rates to be prepaid by stamps affixed to each message by the sender.

Other sections of the bill provide for the creation of a Telegraphic Bureau in the Post-office Department ; the appointment of a "Director-General," at a salary of $6,000 per annum, and such other assistants and clerks as may be found necessary ; the extension of the telegraph to every post-office in the United States, the annual gross receipts of which for postage are not less than one hundred dollars ; the authorization of special service for the newspaper press ; the negotiation of contracts with foreign companies for the interchange of international messages ; and, finally, with a view of securing for the Government the aid of efficient and intelligent employés, that no removals shall be made from offices created by the Act except for satisfactory and sufficient cause, and that all promotions shall be regular from the grades next subordinate.

THE SECOND OR "HUBBARD" PROPOSITION.

The second proposition in respect to the future of the telegraph in the United States, which has been brought before Congress and the country, is best known as the "Hubbard" proposition, from the circumstance of its origination and special advocacy by Gardiner G. Hubbard, Esq., of Boston, and has its most recent embodiment in a bill reported to Congress by the House Committee on Appropriations, December, 1872, entitled "*A Bill to connect the Telegraph with the Postal Service, and to Reduce the Rates of Correspondence by Telegraph.*" This proposition, it is to be observed in the outset, is not like the first—a purely Government enterprise, in which the telegraph is to be managed exclusively by the Post-office Department; but, on the contrary, proposes the incorporation of a private Company, which, in consideration of certain special and extraordinary privileges, to be granted by the Government, agrees to contract with the Post-office

●Note.—In his report for December, 1872, the Postmaster-General proposes that the tariff on all messages transmitted by the Government shall be at the outset at an average of *thirty-three* cents for each twenty-five words throughout the United States, to be reduced, after a "thorough renovation of the lines, to an average of *thirty* cents."

Department for the transaction of the telegraphic business of the country at certain specific rates, claimed to be more favorable than those now existing. In other respects, the essential features of this second proposition (as reported to Congress prior to the present session) are as follows :

First. The Postmaster-General is *required* to contract with the Company authorized by the Act, for a period of ten years, for the transmission *only* (not reception or delivery) of telegraphic messages, at a rate which shall not exceed twenty-five cents for a circuit of two hundred and fifty miles, fifty cents for a circuit of five hundred miles, and twenty-five cents for every added circuit of five hundred miles, for each twenty words or figures, including date, address, and signature; the rates, in all cases, to be prepaid by stamps. The right to charge extra rates for messages, the senders of which are willing to pay for "*priority of transmission,*" or, in plain English, the right to put one message ahead of another for a consideration, is also expressly stipulated and provided for.

Second. The Postal Telegraph Company shall provide lines of telegraph to every city and village where telegraph stations are now maintained, and to all other places which may have a population of three thousand, and to the capital of every State. The United States, on the other hand, are obligated to furnish suitable and convenient accommodations at each postal station for all officers and instrumentalities required by the company for the transaction of its business, including, by specification or legitimate inference, fuel, lights, clerical service, stamps and stationery; and shall also assume the expense, responsibility and business of receiving messages, and also of delivering by messengers or mail all such as by the wires may have been transmitted.

Third. The compensation to be paid to the Company by the Government shall not exceed ten per cent. per annum on its authorized stock capital, over and above all operating expenses; and in case the receipts for the transmission of messages are in excess of the requirements for such payments, the rates for the transmission of messages shall be reduced proportionally. And in case the Company is assessed for any tax or license in any

State or Territory, the Postmaster-General may increase the rates on each telegram between the offices in such State or Territory "until the increased amount equals such tax or license."

Fourth. The Postal Telegraph Company shall have power to make special contracts with railway companies relative to railway service, and with the press for the transmission of news; the rates for which latter class of despatches shall not exceed those paid by existing "press associations" for similar service.

Fifth. The capital stock of the Postal Telegraph Company shall, at its organization, consist of 10,000 shares, of the par value of $100 each—total $1,000,000—to represent "the expenses of organization and connection of its lines with postal telegraph offices;" and, in addition, the Company may from time to time issue new stock, to represent the actual cost of lines that may be purchased or constructed.

Sixth. The Postmaster-General may, at any time after the expiration of five years, purchase the property and franchise of the Company, either by agreement or appraisement, or " upon paying to the Company the actual cost, together with interest thereon at the rate of ten per cent. per annum, deducting therefrom the full amount of any moneys paid to the stockholders for or on account of dividends, interest, or earnings."

REASONS WHY A CHANGE IN THE EXISTING SYSTEM IS ADVOCATED.

Having thus given the essential features, as expressed in the form of bills reported to Congress, of the two propositions which look to an entire change in the existing telegraphic system of the country, the question which next naturally suggests itself is—why is any change to be regarded as expedient?

On the part of those who advocate the exclusive possession and operation of the telegraph by the Government, it is said in general " that the post-office and telegraph have but one and the same object, and that it is for the interest of the people that their management should be in one and the same hands." The example of Europe is also appealed to in support of this theory, in every State of which, with the exception of Great Britain, the telegraph has, almost from the outset, been a Government monopoly, and in Great Britain itself has also recently become so through the sanction of Parliament, and the compulsory sale to the Government of the property and franchises of all privately organized and preëxisting companies. Other reasons, regarded perhaps as even more immediate and important, and semi-officially put forth by the Government through its advocates,* are : that "the press demands a reduction of tariff for its news reports, and a relief from the combined monopoly of the telegraph and 'associated press ;'" "that the interests of the Government demand the entire control of the wires for the proper transmission of the weather reports, and other public business;" and, finally, "that the interests of the people demand the extension of facilities, impartiality in the trans-mission of dispatches, and the reduction of tariffs to the mini-mum consistent with profitable working."

On the other hand, the sum and substance of the reasons put forth in support of the so-called "Postal Telegraph," by Mr. Hubbard and his associates, may be concisely stated as follows :

Protesting, in the first instance, against an exclusive posses-sion and control of the telegraph by the Government, as a measure wholly "opposed to our institutions," but "in har-mony with the principles of arbitrary and monarchical Govern-ments," they, nevertheless, take the position that a partial ownership and interference by the State would, on the contrary, be both wise and beneficial. Professing further a deep interest in the public welfare, and profoundly impressed with the necessity that the people should enjoy greater and cheaper telegraphic facilities than they now do, Mr. Hubbard and his friends claim that this latter result can only be attained through a coöperative union and partnership of the Post-office Depart-ment on the one hand and the Postal Telegraph Company on the other, according to the manner and conditions specified in the abstract of the bill before noticed.

Such, then, in brief, are the reasons put forth to the public in support of the general theory that a change in the existing telegraphic system of the country is immediately expedient.

---

* See speech of R. B. Lines before the House Committee on Appropriations, April, 1871.

The test and analysis of the validity of these reasons comes next in the order of this investigation, but before doing so it seems desirable to present a clear statement of the manner in which the telegraphic service of the United States has been and is now executed.

THE TELEGRAPH IN THE UNITED STATES—PAST AND PRESENT.

It is curious to note that, at the inception of the telegraph, the whole subject was regarded by Congress as one hardly worthy of its serious consideration, and that when it was proposed in the House of Representatives that an appropriation of $30,000 should be made by the Government to test and promote the invention, an amendment that one half the sum asked for should be devoted to experiments in mesmerism was declared by the presiding officer to be wholly germain to the subject. Subsequently, when the first line had been constructed, and the practicability of transmitting messages demonstrated, a *bona fide* proposition by Professor Morse that the Government should purchase the whole invention for the sum of $100,000, was unceremoniously rejected ; the Postmaster-General, Hon. Cave Johnston, to whom the proposition was referred, reporting as follows : " *That the operation of the telegraph between Washington and Baltimore had not satisfied him that under any rate of postage that could be adopted its revenues could be made equal to its expenditure.*" And when, more than twenty years afterwards, a proposal was made to Congress to unite the postal and telegraphic systems, Hon. William Dennison, the then Postmaster-General, as the result of a careful investigation, submitted a report, of which the following is the concluding paragraph : " *As the result of my investigation, under the resolution of the Senate, I am of opinion that it will not be wise for the Government to inaugurate the proposed system of telegraph as a part of the postal service, not only because of its doubtful financial success, but also its questionable feasibility under our political system.*"

Thus formally and decisively neglected by the Government, at a time when help and supervision, if ever to be given, was most needed, the enterprise of telegraphic communication in the United States, with all its risks and then unforeseen contingencies, was taken up by individuals, and, through the personal energy and private capital of comparatively few men, has been expanded to dimensions which find no parallel in the experience of any other one nation, and are surpassed only by the aggregate constructions of all the States of Europe.

In the outset the telegraphic service of the United States was performed by a very considerable number of companies, which were gradually organized under charters granted by the several States; but by 1866 most of the competing and connecting lines had become consolidated under the one charter of the Western Union Company. Since 1866 eight other rival companies have been organized, the lines of one of which stretch across the continent. Congress, on the other hand, except to authorize the building of lines across the public domain, whereby.Government communication with the Pacific Coast and the various military stations of remote territories might be facilitated, has hitherto steadily declined to pass any acts of incorporation, or to legislate in favor of any one Company as distinct from the rest, and has thus, to all intents and purposes, distinctly recognized the policy of leaving the creation and control of telegraphic companies exclusively to the States.

Any review of the experience of the telegraph in the United States would, furthermore, be imperfect, which omitted to call attention to the circumstances that; while the railroad system of the country has grown up under the stimulus of grants by Congress of money and of millions of acres of its public lands, superadded to subscriptions, bounties and exemptions innumerable from States, counties and municipalities, the telegraph has given rather than received favors from the public. For if we add to the trifling donation made by Congress in the outset to Professor Morse, the highest estimated money value of all the privileges since granted by the Government to all the Telegraph Companies, namely—the right to string wires along military and post roads, to cross the wilderness of the plains, to preëmpt land for actual occupation*—a right granted to every citizen—it is capable of direct proof that, through work performed for the Government and never paid for, and through services rendered to the public in time of war, flood, pestilence

* Not an acre has been preëmpted.

and conflagration, to the coast survey and science generally, for all of which payment was never asked or expected, the Western Union Telegraph Company alone has made to both Government and the public a compensation which, to say the least, has been in the nature of a fourfold equivalent.

TAXATION OF THE TELEGRAPH IN THE UNITED STATES.

Again, while in all other countries the capital, franchise and business of the telegraph has been carefully exempted from taxtion, in the United States, on the other hand, a rule of an exactly opposite character has been recognized. Thus, from 1865 to 1871 the several Telegraph Companies of the United States paid directly to the Federal Government, in the form of internal revenue taxes, an aggregate of $1,549,000; and this, too, in addition to onerous State and local taxes, and a system of national customs taxes on materials of construction and operation, which last, in the case of wire alone—the leading article of telegraphic consumption—enhances its cost *sixty-two per cent.* (on a gold basis) beyond what is paid for identically the same article in either Great Britain, Belgium, Switzerland or Holland.* And, although at the present time the national internal revenue taxes on the receipts of Telegraph Companies have been repealed, the aggregate of local† and customs taxes yet enforced are, in the case of the Western Union Company, equivalent to *ten per cent. on full one ninth* of its total annual gross receipts for the transaction of business. And yet we find the Federal Government, which in part upholds and justifies the continuance of such taxation, assuming through its representative the position of a complainant, and virtually saying to the several companies, " Because you do not transact your business cheaper we ought to deprive you of the privilege of doing business at all."

DEVELOPMENT SINCE 1866.

Since the final consolidation of 1866 the telegraph facilities

---

* If we include premium on gold, freights, commissions, &c., the cost of wire in New York is at least double the price for the same article in England.

† In some instances the Western Union pays a tax as high as one thousand dollars for the privilege of doing business within the precincts of a single municipality.

of the United States have been increased by the construction of more than 30,000 miles of additional line, 75,000 miles of wire, and by the opening of more than 3,000 new stations, at which messages can be transmitted and delivered. The expenditure rendered necessary for this developement has been about *twelve* millions of dollars, of which the Western Union Company has paid about *five* millions, in addition to the contributions of railway companies included in its system, which amount to about two and a half millions—the increase during the year ending June 30, 1872, under the auspices of the Western Union alone, having been 6,000 miles of line, 16,039 miles of wire and 631 offices.

REDUCTION OF RATES.

During the time referred to, moreover, not a single year has elapsed in which there has not been a marked reduction of rates; so that at the present time the average sum charged for the transmission of messages is not in excess of one half that required in 1866 for the performance of similar service.

The assertion made by the Postmaster-General in his recent report, that the average receipt per message of the Western Union Company "has been increased *eleven* cents, or nearly 20 per cent. since 1867, notwithstanding the undoubted reductions of tariff between important points," although finding some warrant in the publication of imperfect data in 1869, is nevertheless entirely incorrect and deceptive—the average annual tariff on all messages, excluding press and market reports, and all railway and company service since 1868, having been as follows:

1869, $0.92; 1870, $0.77; 1871, $0.73; 1872, $0.62.*

As a contribution to economic science, it may be further stated that the average *charge* at which telegraphic messages are now transmitted in the United States for the public is less than the

* The statistics published during the years immediately succeeding the consolidation of the various lines in 1866, and used in all the earlier discussions respecting the working of the telegraph in the United States, are now known to have been exceedingly imperfect—necessarily so through lack of an organization like that now existing, which has required years to perfect and develop. The averages above given—the result of the most recent and careful investigation—are believed to be as accurate as it is possible to state them.

average *cost* for doing equivalent work in 1866, although since that period there has been a marked advance in the wages of employés in almost every department of service, and a very great increase in the cost of wire, telegraphic poles and some other materials. Thus, for example, it costs more at the present time to transport telegraphic poles from the upper lakes to Chicago than it cost four years ago for the poles delivered at Chicago. The size and weight, and consequently the cost, of the great portion of the wire now used for telegraphic construction is also considerably greater, on a gold basis, than it was in 1866 and the years anterior.

Attention is also asked to the fact that, in nearly every instance in which the Western Union Company has made a reduction of rates, it has been done with a full knowledge of the fact that such a reduction would be accompanied by an absolute decrease of net revenue. Thus, when, in 1869, the present system was adopted of estimating telegraphic distances by an "air line," rather than by the route actually traversed, resulting in an average reduction of all rates of about 15 per cent., the loss in net earnings during the succeeding seven months was $419,295; and again, when, in 1870, in addition to other reductions, a system was adopted of allowing messages to be sent at night on all lines in the United States and Canada east of Omaha, at rates one half less than those charged by day, the net receipts of the Company declined in the succeeding twelve months from $2,748,801 to $2,227,965, thus entailing a loss in a single year of over a half a million of dollars. That such reductions are likely to prove ultimately advantageous to the Company, as well as to the public, is not to be disputed; but the fact that the Western Union Company have been willing, deliberately, and in repeated instances, to submit to a very large and immediate loss, with the expectation of future gain, through an increased use of the telegraph by the people, consequent upon reduced charges, shows an amount of practical wisdom in dealing with the public interests, strikingly in contrast with the reluctant slowness with which those intrusted with the government of the United States have met every proposition for the reduction of taxes, which only the exigencies of an active war could furnish an argument for continuance. The further circumstance should almost be overlooked, that in the memorial addressed to the Senate of the

United States, under date of February, 1872, the Western Union Company state that work has been in progress for some time by this Company preparatory to a reduction of rates, additional to those already effected.

TELEGRAPH STOCK AS AN INVESTMENT.

As a further contribution to the recent history of the American telegraph, it should be stated that, during the period of development under consideration, or from 1866 to 1872, the amount paid in dividends to stockholders in the telegraph companies of the United States has been about five millions, or less than ten per cent. on their present aggregate stock capital, estimated at $60,-000,000. If it be said that the actual value of the franchises and property of the several companies is less than the par value of their stock, attention is asked to the circumstance that the Government of Great Britain, three years ago, paid more than thirty-seven millions in gold for a system of telegraphs in that country, operating 29,740 miles of line, and 2,000 offices, as compared with a present aggregate in the United States of 80,000 miles of line and 6,300 offices. One million of dollars per annum again would be ten per.cent.—the rate contemplated in Mr. Hubbard's bill—on ten millions of capital ; but this is less by two millions than the sum actually expended by the telegraph companies of the United States, independently of or in connection with railroads, during the last six years, for improvements and construction. And if it be replied to this, also, that the amount derived from receipts and expended in improvements and construction represents profits equally with the dividends paid directly to the stockholders, it is a good and sufficient answer that, if it be so, it is profit that up to the present time has accrued wholly to the public and not to the stockholders, and that for an indefinite future a large annual expenditure for similar purposes will be absolutely indispensible to meet the demands of an increasing population and new areas of territorial occupation. That the companies have been willing to exercise this forbearance of any immediate returns from their investments through an expectation of large future gains, as the country increases in wealth and population, may be regarded as a correct assumption ; but the

2

fact that this is so, would certainly seem to constitute in itself a valid bar to any immediate demand for a change on the part of a public which, for the present at least, is profiting exclusively from such forbearance. But be this as it may, it is a matter of certainty that the capital invested in telegraphs in the United States is not now, and for the last six years has not been, in the receipt of adequate compensation; that any profit under the Government scheme will be impossible; and under the Hubbard bill, except at the expense of the Government, a matter exceedingly problematical.

As a further illustration of this position, take the financial exhibit of the Western Union Telegraph Company for the year ending June 30, 1872. Gross receipts, $8,457,095.77; total expenditures, $5,666,863.16; apparent net profit, $2,790,232, or $6\frac{8}{10}$ per cent. on a capital of $41,000,000, or $9\frac{3}{10}$ per cent. on a capital of $30,000,000. But out of this net gain or profit the company constructed or purchased over 16,000 miles of wire additional, all of which was nearly as essential to the accommodation of the business and social interests of the country, as was the expenditure (not included in the surplus) of $930,000 during the same time for the maintenance and repair of lines previously existing. That the stockholders in the Western Union and other telegraph companies may receive something better in the future is certainly to be hoped; for if they do not the public may feel assured that either the average of existing tolls will have to be advanced, or no more lines will be built by private capitalists looking to an average rate of interest on investment.

TELEGRAPH FACILITIES IN EUROPE AND THE UNITED STATES.

As has been already stated, the telegraph service of Europe, with the exception of the various submarine lines, has from the outset been mainly under the ownership and control of Government. On the contrary, in the United States the construction and operation of the telegraph has been left exclusively to private enterprise. Under such different circumstances of development the comparative results have been as follows: In Europe, with a population approximating 300,000,000, the telegraph system in 1871 embraced 175,490 miles of line, 474,000 miles of wire, and 15,500 offices.

In the United States, with a population which may be estimated at 40,000,000, there are about 80,000 miles of line, 180,000
miles of wire, and 6,300 offices.

The ratio of telegraphic facilities to the population in Europe
and the United States may therefore be approximately indicated
as follows:

				EUROPE.	UNITED STATES
Number of inhabitants to each mile of line				1,708	500
"	"	"	" wire	631	222
"	"	"	office	19,351	6,365
"	"	"	messages sent	9	3

✓ It will thus be seen that, as regards the facilities for telegraphic
communication furnished in Europe and the United States, the
latter are very far in advance of the former.

COMPARATIVE RATES OF CHARGES IN EUROPE AND THE
UNITED STATES.

The average charges for the transmission of messages in Europe
and the United States also constitutes an important element in
any comparison that may be instituted in respect to the relative
merits of the two systems. On this point we quote the testimony
of George B. Prescott, Esq., the best recognized authority on
telegraphic statistics in the United States. He says : " The tolls
for the transmission of messages are not the same in any two
countries in Europe; nor are they uniform for all classes of messages in any one country. Telegraphic correspondence in Europe is divided into two general classes, called 'internal' and
'international' messages. The internal are those which are received, transmitted and delivered in the same country ; the international are those which are received in one country and transmitted into another country. ✓As a general rule a low rate of
charges is adopted for the transmission of 'internal' messages,
while a high tariff is imposed on 'international' messages. The
telegraphic tolls in continental Europe in 1869 averaged 36⅔
cents for internal messages, and $1.01 for international messages,
which is a higher average charge than is imposed in this country,
although it is well known that skilled labor is much more expensive here than in Europe."

It would seem as if an exhibit of such a character as above

given would prove reasonably satisfactory to the public, and be also regarded by them as embodying so much of promise for the future as to warrant, at least for the present, a general opposition to any radical and sweeping interference with the existing system. That the public, furthermore, are either not dissatisfied with the manner in which the telegraphic service of the country has been performed, or take but comparatively little interest in the subject, is sufficiently shown by the circumstance that up to the present time not a single memorial or petition has been presented to Congress from any Chamber of Commerce, Board of Trade, Municipal Organization or Press Association which sets forth the necessity or prays for the provision of any new system, or which complains of and seeks redress for any existing grievances. But as, nevertheless, a change of a certain character has, on the one hand, been recommended by the President of the United States and some of his principal advisers, and as, on the other, certain citizens, of acknowledged ability and enterprise, seek from Congress aid and authority to inaugurate a system of an entirely different character, it is important to next subject to analysis the elements of the respective propositions, and see how far they are worthy of popular consideration and endorsement. And first as regards the Government proposition.

REVIEW OF THE GOVERNMENT PROPOSITION.

First.—As the Fifth Amendatory Article of the Constitution of the United States provides that private property shall not be taken for public uses without just compensation ; and as the act of 1866, in addition, specifically stipulates that if at any time the United States shall decide to take possession of the telegraphic system for military, postal or other purposes, it shall purchase all lines, property and effects of existing companies at a fair appraisement, it is legitimate to assume that the people of the United States will pay, at least, a fair market price for whatever they propose to take possession. But how much will that price probably be ?

In answer to this question we have first the result of an investigation, submitted to a Select Committee of the House of Representatives on the Telegraph, by Gardiner G. Hubbard, Esq., who, as the principal advocate of a company contemplating a similar purchase, would not naturally present an exaggerated estimate. This gentleman's figures of the total primary cost likely to be incurred by the Government, as a consequence of the proposed adoption of the telegraph, are as follows:

Estimate of appraisement of existing lines, $30,000,000.

But with a reduction of the rate of charges, as proposed under the Government system—namely, twenty-five cents for every twenty-five words—it is certain that the number of despatches offered for transmission would largely increase, and to meet this increase new facilities in the shape of additional wires would be needed. Mr. Hubbard estimates such extensions as requiring 270,000 miles of new wire, at a cost (at $100 per mile) of $27,000,000. Mr. Orton, of the Western Union, on the other hand, as the result of the experience of that Company, says 330,000 miles would be needed, at a cost per mile which will approach much closer to $150 rather than $100. Then, again, the bill for telegraphic absorption by the Government, endorsed by the Postmaster-General, proposes to establish a telegraph station in connection with every post-office in the country, the gross receipts of which for postages are not less than $100 per annum. The estimate for such further extension is fixed by Mr. Hubbard at $6,000,000 additional, making the total first and minimum cost to the Government of the proposed scheme not less than $63,000,000.

It should, however, be stated that the Postmaster-General, in his recent report, December, 1872, expresses an opinion, as a result of his investigations, that a new system of telegraph, " equal in extent to the present " one, could be constructed by the Government for a total cost of $11,880,000. But the utter absurdity of this official estimate becomes at once apparent, when it is considered that at least an equal sum has been expended by the various telegraph and railway companies for simply so much of the existing telegraphic system of the country as has been constructed since the year 1866, and that the cost of such labor and material as would be required in any new construction has not since experienced any decline, but, on the contrary, in some respects has been augmented.

In a report submitted to the House of Representatives, December 20th, 1872, the Committee on Appropriations, on the other hand, in discussing this subject, use the following language: "The purchase and extension of lines necessary to transmit annually the 30,000,000 messages contemplated by the Post-master-General would involve the necessity for appropriations or a bonded indebtedness which has been estimated to equal, at least, $75,000,000."

To meet now the probable large expenditure which would be necessary, a new national loan would therefore have to be authorized; the Government would be again placed in the position of a borrower; the whole necessitating a new issue of bonds, new syndicates, new suspicions of partisan and Federal patronage and commissions, and an unavoidable further continuance of that interference with the financial interests of the country which has already given to the Treasury Department a power and an influence which the framers of the Constitution never anticipated or intended. And, as illustrating further how one interference by the Government with business that does not legitimately pertain to it naturally tends to suggest and open the way for another, it may be mentioned that it has been proposed (unofficially) to establish savings banks all over the country in connection with the post-office, and then use the deposits to defray the expenses of tele-graphic purchases and constructions—a scheme which has the taint of small, if not of fraudulent speculation, which involves the dispensing of new patronage, and which would undoubtedly cost the Government far more than any loan it could otherwise negotiate.

It is also a matter of interest to review, in this connection, the recent experience of so practical a nation as Great Britain in ab-sorbing by purchase the telegraphic system of that country. When the project was first brought before Parliament, the estimate of cost, founded on the judgment of experts, was " twenty years' purchase" of the net profits of the several British com-panies for the years 1867-8, predicated in the aggregate at £2,-200,000 or $11,000,000; but when the contract was once made, and the actual results determined, it was found that the Govern-ment had in reality obligated itself to an expenditure of £7,518-955, or *nearly forty millions of dollars.*

Second. In the bill reported by Hon. C. C. Washburn from

23

the Select Committee of the House on the Telegraph, July, 1870, and which, at the time mentioned and subsequently, received the approval of the Post-office Department, the rate for which the Government proposed to undertake the transmission of messages was 25 cents for each 20 words or figures, for all distances within the territory of the United States. The opinion of Mr. Orton, Mr. Prescott, Mr. Hubbard, and almost every other person who had made study of the telegraph in the United States a specialty, was, however, to the effect that the sum named could not by any possibility reimburse the Post-office Department for the expense of operating the telegraph as a system, to say nothing of the interest on the original purchase and investment. | Mr. Washburn, as the result of his investigations (claimed to be most thorough), thought differently, and in his report made use of the following language : "The Committee do not expect that on extreme distances the low rate of 20 or 25 cents will be self-sustaining, but they do expect that all such differences will be made up on shorter lines," and "they have made a calculation, *based on reliable estimates*, showing a small profit." (Report H. R. No. 2,365, p. 34.) And again, on page 54 of the same report, Mr. Washburn unqualifiedly asserts "that by Government management and connection with the postal service a large saving can be made in expenses, and a reliable system established, which, at a uniform rate of 25 cents for any distance, will be self-sustaining." And yet, notwithstanding these calculations, "based on reliable estimates," we find the Postmaster-General, as the result of two years' additional experience, now proposing that the Government rate at the outset shall be 33½ cents, to be reduced, after a "thorough renovation of the lines," to 30 cents. It is, therefore, obvious that the assumption of the Postmaster-General, if correct now, places Mr. Washburn in the position of urging in 1870 a scheme upon Congress, "based upon reliable estimates," which, if adopted, would have entailed upon the Government an average loss of from 8 to 13 cents on every telegraphic message of which it undertook the transmission.

CHEAP TELEGRAPHIC SERVICE UNDER THE GOVERNMENT AND INCREASED TAXATION OF THE PEOPLE CORRELATIVE.

But that the idea of making the telegraph, any more than the

Post-office, self-supporting in the hands of the Government does not really enter into the plans of those who advocate the scheme of Federal interference, it is to be called to mind that, in one of the earliest bills brought before Congress and earnestly advocated, namely, that reported by Hon. B. Gratz Brown in 1865, it was seriously proposed that the Government should construct telegraph lines and work them in connection with the Post-office at a uniform rate of three cents per message—a proposition—then, equally as the one now advocated, equivalent to saying, that the necessity of affording to the people of the United States cheaper telegraph service is so imperative and apparent as to demand that the Government shall annually add to the already heavy burden of taxes on the people a large additional burden, in order that so desirable a result may be effected. But it does not seem to have occurred to any or all of these gentlemen, whose bosoms swell so readily with the idea of Government philanthrophy, that the Government has never anything to give to the people in the way of pecuniary aid or bounty other than what it has previously taken from them under some form of taxation, with some eight per cent. additional, to pay for the cost of the taking. And again, that if it is to be an accepted principle of our national policy that the Government is to furnish to the people such things as are acknowledged to be necessary, it stands to reason that such service should commence with those things which are of prime necessity rather than with those which are secondary ; and that food and raiment, fuel, shelter, and education belong to the first class, and telegraphic service to the latter. What the annual deficit to the Government, transmitting telegrams at the rate of *three* cents per message, would have amounted to neither Mr. Gratz Brown or any other person has definitely stated ; but on the basis proposed by Mr. Washburn, with the concurrence of the Post-office Department, of 25 cents per message, Mr. Hubbard has presented to Congress the following estimate :

First.—interest at 5 per cent. on national bonds representing the cost of the lines, $3,150,000.

Second.—In Europe the cost of transmitting telegrams ranges, according to Mr. Hubbard, from $15\frac{1}{10}$ cents *gold*, ($18\frac{1}{10}$ currency) in Belgium to $1.18 in Russia. (Report H. R. 41st

Congress, 28th Session, No. 2365, p. 146.) And he adds: "The cost of transmission increases with the length of the message and the distance of its transmission, though not in the same proportion." In Belgium and Switzerland, the two countries of Europe where the charges for telegraph service are least, the average distance to which messages are transmitted is fifty miles, but in the United States the average is *three hundred miles*. " To ascertain, therefore," continues Mr. Hubbard, "the cost in America, it will not be safe to add less than fifty per cent. to the cost in Belgium for the extra length and distance;" which moderate assumption would give $27\frac{7}{10}$, currency, as the cost to the Government of each message transmitted, and involving, on the basis of 25 cents per message, a direct loss of $2\frac{7}{10}$ cents on each message, or of $1,080,000 per annum on the estimated volume of business. To this must be added the annual expenditure on account of extensions, improvements and repairs, also estimated by Mr. Hubbard at $2,560,000—making an annual aggregate deficit of $6,290,000.

But it must be borne in mind that when Mr. Hubbard takes the experience of Belgium as his basis of comparison, he selects a country which, if we exclude Switzerland, is altogether exceptional in Europe, and one in which the wages of skilled labor, and the cost of all the elements that enter into telegraphic construction and operation, touch a very low figure. And, as strikingly illustrative of this exceptional character of Belgium, we have the fact that while wages and the cost of material are equally cheap, if not cheaper, in Bavaria and Austria, the average cost of a telegraphic message in the first of these countries is twenty-two cents gold, and in the latter fifty-seven cents, and that in neither Bavaria nor Austria do the total annual receipts from the telegraph approximate the aggregate annual requirements for telegraphic expenditure : the deficit in Bavaria for 1870 having been 75·1 per cent., and in Austria 28·2 per cent. (See appendix to the Review, marked B.) A more reasonable estimate of the average cost of transmitting Government telegrams in the United States, founded on European data, would, therefore, more probably give us one hundred, rather than fifty per cent. in excess of the average of Belgium—carrying up Mr. Hubbard's estimate of the cost of each message from $27\frac{7}{10}$ cents to $36\frac{2}{10}$ cents, currency; and the loss on the same from $2\frac{7}{10}$ cents to $11\frac{2}{10}$ cents, or $3\frac{2}{10}$ cents on latest basis of 33 cents, advocated by the Postmaster-General. But this average is not so favorable as has been already attained to by the Western Union Telegraph Company, when it operates under conditions similar to those existing in Belgium, namely, over limited areas, and through and between dense centres of population, the charge for a message from New York to Boston (a distance of 234 miles), or between New York and Philadelphia, being at present but thirty cents currency, with a reduction of one half for messages transmitted by night. It is curious to note, also, in this connection, how narrow is the margin between surplus and deficit under even Belgian conditions and economy. Thus M. Vinchent, the Director of Belgian telegraphs, in a recent exhibit of the ten years' experience of that kingdom, prior to and including 1869, shows that the excess of receipts over expenditures during that time, for telegraphic operation, construction and repairs, was only 581,844 francs ($116,000), out of an aggregate of receipts of 11,295,773 francs, or at the rate of $11,600 per annum. And that this small but favorable annual average has not since been maintained, is proved by the Belgian statistics of 1870 (the last available), which give an aggregate of $310,938 telegraphic receipts, and $305,730 telegraphic expenditures; and out of this last sum only $18,030 is credited to construction and contingencies.*

If we turn now to other countries in which, although possessing all the advantages of a strong centralized Government, the same system, economy and intelligence which characterize Belgium do not prevail, the results of telegraphic operation under the exclusive auspices of the State are much more significant. Thus, including in the annual expenditure the sums disbursed for constructions and repairs, as well as for operating, the accounts for the year 1870 exhibit the following results:

NORTH GERMANY. — Receipts, $1,621,501 ; expenditures, $1,721,855 ; deficit, $136,215, or 8·3 per cent.

---

* M. Jamar, Minister of Public Works in Belgium, in a recent report, also makes this statement, that " the net product of the Belgian Telegraphic System has been diminishing for several years, and was reduced to a point at which there was scarcely any profit in 1868."

BAVARIA.—Receipts, $162,248; expenditures, $284,835; deficit, $122,587, or 75·1 per cent.

DENMARK.—Receipts, $104,280; expenditures, $113,540; deficit, 8·8 per cent.

SPAIN.—Receipts, $289,340; expenditures, $715,109; deficit, 147 per cent.

AUSTRIA.—Receipts, $929,221; expenditures, $1,375,407; deficit, 28·2 per cent.

In Great Britain, where the Governmental system is claimed to be a success, the fiscal exhibit of telegraphic service for the fourteen months prior to March, 1871, was as follows : Total receipts, £798,580 ($3,992,900); total expenditures, £1,397,389 ($6,-986,945); deficit, £598,809 ($2,994,045). The expenditures here are returned in two classes, namely, capital expenditure, £926,-894, and working expenditure, £470,495 ; but under the head of the former is included an expenditure of £346,449 for poles, arms, wires, insulators, instruments, batteries and tools ; and also the sum of £377,449 for engineering, salaries, alteration of buildings, examining accounts, law expenses, telegraphic instruction, and the like—all of which would seem to be annually essential to the working of a system as large as that of Great Britain, so long as it is maintained in a condition of effectiveness.

Of other telegraphic systems under Government control, those of Hungary, Norway, Sweden, Holland, Portugal, Roumania, the Indo-European line, and the lines of British India, all in like manner exhibit, for the year 1870, a deficit of receipts as compared with expenditures ; while only in Russia (where the average charge for the transmission of messages is $1.52), Belgium, Switzerland, Italy and Turkey, is there a claim preferred that the annual receipts from messages are equal to or in excess of the expenditures necessary to work, maintain or extend the lines necessary to transmit them.*

* Sir James Anderson, in a paper read before the Statistical Society of London, June, 1872, presents the following statement of profit and loss contingent upon the Government maintenance of the telegraph during the year 1869 in the following States of Europe—interest for construction only (and not average annual expenditure for construction) being included:

PROFIT.—Bavaria, £7,657 ; Belgium, £2,901 ; Italy (no data relative to construction being obtainable since 1861), £25,966 ; Russia, £120,010 ; Switzerland, £2,541.

LOSS.—Austria and Hungary, £22,067 ; Baden, £505 ; Denmark, £7,219 ; France,

With such evidence illustrative of Governmental management of the telegraph in the Old World, what must be the economical results of a similar system in the United States, where the Government, as a general rule, always pays from *twenty* to *fifty* per cent. more for whatever it purchases, in the way of service or material, than private citizens ; and where, with the possible exception of the manufacture of small arms, no work that it has ever undertaken, from the building of a ship to the printing of a book, compares favorably in point of quality and economy with the similar work of individual ? The total deficiency of six millions, which Mr. Hubbard estimates the people must be annually called upon to pay by taxation, under Mr. Washburn's bill, for the luxury of having the Government own the telegraph, will, in all probability, have to be multiplied by two—possibly by three—to represent the figures which will approximate the truth, and all for the benefit of not over *one thirty-second* part of our population ; that being the proportion which Mr. Palmer, of the Committee on Telegraphs, reported to the House of Representatives, as likely to use the telegraph at the rate of three messages per month, provided that, under the reduction of rates by the Government, the whole number of messages should increase to the extent of 40,000,000 per annum.*

It may be, however, that to some the addition of *six*, *twelve*, or even *eighteen* millions to a present annual national expenditure of about three hundred millions, will appear insignificant in comparison with the results promised or anticipated. If there be such, the startling fact is commended to their attention, that at the present time the ratio of increase in our national expenditures, for what may be called the civil service, is in excess of that of any of the Governments of the Old World—and since

£34,520; Germany (north), £57,888; Great Britain (Indo-European), £57,688; Greece, £11,688; Holland, £23,627; Norway, £6,667 ; Roumania, £13,209; States of the Church, £1,687 ; Sweden, £1,782.

* Excluding press reports, the largest number of messages sent in any one year (1872) was probably not in excess of thirteen millions. This aggregate, apportioned to a population of 39,000,000, would give one telegraph message once a year for every three persons, at an average cost to each of about 21 cents; and yet it is for the purpose of relieving the people of this great burden that the Government proposes to incur an expenditure of over $6,000,000 per annum.

1864 has been, on the average, in excess of *eight per cent. per annum*, while during the same period the ratio of increase of population has not been equal to three per cent. per annum. And also, as illustrating the influence of the present burden of taxation on the strictly agricultural interests, the facts brought out by recent investigations in New Hampshire; which show that in one of its most fertile and, at the same time, favorably situated districts in respect to markets—Rockingham County— the present average annual tax for State, county and local purposes, apportioned to each farm producing on an average an annual product of $680.40, is about fifty dollars, or, in-cluding national taxes, direct and indirect, approximately one hundred dollars—causing a continued decrease in the value of all real property, and a steady decline in population ; or that other circumstance, that to-day the future title to no inconsider-able part of the real estate of one entire State—South Carolina —bids fair to be a title derived from the Sheriff for sales in default of ability on the part of the landowners to pay the taxes assessed upon them. Surely, in view of such facts as these, it is a matter worthy the most serious consideration of both Congress and the people, whether there are any circumstances, short of the preservation of the national honor or existence, which can justify the smallest particle of increase in the weight of any existing national burden.

In one respect, it must be admitted that the Federal Gov-ernment would have advantages in constructing telegraph lines not possessed by individuals or incorporated companies ; for it could purchase its wire sixty-two per cent. cheaper at the port of importation; have its poles delivered at twenty per cent. less on the borders ; and be freed from the necessity of paying annual taxes and licenses to the various States and municipal-ities. But what sort of consistency or, to use a stronger word, "decency" is there in a Government justifying, on the grounds of expediency or necessity, the continual imposition and main-tenance of such burdens on its citizens, and then not only refus-ing to be bound by them itself, but even pleading the privilege of such exemption as a good and sufficient reason why it should interfere with the business of such citizens.

There is another point of similar significance in this same connection. Thus, for a period reaching back, at least, to the inception of the war—the one policy which more than almost any other has characterized the Federal Government, has been, that all legislation should be in the direction of maintaining a higher standard for the wages of labor in the United States than is maintained in Europe.

Now, out of the whole amount paid by the Western Union Company during the fiscal year 1872 for operating the telegraph, nearly three fifths were disbursed on account of wages or salaries; which wages or salaries were from two to four times in excess of what are paid for similar services in Europe. Thus, for example, while the London telegraph offices are operated by females, at wages ranging from eight to twenty shillings per week, the wages paid to the fifty female operators in the office of the Western Union Company at New York range from $40 to $65 currency per month, or, in more direct comparison with the wages of the English female operators, from 40 to 66 shillings per week. And what is true in respect to comparative wages in this department of the telegraph is true of every other; and yet the Federal Government now makes this very state of affairs, which all its recent legislation is claimed to have occasioned, the main cause of complaint against the existing Telegraph Companies for not providing cheaper service; and proposes, by absorbing the telegraph and making the postmasters do duty as operators, to further condemn in practice what it still justifies in theory.

THE QUESTION OF GOVERNMENT EFFICIENCY.

Third—But granting that the proposition put forth by the advocates of the absorption of the telegraph by the Government be true, namely, that the people are in present and urgent need of cheaper and greater telegraphic facilities, the question is a most pertinent one, whether the ends sought for are in any degree likely to be attained through the agency of the Government? That increased cheapness is only likely to be reached under Government, through increased taxation, has been already demonstrated; but how about greater efficiency? To this question a full and sufficient answer would seem to be afforded in the past and present record of the business which Government has already monopolized. Take as one illustration the Post-office itself—the department which now proposes to extend its business by absorbing the telegraph. Does not every one know that in point of efficiency, trustworthiness, and attention to the interests of the public, the Post-office in the United States is far inferior to the postal systems of Great Britain, Belgium or Holland? Are there any towns in Great Britain, of from 500 to 1,500 inhabitants, in the midst of a densely populated district, which, like similar towns in New England, have mail facilities limited to three times a week? Is there a case parallel under any of the more highly civilized governments of the world like that which now, and for years past, has existed on the Pacific coast, of a whole community conforming to the strict letter of the law by placing an U. S. postage stamp on their more valuable letters, and then, at eight times additional cost, confiding the same letters to a private express company for transmission and delivery? What a commentary on the honesty of its officials, and the integrity of its civil service, does the Post-office Department itself confess when it authorizes everywhere the publication of the following notice: *"Valuable letters should invariably be taken to the Post-office and registered. The registry fee to all parts of the United States is 15 cents"* postage in addition.

Postage at one penny, and the abolition of the franking privilege, became established facts in Great Britain as far back as 1840; but it was not until 1863, or twenty-three years subsequent, that the Post-office Department of the United States could see its way clear to the adoption of a uniform rate of *three* cents on every half ounce letter to all portions of its territory. During the session of Congress which adjourned in May, 1872, the use of the so-called " postal cards"—a roundabout device for effecting a reduction of postage without meeting the question manfully, and withal equivalent to saying to the people of the United States, " If you will write your letters so that the Post-office officials may read them, the postage shall be one cent, but if otherwise, three"—was authorized by Congress; and yet up to the present writing, December, 1872, the public have derived no benefit from the authorization; and simply for the reason that the experts of the Post-office Department, after a year or more deliberation on the subject, forgot to have the bill accompanied with the essential provision of an appropriation necessary to put the device into operation.

And what is true of the business of the Post-office is true of the business of almost every other department of Government; the appraisement of goods liable to customs duties, the system of entries and withdrawals, of storage in bond, the inspection of vessels, the collection of customs revenue—in all of which the administration of imperfect, and what in most countries are obsolete laws, seems always in the direction of needless obstruction and expense to the business interests of the community, and rarely, if ever, in the direction of economy and convenience; added to all of which is a tacitly recognized system of adjudication between citizens and the several executive departments of the Government, which in all questions of doubt uniformly applies the benefit of the doubt to the Government, and rarely, if ever, to the individual.

In short, were any individual or corporation to undertake to do business in the same dilatory, expensive and vexatious method as the Government of the United States to-day discharges all of its functions having relation to the production, distribution and consumption of the country, their existence, so far as public patronage was concerned, would be exceedingly limited ; and yet it is under just such circumstances that the public are asked to seriously consider the expediency of transferring the entire telegraph system of the country to an agency whose present business capacity is utterly inadequate to the proper discharge of its present business responsibilities.

UNRELIABILITY OF THE GOVERNMENT ESTIMATES.

It is certain, furthermore, that if any additional evidence was needed in support of these conclusions there could be no better field to search for it than in the several reports which have been made in favor of the Government theory of the telegraph, since its original conception in this country and first presentation to the public; for no one can candidly examine these reports, from the one made by Hon. B. Gratz Brown, in 1865, down to the last by the present Postmaster-General, without being most painfully impressed with a conviction that the Government is being urged to take action upon a most important, financial,

33

political and social question, in respect to which its advisers
have only the most indefinite and inadequate information.
Thus, in 1865, Mr. Gratz Brown advised *three cents* per message,
for all distances throughout the United States, as the proper
tariff to be adopted by the Government in the operation of the
telegraph. In 1868, Mr. E. B. Washburne proposed *one* cent
per word, exclusive of date, address and signature, with *three*
cents for postage, and two cents for delivery of each message.
In 1870, Mr. C. C. Washburn was confident, " from a calculation'
based on reliable estimates," that a tariff of from twenty to
twenty-five cents per message, inclusive of date, address and
signature, would afford the Government a small profit. In
April, 1872, Mr. R. B. Lines, of the Post-office Department,
in advocating the theory of Government ownership before
the House Committee on Appropriations, expressed an opinion
that " no reduction at all should be made until the lines had been
in possession of the Government for, at least, a year," and that
then discretion should be " left to the Postmaster-General to
regulate the rates within certain limits, according to the course
of business as shown by the books of the Department." And
now, in December, 1872, comes the Postmaster-General himself
with a proposition to make the rates at the outset thirty-three
cents on all twenty-five word messages within the United
States, and " after the lines have been renovated," thirty cents.
It is also to be noted that Mr. Hubbard, who first proposed
25 cents under his system, for a circuit of 500 miles, now
thinks 25 cents for a circuit of 250 miles a more prudent
assumption. Now, it should not be overlooked that each of
these gentlemen has assumed to speak with authority derived from careful investigation, and that all have pro-
fessed confidence, based on "reliable estimates," that if
the Government should adopt the rates by them recommended, the realization of a profit on the business transacted would be reasonably certain. It is clear, therefore,
that somebody has blundered; but as the blunders involve
losses of only a few millions, and that to the National Treasury,
the matter may be passed over in these days of large taxes and
corresponding expenditures as of comparatively little consequence.

3

Coming next to the report of the Postmaster-General for December, 1872, we find that while he has found sufficient room to present to the American public extensive tables of European telegraphic statistics, he has not been able to afford space in the same report for the statistics of the last year's business of the largest company in the United States, which were furnished promptly and in detail to him on application. He has, however, furnished a table, professing to exhibit the condition of the telegraph systems of the United States and Europe, of which the following is a partial analysis:

Under the head of Great Britain will be found the following: *"Complete returns for previous years not having been received, the estimates of the British Post-office for the year ending March 31st, 1873, are used instead;"* and this in the face of the fact that complete returns of the British Government system for the first fourteen months of its existence were officially published in the summer of 1871, and have ever since been readily accessible.

Throughout the whole of this table, moreover, there runs the mistake of adopting one standard of comparison for stating the telegraph business of Europe, and another and different one for stating the telegraph business of the United States. Thus, while in the United States a message is only counted once, whether it is transmitted one hundred or one thousand miles, it is counted in Europe over and over again, in each petty State through which it is transmitted. In this manner the apparent number of messages in Europe is greatly increased above the number actually transmitted; and by not recognizing this fact the tables of the Postmaster-General are made to present statements that, to say the least, will not sustain investigation. Thus, for example, the average receipt for messages in Bavaria, for 1870, is stated by the Postmaster-General to be sixteen cents; but the official report of Bavaria for that same year gives the following figures: Internal messages, 295,170; international, 197,016; total, 492,186. The receipts being $162,243, the average per message of every kind was, therefore, not 16, but $32\frac{9}{10}$. But by including in the aggregate 219,992 received messages, 212,067 transit messages, and 85,920 free messages, the Postmaster-General's table swells the total number of messages to

1,010,176, and thus reduces the average from thirty-two to sixteen cents.

In Baden, according to Mr. Creswell's table, there were transmitted, in 1870, 629,201 messages for $85,008, being an average of thirteen cents per message ; while the actual number of messages sent in that country, exclusive of Government messages, was 337,442 ; and had Mr. Creswell had before him the " *Tariff Général des Correspondances Télégraphiques*," published at Berne in 1869, by the Convention Télégraphique International—and without which important table his means of information must have been singularly deficient—he would have read that the lowest price at which an internal message can be sent within the small State of Baden is eighteen kreutzers for ten words; or at the rate of 24.4 cents for twenty words, while for International messages another and still higher rate is adopted.

In Italy, also, according to the Postmaster-General's table, there were transmitted, in 1870, 2,378,119 messages, upon which the tolls amounted to $945,234, making an average rate per message, as stated in the table, of thirty-two cents; but which, according to the ordinary rules of arithmetic, should give thirty-nine and eight-tenths cents per message.

The main object of the Postmaster-General, in common with all the other advocates of the proposed plan of Government absorption, is to show that the rates for telegraphic correspondence in the United States are, as compared with those of Europe, extremely and unnecessarily high ; but they either omit or fail to give prominence to two circumstances, which are absolutely essential to the determination of any correct conclusions. The first of these is, "that while there are in the United States but one kind of messages, there are in Europe three classes, called, respectively, internal, international and transit. The internal messages are those which are transmitted, received and delivered in the same country. The international messages are those which are transmitted from one country into another. The transit messages are those which are neither sent nor received in the country in which they are reckoned, but are simply shot through it in going from one State to another. In this way small States like Bavaria, Belgium, Baden, etc., which really send but a small number of messages, are able to show an apparently large annual traffic. Countries so situated in Europe, as a rule, have adopted a low rate of charges for their internal messages, the deficit being made up by a tax upon international and transit messages paid by surrounding States. Thus, for example, Belgium charges a minimum rate of half a franc for the transmission, receipt and delivery of a message within her own territory, while she imposes double rates upon both international and transit messages, one class of which requires only one half the service of an internal message—being simply either sent or received from or into the country—and the other class requiring no service at all, being simply sent through the air on its way from one neighboring State to another. The case would be analogous to that of one of our States which should set up an independent telegraph system of her own, and should charge a low rate for the transmission of messages within her own territory, and impose a heavy tax upon messages passing through her territory between the other States of the Union. Suppose the State of New Jersey, for example, was to establish an independent telegraph system, and fix the rates for messages passing within her own territory at the Belgian rate of ten cents, and then charge twenty cents for every message passing through her territory. The result would be very favorable to the finances of New Jersey, as the tax upon the correspondence between New York and Washington alone would more than pay the entire cost of her own system."

The second circumstance, to which the advocates of the Government theory fail to give prominence, is the difference in the relative cost of the telegraphic systems of Europe and the United States—a difference which may be succinctly expressed by saying that, as a general thing, owing to distances in the density of population and area of geographical occupation, it requires the construction of ten miles of wire in the United States to one in Europe to do the same business, and that the cost of everything in the United States, in the way of telegraphic construction and operation, is on an average, full fifty per cent. greater than in Europe. How entirely, however, the Postmaster-General puts a different complexion on this last proposition is evidenced by the statement of his tables, that while the cost of constructing each mile of telegraph line in the United States is $120, and of each mile of wire $80, the cost in Great

Britain is $164 for each mile of line, and $41.22 for each mile of wire.*

To show now the unreliability of all this, it is only necessary to call to mind that the greater portion of the telegraph wire used in the United States is made in England, and that England is to-day the cheapest place in the world in which wire can be purchased—the relative cost of No. 8 "*extra best best*" galvanized iron wire being at present 5½ cents *gold* in Manchester, and 10½ cents *currency* in New York; and, also, that not a little of the wire now in use in the United States, erected during the war, has cost, from causes over which the telegraph companies could have no control, as much as twenty cents per pound; and that if the United States Government were now to construct new lines, it would find that the simple conveyance of the wire to not a few localities would require an expenditure equal, or more than equal, to what the wire originally cost at the port of importation. The impossibility of instituting a fair comparison —such as Mr. Creswell attempts—between the cost of telegraphic lines in Europe and the United States, is further shown by the fact that while the sizes of telegraph wire used in the United States are of 6, 7, 8 and 9 gauge (none being employed smaller than the latter), the wire used very largely in Europe is of No. 11 gauge, weighing but one half as much as No. 8, and costing proportionately less. No. 6 wire, of which there is a considerable amount used in this country, weighs 550 pounds per mile, and costs $57.75 per mile, delivered in the city of New York. No. 8 wire weighs, in round numbers, 400 pounds per mile, and, at 10½ cents per pound, costs $42 per mile. No. 9, the smallest wire used in this country for telegraph lines, weighs 340 pounds per mile, and costs, at the place of importation, $35.70 per mile. It is, therefore, somewhat difficult to see how it is that Mr. Creswell is able to state that wire costing from $35.70 to $57.75 per mile at the place of importation, can be transported all over this broad continent, and erected along the lines of the railway and post roads, at an average cost of $30

* In a note at the bottom of the Postmaster-General's tables it is stated that the cost of the lines and apparatus of the English lines ($164) is "estimated at the average of Continental lines;" but if reference is made to the estimated cost of Continental lines in the same table, the sum given will be found to be $170.72, and not $164.

per mile, to say nothing of the insulators, cross-arms and other appurtenances necessary to its maintenance and operation.*

In the United States, according to Mr. Creswell's tables, the whole number of messages transmitted by all the telegraph companies doing business in 1872 was 13,700,000, (including nearly 2,000,000 press messages), for which the receipts were $9,590,000, or at an average of 70 cents per message. But in the statistics furnished to the Postmaster-General by the Western Union Telegraph Company (but not published) it was shown that this single company transmitted in 1872 10,933,318 messages, exclusive of press and weather reports, for which was received $7,040,803.53, less $220,395.75 refunded to other lines and uncollectable; or, $6,820,407.76, being an average of 62 cents per message; and for the transmission of 1,512,361 estimated press messages, $979,088.71, making a total of 14,444,100 messages, and $7,799,-

---

* The following analysis of the Postmaster-General's estimate of the past and prospective cost of the telegraph system of the country is copied from the *Journal of the Telegraph:*

"The majority of lines in this country," says Mr. Creswell, "have been built very cheaply; their entire cost, including patents, being probably much less than $10,000,000. Data in possession of this Department show that many lines have been lately built, probably not of the best quality, but fully up to the average standard, for not more than $115 per mile of single wire line, and $30 per mile of additional wire. For equipment an allowance of $5 per mile is ample. Were all the wires to be strung at the same time, as they would be were the present system to be duplicated by the Government, the cost would probably be much less. The cost of a new system, equal in extent to the present, would, at the above rates, be $11,880,000."

The extent of the system which Mr. Creswell states could be reproduced at a cost of $11,880,000 embraces about 80,000 miles of line and 200,000 miles of wire.

The only estimate accompanying the Postmaster-General's Report, going to show the cost of constructing a similar system in the United States, is one furnished by Mr. Charles T. Chester, of this city. In this estimate Mr. Chester gives the cost of constructing 75,000 miles of line and 175,000 miles of wire, including equipments, at $18,253,625; *provided the wire is imported free of duty.* This estimate, which, by the way, *is not footed in Mr. Creswell's report,* does not include cables for river crossings, of which the Western Union Company, alone, has in operation 234½ miles.

Mr. Chester has achieved some notoriety as the manufacturer of a certain style of telegraphic apparatus, but, we believe, has never had any experience in constructing telegraph lines, with the single exception of the fire alarm telegraph of the City of New York. This system is embraced in the following inventory, for which we are indebted to the President of the New York Fire Department:

INVENTORY OF LINES AND APPARATUS BELONGING TO THE NEW YORK FIRE DEPARTMENT.

625 Miles of wire.
2,650 Telegraph poles.
2,500 Feet of submarine cable.
549 Street boxes.
84 Gongs.

491.49 in telegraph receipts. Now, deducting the messages sent
by the Western Union Company from the total number stated in
Mr. Creswell's table as having been sent by all the companies in
the United States, and deducting also the telegraph receipts of this
company from the total telegraph receipts of all the lines, we have
the following most curious and remarkable result, namely: that
the several lines in the United States, in opposition to the Western
Union, sent during the year but 1,255,501 messages (of which
nearly 500,000 were press messages), for which they received
$1,790,508.51, being an average of $1.42 per message. But
as the various opposition lines extend mainly over short routes,
where competition is supposed to have reduced the rates to a
minimum, the value and logical correctness of Mr. Creswell's
exhibit become sufficiently evident.

The disingenuousness of the Postmaster-General in discussing

16 Dials.
41 Keys and bells.
1,189 Cells of battery.
1 Recording register.
2 Repeaters.
2 Switch boards.
1 Testing instrument.
1 Wheatstone's measuring instrument.
60 Galvanometers.
175 Lightning arresters.
61 Morse relays.
61 Morse keys.
2 Police dials.
9 Sets (Morse key, relay and bell).

For the construction and equipment of the above system Mr. Chester rendered a
bill against the City of New York, as we are officially informed at the Comptroller's
office, of $850,000.
Now, if 625 miles of telegraph wire costs $850,000, then 175,000 miles would
cost $238,000,000.
625 : 850,000 :: 175,000 : 238,000,000.
If, however, we suppose that the estimate which Mr. Chester has rendered to the
Postmaster-General is a correct one, and that 175,000 miles of telegraph wire costs
but $18,253,625, then 625 miles would cost only $65,187.
175,000 : 18,253,625 :: 625 : 65,187.
In Mr. Chester's estimate for constructing Government lines, which he proposes
to erect for $104.30 per mile of wire, he includes 75,000 miles of poles, averaging
33 per mile, and making a total of 2,475,000 poles. In the line which he constructed for the City of New York, for which he charged $1,360 per mile of wire,
he used only 80 miles of poles, averaging 33 per mile, or a total of 2,650 poles.
For the Government line the estimate embraces an average of 14 poles per mile
of wire, and the average cost of the line per mile of poles is $243.38.
The line constructed for the City of New York, however, averages but a fraction
over two poles per mile of wire, and the bill rendered for it is at the rate of
$10,625 per mile of poles. On this basis the cost of constructing 75,000 miles of
line would be $796,875,000.
We leave the Postmaster-General and Mr. Chester to settle the discrepancy
between the two estimates.

this whole subject is also shown in the manner in which he refers
to a recent communication made to the Postmaster-General of
Canada, by the President of the Montreal Telegraph Company,
in reference to the recent adoption in the " Dominion of Canada"
of a uniform tariff of " 25 cents for ten words, and one cent for
each subsequent word, irrespective of place or distance"—a rate
which at first glance seems to be very low, but which on twenty-
five words, the proposed standard of the United States Government, would be 40 cents. From this Mr Creswell, as will be
seen by reference to page 32 of his report, quotes in his argument only so much as passes for an endorsement of the views
which he desires may be accepted by Congress and the country,
and omits the following of much greater significance : "It will
be necessary for you, however, to remind the Postmaster-General
of the United States that though this system has been entirely
successful here, it could scarcely be put in operation in the
United States, except under the control of the general Government, owing to the onerous charges to which the business there
is subject. Telegraph wire and all other material used in telegraphing are admitted into Canada free of duty, but are subject
in the United States to heavy duties, averaging probably 60 to
70 per cent. The expenses of living being greater in the United
States than in Canada, salaries are necessarily higher. Taxation
is also more burdensome, and every article in use is dearer. It
is true that against this must be placed the more dense and probably more active population of the United States, and the larger
amount of business transacted ; but the distances are so great
that I doubt if a uniform 25 cent tariff (' i. e., for 10 words, or 40
cents for 25 words') all over the country would maintain the
business in an efficient manner at present."

In a subsequent paragraph the writer expresses an opinion
that the Canada rate—i. e., 40 cents for 25 words—may, in the
course of a few years in the United States, through an increase
of business, "become self-supporting ;" but if this should be the
case, is it not altogether probable, in view of the very great reductions made by the Western Union since 1866, that such a
result will be attained equally soon, if not sooner, by this
company than by a Government Department, which could
not see its way to a uniform rate of postage until Great Britain
had for more than twenty years furnished an example, and

which even now expends, in the city of New Orleans, *five* cents in the delivery of each single letter, which may be carried from any point in the United States to that city for the sum of three cents.

One other matter made much of by the Postmaster-General in his report may also be appropriately noticed in this connection, namely—the alleged " enormous and dangerous" abuse of the " free message business." If the Postmaster-General had taken the trouble to inquire, instead of trusting hearsay and rumor, he would have found that for the last fiscal year the whole number of free messages transmitted over the wires of the Western Union, would, if paid for at regular rates, have returned the sum of $750,000. Such a result on its face is unquestionably somewhat startling; but its importance vanishes in view of the further statement, demonstrable from the books of the company, that out of this large aggregate, full 70 per cent. was on account of messages transmitted for railroad companies, from whom the telegraph was receiving an equivalent service in the way of maintenance and repair of its lines; and that of the remaining *thirty* per cent. a very large proportion was in the nature of compensation to hotels, express companies, &c., for the rent of offices or accommodations afforded the company.

The statement, therefore, made at the commencement of this review, that the Government was undertaking to deal with a subject of great financial, political and social importance, without being in possession of either accurate or adequate information, is abundantly confirmed by the evidence which has been cited.

TELEGRAPH OWNERSHIP BY THE FEDERAL GOVERNMENT INCON-
SISTENT WITH THE THEORY AND MAINTENANCE OF RE-
PUBLICAN INSTITUTIONS.

But a more important and conclusive argument against the absorption and control of the telegraph by the Government is to be found in the fact, that the adoption of such a policy is in direct antagonism with and destructive of the fundamental principles upon which the Government itself has been established. We are a nation of forty millions, made up of individuals representing almost every nationality and human variety, and increasing at such a ratio as will give us at the close of the present century, or within a period of thirty years, a population approximating a hundred millions. The area of country inhabited embraces extremes of over 2,500 miles in direct distance; while the diversity of character and interest, among the people of the different sections, growing out of differences of soil climate, pursuits and education is even greater comparatively than the distances by which they are separated. Language excepted, the different States of Europe do not differ so much among themselves as New York differs to-day from Texas, or South Carolina from California. The problem of greatest moment, therefore, presented to us as a nation, is to harmonize these varied and conflicting interests, and to unite them all under one firm and stable Government. The solution of a similar problem has been essayed before—in Old Rome and in modern Austria and Russia—under conditions of the most centralized imperialism; but its attempt under a republic with universal suffrage and with no standing army is something for which, apart from our own experience, there has been no precedent for success. Whether those who framed our Constitution were men of superior wisdom, and clearly foresaw the conditions under which their work was to be tested, is a matter which is here unnecessary to discuss ; but that they originated or adopted the only theory under which, through recognition, our past success has been mainly dependent, seems certain ; and that was, that while it is the essential feature of every imperial and centralized government to think for, act for, and, as far as possible, direct the pursuits and even the creeds and amusements of the people, it is, on the contrary, the essence of a republic, composed of a union of separate independent States, to concern itself as little as possible with the internal affairs of the nation, and to do nothing whatever for the people which the people are willing or capable of doing for themselves. And if this theory be correct, the conclusion is irresistible, that a measure like the one contemplated, of absorbing and operating the telegraph by the Government, is a step away from republicanism and towards imperialism, to be especially resisted by all those who believe that whatever there is of danger threatening the vitality of our institutions is due mainly to the tendency of the Federal Government to enlarge the sphere of its functions, and to exercise powers that were originally never intrusted to it.

43

INCREASE OF FEDERAL PATRONAGE. .

The increase of Federal patronage incident to the adoption of the measure under consideration constitutes a further most striking illustration in the same direction. The number of officers and agents, other than soldiers and sailors, and employés in Government workshops, who are at present in direct receipt of compensation for services from the National Treasury is estimated at upwards of sixty thousand—the number engaged in the Post-office Department alone being 44,655 ; all of whom, and as many others as by reason of social relations have a community of interest, together with all such as under our system of " rotation in office " are expectants of office, may, as all experience shows, be relied on to support any policy or any nomination which any administration controlling their official existence may favor under the plea of public utility or necessity. Of this the story of the " Plebecite" in France; the subserviency of all Federal officials prior to the rebellion to the interests of slavery, and the experience of all our recent presidential elections, are in themselves sufficient of illustration and evidence.

Under such circumstances it is now proposed to augment the number of recipients of Federal patronage according to the following approximative estimate.

The number of persons at present in the exclusive service of the Western Union and other telegraph companies, in the capacity of operators, clerks, messengers, superintendents, contractors and repairers, is over 10,000—a number much smaller than it would be, were there not such a coöperation of service and proprietorship between the leading lines of railway and the telegraph as admits of the employment of railroad officials by the latter, at little or no expense, as operators or repairers. But under the proposed Federal system all of this economy of copartnership must disappear, for, as a recent report of the Post-office Committee of the House of Representatives has it, " the functions of the Government are exclusive, and whenever it formally undertakes any service, as proper to be exercised by it, private parties must necessarily be excluded from the performance of the same service."

Again, an essential feature of the Government scheme is, that the Post-office Department shall, as soon as practicable, establish a telegraph office at every post-office in the United States, the gross receipts of which are not less than $100 per annum, to be accompanied by a free delivery by carriers of all messages within a circuit two miles in diameter; which free delivery, in the case of letters, now pertains to less than one hundred offices in the whole country. The number of post-offices whose annual receipts are of the amount above specified is at present about 12,000; and as it is not unreasonable to estimate that if the *average* number of Federal telegraphic employés, at the outset, was not two to each office—an operator and a messenger—it would not be long before at least that number would be regarded as the lowest standard of Governmental necessity.

That, in the course of time, the office of postmaster and telegraph operator would, in many small towns, come to be filled by one and the same person, thus reducing the number of additional employés in such places to a messenger and occasional repairer, is not unlikely; but that, in view of the pressure incident to American politics to create and maintain offices for political reasons, any such practice is likely to become general, is something altogether improbable; and, as showing further how unmistakably the drift of political management is at present in respect to such matters, the following incident may be related: During the past summer an application was made to one of the bureaus of the Government, having in charge a branch of manufacturing, to purchase and introduce a new labor-saving machine, which private enterprise was everywhere adopting. The proposition was declined for the very same reason that it was made—namely, that it would occasion a reduction in the number of those receiving employment, the officer in charge adding that the policy forced upon him was to employ as many, and not as few men as possible, and that any deviation from it would occasion him annoyance, and possibly a forfeiture of his situation.

It will also readily suggest itself that whatever is likely to be gained from the employment of postmasters in small towns as telegraph operators, is likely to be far more than compensated by the very great increase of force necessary to meet the requirements contingent on the expected increase of business under Government rates and management. This increase the Postmaster-General thinks would, after one year, be from 13,700,000

messages (the present estimate) to 30,000,000 ; Mr. Washburn
and others say 40,000,000 ; while the experience of the Western
Union shows that for every additional 400 messages per day
passing between any two points there must be an additional
wire, and an entire new set of operators and messengers.*

It is, therefore, altogether reasonable to assume that, if the
Post-office Department takes possession of and directs the telegraph service of the country in the manner proposed, the number of additional offices which will at once, or in a short time,
be added to the roll of Federal patronage will equal or exceed
25,000.† And if the theory of the Government be correct, that
the people need the telegraph, and that it is essential to civilization and the spread of intelligence that they should everywhere
enjoy its use cheaply, there can be no good reason assigned
why it should not be made co-extensive with the Post-office;

* The largest business ever done in one day at the general office of the Western
Union Company in the City of New York was on November 11th, 1872, when
21,132 messages and 95,490 words of press matter were sent and received.
Estimating the latter at 30 words per message, the aggregate would represent a
total of 24,315 messages.

Sixty-two wires were employed in doing this work—six of them being doubled by
the use of Stearns' Duplex Telegraph, making an average of 392 messages per wire.
The wires were all worked to their full capacity until very late at night, and many
of them all night. The weather was fine and the lines in excellent order, so that
the work done may be regarded as practically exhibiting the maximum capacity
of the wires under the most favorable conditions.

† " The supposed economy of uniting the two services will probably be found in
practice in a large measure delusive. A few clerks and letter-carriers in the Post-
office may be able to take upon themselves additional duties, but, as a general rule,
it will be found in this, as in other cases, that any additional work requires additional workmen. A clerk cannot be assorting the mails and receiving telegrams
at the same time: the two functions will unavoidably interfere with each other.
Neither can much economy be effected in the matter of rents."—*Report of
Committee on Post-offices and Post-roads, House of Representatives*, 1869.

Mr. Palmer, of the Select Committee of the House of Representatives, in a
report made July, 1870, estimated that the number of additional employés which
would be required by the Government to manage the telegraph at from 20,000 to
25,000. Mr. Beck, of the Committee on Ways and Means,* in January, 1872, reported to the House, as the result of his investigations, that he was satisfied " it would
require not less than 25,000 additional Government officials to manage and control
the telegraph system of the United States under the bill of General Washburn,
and the number would increase every year."

* Beck was on Washburn's Special Committee.

or why a post-office district whose annual receipts are $100 should have a wire and an operator, and another contiguous district, whose receipts are only a little less, should be deprived of similar privileges. The plea that *one* office would be remunerative and the other would not could not be consistently offered, for in neither case would the receipts from business be likely to defray more than a fraction of the expenditures; and the fundamental idea, moreover, with which the Government enters upon its scheme is, that necessities, and not expenditures, are to have the prime consideration. The scheme of telegraphic ownership once entered upon, the logic of the case, and the desire of every member of Congress to please his constituents, would therefore soon lead to the extension of the wires to every post-office, except the very smallest, and consequently augment the number of new officials very far beyond the number already indicated.

Does it not also occur to the Postmaster-General and others, who with him are so strenuous for the Government appropriation of the telegraph, that every argument they can bring forward in support of their pleaded necessity, namely, protection against corporate monopolies, the urgency of cheaper service, the requirements of the State in time of war, can be made to justify equally the Government appropriation of the business of the railroad and express. Nay, more, do we not find that in Continental Europe, whose experience in respect to the telegraph is commended to us for imitation, that the railroad and express, equally with the telegraph, have passed under the control or ownership of the Government, and that the reasons which have influenced to such action in the one case have been regarded as equally applicable to the others. In 1869 the Government of Great Britain took possession of the telegraph, and, as a sequence of such policy, a Committee of Parliament, within a very recent period, have reported in favor of a similar ownership by the Government of all the railways of the United Kingdom.

THE EXTENT OF GOVERNMENT INTERFERENCE INVOLVED IN TELEGRAPH OWNERSHIP.

But there are other aspects of the case which, when subjected to examination, would seem to still less commend themselves to the approbation of the public.

The proposed Governmental system, as has already been pointed out, makes all other telegraph competition unlawful, and prescribes punishment by a fine for every offense of transmitting or receiving messages without official permission. Now, when we consider that within the circles of population and business which employ the telegraph, its use is daily becoming more common and familiar; that besides the public offices for the transmission of messages from town to town and from city to city, the telegraphic instrument has become the indispensable adjunct of every police station, fire-alarm, stock and produce exchange, and underwriters' agency for the reporting and relief of vessels; that in the free hand of railway officials it regulates the movement of every train, and in those of merchants and manufacturers it communicates between office of sale and places of production; that it is already sold as a toy for children to play with it, and that the improvements of every year tend more and more to simplify and extend its operation and agency, does it not become obvious that the proposed Government control of such an instrumentality embraces a great many more interests than those represented by the Post-office? and further, that to keep that control exclusive will require a system of law and espionage so foreign to our people that practically it can never be executed? Indeed, it is much the same thing as if the Government, for the reason that it desired to use the power of steam for the exclusive transmission of the mails, should make its use for all other purposes a matter subject to official permission. It is possible that no injury might actually result therefrom to the business of the country, but it is certain that such a system would engender complications and a spirit entirely foreign to the atmosphere of this last half of the nineteenth century. As a more specific illustration to the same effect, take the so-called "gold and stock" telegraph of the city of New York. Here is a system by which upwards of 1,000 separate offices receive uninterrupted messages during business hours relative to prices and sales, the telegraph company furnishing the operators and the instruments, and the officers of the "Stock Exchange" the information. The Government, however, under the new system, would furnish both the information and the instrumentality, interpose its official representative into the center of the financial market, and make

the character and quality of the information transmitted dependent on other considerations than the business interest immediately interested. If it be said that in Europe, where the telegraph is a Government monopoly, none of these complications
and embarrassments to business have been experienced, it may
be replied that in London the first effect of the Government
possession of the wires was to break up the use of the
telegraph by the Stock Exchange; and that, furthermore,
nowhere in Europe, and not even in London, is there any such
use made of the telegraph as has come to prevail in the United
States.

A GOVERNMENT SYSTEM OF TELEGRAPH PROVOCATIVE OF ES-
PIONAGE AND INTERFERENCE WITH THE RIGHTS OF
CITIZENS.

The probability if not necessity, of a system of espionage, in
order to make the proposed exclusive control of the telegraph by
the Government effective, has been touched upon ; but the subject is too important to be dismissed with an allusion. Necessarily the possession of the telegraph brings those who manage and
operate it into very close connection with the finances, the commerce, the press, the politics and the social relations of the
country. Under the present system the pecuniary interests of
the companies imperatively restrain them from favoring any
party or interest. In addition to this there is always the im-
pending peril and threat of heavy money penalties, recoverable
at law, for any breach of trust or neglect of duty ; and how
often judgment is rendered for errors acknowledged by the
complainants to be unintentional the records of the courts abundantly testify. How honorably, furthermore, the existing companies have discharged their trust to the public is proved by
the circumstance that, among all the reasons advanced for a
change of system, "breach of faith" has not been specifically
cited in a single instance. A Governmental system, on the
contrary, which, as in the Post-office, will assume no responsibility for the dishonesty, incompetence and mistakes of its
agents, and one, moreover, in which its agents know that their
station and salary, if not their permanence in office, is more
dependant on the favor of superiors than on good behavior, can

but be provocative of carelessness and indifference. Differing from communications by mail, there can be no secrets, except through the use of ciphers, to those who operate the telegraph, and when responsibility is lessened the temptation to violate privacy will most assuredly be increased. Are the American people ready to accept the idea that all that passes over the wires, both at the time of transmission and ever thereafter, is liable to be inspected and used by the changing officials who may fill the departments at Washington—for a paragraph in the Government bill reads: "*that the originals of all messages shall be transmitted to Washington, to be preserved for reference?*" Are the public willing to place further facilities in the way of the exercise of the prerogative already claimed to be possessed by committees of Congress, of taking possession and using such re- cords—a claim noways different in principle from the opening and reading of letters intrusted to the Post-office—and for the resistance to which the manliness and integrity of the officers of the existing telegraphs have as yet proved the only effectual ob- stacle ? On the Continent of Europe there is not a government which does not regard the telegraph as an adjunct of the police, and which does not claim and, probably, exercise the power of interfering with the transmission of any message which it may regard as prejudicial to its own interests ; and even in England, liberal as her government is in comparison with those upon the Continent, the right to delay or withhold telegrams for the press has been claimed and exercised by her officials within a very recent period. It should not be forgotten, furthermore, that in the period of anti-slavery agitation the action of United States officials was precisely similar, in respect to the transmis- sion and delivery of the so-called " Abolition Documents" by the mail, and that this action was justified and defended by those who were then in control of the Post-office Department; and also that within the last month we have had the curious spectacle of the Postmaster-General—an American lawyer— asking the Attorney-General of the United States—another lawyer—whether it be permissible for postmasters to open sealed letters, and detain them on suspicion that their contents were made up of something morally objectionable. One is almost tempted to ask whether the official making the inquiry referred to, knows that we are living in the nineteenth century, and that the form of government he helps to administer is a Republic and not a despotism ?

In an exciting political contest, like that which the country has just passed through, can it be doubted that the telegraph, if in possession of the Government, would be used for political purposes—for the perpetuation of its own power, or for the assistance of its friends. And even if this should not be the case, and the Government should keep itself immaculate, the very fact that very great facilities for the use of the telegraph for partizan purposes existed, and that detection was almost impossible, would of itself be provocative of such a distrust as would limit the use of the wires for political correspondence almost exclusively to those in sympathy with the then existing administration.

There is still another point in this connection well worthy of public consideration. Suppose, in the heat and excitement of a national political contest, in which the result was acknowledged to be close and doubtful, a general suspicion should be excited—groundless or otherwise—that the telegraph had been or was likely to be used by an administration for its own political advantage, would not, from that very moment, the utility, nay, even the continuance of the system as a whole, be impaired or totally interrupted ? A fine copper wire, carried from the line down a crack of the telegraph pole to the ground, effectually interrupts the current; trees can fall conveniently in the woods in many different localities ; and although there are instruments which will enable a boy sitting in a central office to determine within a half a mile the location of a break in a line of telegraphic wire stretching over a distance of from two to three hundred miles and upwards, there can be little information got out of such instruments when nothing remains of a circuit but numerous detached fragments. At the outbreak of the war in 1861 it will be remembered that the telegraph and express continued to operate in the hostile districts of the South long after the Post-office had ceased to discharge its functions; and simply because it was understood that the agency in one case was Federal and official, and in the other private and inferentially neutral.

FEDERAL TELEGRAPH OWNERSHIP AND CIVIL SERVICE
REFORM.

" Civil service reform " and the restraint of great "monied
monopolies " are things much talked of late, as among the necessities of our national situation ; but what civil service reform or
any other beneficial reform is to be expected in national affairs,
if the Government is to be invested with the reach of power over
the business, wealth, politics and press of the country, as this
scheme contemplates? Or what the restraining influence on
monopolies, when the Government itself has become the mono-
polist, and has added to the patronage which it now possesses
all that pertains to the corporations which it proposes to digest
and assimilate? Is it too much to affirm that an administration
once in power, with such influences at its control and disposition, could make its tenure of existence commensurate only with
its inclination ?

The true idea of civil service reform—the only one which will
ever prove truly effective—is to be found in carrying out the original theory, that the Federal Government should be restricted to
the most limited sphere of action consistent with its own safety
and existence, and in reducing the patronage at its disposal to the
minimum; and not in first increasing the amount of patronage
and then making rules to prevent abuse in its distribution—a
process very like praying to be led into temptation and to be
delivered at the same time from its influence. And yet, as
showing to how small an extent this idea finds popular acceptance, we have the Postmaster-General of the United States urg-
ing, as one principal reason why the Post-office should absorb the
telegraph, that, if it is not done, the telegraph, under private
management, will absorb the Post-office. The assumption
of the Postmaster-General is in the first place wholly
unwarranted, for all the evidence, both in this country and in
England, is to the effect that correspondence by mail increases
nothwithstanding the increase of telegraphic facilities, and
from the nature of the case necessarily must do so; the Western
Union Company, for example, notwithstanding its unsurpassed
facilities for using the wires, being the greatest single customer
for postage stamps in the United States; and secondly, if the
contrary were true, it does not seem to have occurred to the

Postmaster-General, that to most people who have studied the theory of our Government, and the dangers to which it is exposed, any cause occurring naturally which would relieve the Government from the Post-office, with its six million annual deficit and forty-four thousand officials, would be a thing to be rejoiced over and not one to be deprecated.

THE WESTERN UNION COMPANY AND THE SIGNAL SERVICE BUREAU.

How strong is the tendency on the part of Government officials, disconnected with the business of the country, and not dependent on subserving the interests of the public for their continuance in office, to exercise power in an arbitrary and unwarranted manner, is strikingly exemplified in the course recently pursued by what is known as the " Signal Service Bureau " of the Government. This service, as first projected, was in the nature of a scientific experiment, to which the Western Union Telegraph Company freely lent its resources in the absence of any stipulated compensation, at a time when Congress had not sufficient faith to make an appropriation for the Bureau adequate to its necessities. As a scientific experiment, moreover, notwithstanding its results of interest and value, it mainly still is; and yet one of the chief arguments advanced in support of the Federal ownership of the telegraph (we quote the exact words of an official report) is, that " the interests of the Government demand the entire control of the wires for the proper transmission of the weather reports and other public business;" thus conclusively showing that in the thoughts of Federal officers the old monarchical principle has attained full recognition, namely—that the interests of the rulers are to be considered first, and those of the people last; and also that, in the judgment of these same persons, it is of great deal more importance to send over the country by the telegraph, in extended prolixity, the latest statements of what the weather was yesterday and what the wind is likely to be to-day, taking possession, with inflexible routine, if need be, of the only wire which conflagration, flood or tempest have left serviceable, than that the great movements of commerce, of business and of society, which control prices, determine production and regulate the daily life of the nation, should be allowed to pulsate throughout the whole extent of a continent with the minimum of delay and interruption.* (*For further details of the relations of the Signal Service Bureau to the telegraph, reference is made to the appendix to this report marked C.*)

THE RIGHTS OF STATES UNDER A FEDERAL MONOPOLY OF THE
TELEGRAPH.

Another question of interest sure to grow out of the absorption of the telegraph by the Government would be that of the tenure and conditions under which real property, taken from the several existing telegraph companies, would be held by Federal authority within the territorial limits and sovereignty of the different States in which such property may be located. The 17th clause of the 8th section of the 1st article of the Constitution of the United States provides that Congress shall have power to "*exercise exclusive legislation*" over the seat of Govern-

* As the relations past and present of the Signal Service Bureau with the Western Union Telegraph Company are being used to excite prejudice against the management of the telegraph system of the country by private agencies, attention is here asked to the following succinct statement of the exact facts copied from the *Journal of the Telegraph:*

The Signal Service business was new and peculiar. It required the exclusive occupation of from twenty to thirty of the principal circuits, varying in length from 250 to 2,50) miles, three times in each twenty-four hours, and the dropping of the messages transmitted thereon at each signal station. In addition to the occupation of these important circuits, extending throughout the United States, for the transmission of the weather reports, the Chief Signal Officer represented that it was necessary that he should have at his disposal special circuits between Washington and New York, Washington and Chicago, and Washington and New Orleans. These circuits were required to be connected with the Signal Office at 7.45 A. M., 4.45 P. M., and 11.45 P. M., daily, and at such other times as the Signal Officer should call for them. The Signal Service had been in operation but a short time, however, when it was ascertained that these special circuits were being put to other uses than the correction of errors in reports and other matters connected with their transmission. It was found that they were being taken for purposes of display, as well as for the obtaining of trivial information, such as the hours for the departure of trains, the hiring of operators, the procurement of vaccine matter for the prevention of small-pox, &c., &c., during the most crowded hours of the day, when they were most useful to the public, and, therefore, most valuable to the company.

The authority of the Postmaster-General to fix the telegraphic charges for Government messages, under the Act of 1866, was not denied; but the company did not admit the right of that officer to control its wires, to direct when and how circuits should be made up, and to dictate the routes by which messages should be sent to their destination. Nor did it admit the right of any officer of the Government to order its operators to open their offices at unusual and inconvenient hours in the morning, and to keep them open at night until the permission of some other Government official to close them had been obtained. The position of the

ment, and a "like authority over all places purchased *by the* "*consent of the Legislature of the State in which the same shall be,* "for the erection of forts, magazines, arsenals, dockyards and other needful buildings;" and in accordance with this provision the Federal Government has never, heretofore, except in the exercise of " war powers," assumed ownership or exclusive control over any property within any State, except by a consent of the Legislature of such State, formally sought and given. It is also important to note that the words "*by the consent of the Legislature of the State in which the same shall be,*" were unanimously inserted by the Federal Constitutional Convention on motion of Rufus King, of Massachusetts, and Gouverneur Morris, of Pennsylvania, to obviate an objection raised by Elbridge Gerry, of Massachusetts, that without them the clause would confer a power upon the central Government which might prove perilous to the rightful sovereignty, within their sphere, of the States; and that Mr. Madison, in one of the numbers of the " Federalist," subsequently called attention to the great value of this clause, as a check on the possible encroachment of the Federal Government on the powers of the States.

Now, in all the reports and bills advocating or providing for the absorption of the telegraph by the Government, it seems to be taken for granted that the Federal authorities are to be em-

company upon this point was clearly and unmistakably set forth by the president of the company in the proceedings of the Committee on Appropriations at Washington, March 29, 1872, in the following words, which we quote from the report of that committee:

" I have conceded the right of the United States to require anything to be sent by telegraph to anybody, anywhere within the reach of our wires, and at any time that our offices are accessible for that purpose. I distinctly disclaimed the position that there is anything about the messages of the Signal Service that excludes them from the provisions of the Act of 1866. The Chief Signal Officer may file in the Western Union Telegraph Office any number of messages directing them to be sent to as many stations as, in his judgment, it is necessary for the public service that they should reach; and it is competent for the Postmaster-General to fix a rate to every station in the United States to be applied to that business; but then and there his authority in the premises ceases. I take those messages and—exercising the utmost diligence, and being the best judge as to which wires I shall employ to do the work, and what is the most expeditious route between the initial and the terminal stations, or as to how many of several routes shall together be employed for that purpose—I must deliver these messages at their destinations But that we shall keep an office open all night at some places and open half the night at other places, and shall open one at five o'clock in the morning, and another at six, and another at seven, in order that they may all be in telegraphic communication at the same instant, and that we shall connect the War Department or the Signal Office with our main office, and permit its officers to control our wires, is a right which, with great respect to the Postmaster-General, I deny to have been conferred under this Act."

powered by Congress, not only to abrogate at once all State charters under which all telegraph companies are now organized, but also, and irrespective of State permission, to exercise absolute control and ownership, with a concurrent exemption from all taxation, over all real property at present belonging to existing telegraph companies, and wherever situated. And, if this assumption be correct, it follows that either the Federal Government is, at this time, proposing to itself the alienation and transfer from State jurisdiction of extensive properties in a manner not authorized by the Constitution, contrary to all precedent, and wholly subversive of State sovereignty as heretofore recognized ; or, if the contrary be true, and no such procedure is contemplated, that no system of Government telegraph can practically go into operation without the consent of the several States ; and that the opposition of even one State would be sufficient to prevent the scheme from becoming uniform. And, as appertaining to this matter, attention is here asked to the circumstance that, since the commencement of the present session of Congress, a bill has been introduced into the Senate which proposes to transfer the power of condemning private property for public (" Federal ") uses from the Legislatures of the separate States to the Federal courts, and so relieve the general Government from the humiliating necessity they are now under of asking State authority for leave to appropriate State property.

THE REAL ISSUE INVOLVED IN THE PROPOSITION OF FEDERAL
INTERFERENCE WITH THE TELEGRAPH.

Whether, therefore, under the scheme of Federal interference, direct or indirect, the people are likely to obtain more efficient and cheaper telegraphic facilities; whether it is a necessity for the Signal Service to control exclusively the wires for its own purposes, or whether the interests of any particular company are likely to be injuriously affected, are all alike questions of minor importance; inasmuch as the real question involved, the one before which all others shrink into comparative insignificance, is—Will the people consent to the inauguration of a policy, on the part of the Federal Government, which revives the old Mediæval doctrine of the necessity of State interference with the pursuits and business of the people, and every step in

the carrying out of which is a departure from Republicanism
and an approach towards despotism and monarchy?

THE TELEGRAPH AND THE ASSOCIATED PRESS.

One point more in connection with this review needs to be
noticed, and that is the assertion that the Western Union Telegraph Company, through its alliance with the "Associated
Press," constitutes a monopoly obstructive of newspaper enterprise and the free dissemination of news, and as such ought
to be abated. How entirely unfounded, however, this is will
at once appear from the following statement :

The "Associated Press," in its inception, was an organization
having its headquarters in the City of New York, and composed
of representatives of the then principal newspapers of that city,
for the purpose of combining their respective energies and
diverse facilities for the collection of news. This was many
years ago, and in the days of the infancy of the telegraph. Subsequently, as railroad and telegraph facilities extended, and as
the benefit of coöperation became clearly apparent, a series of
similar organizations were formed—East, South, West, and on
the Pacific *—each one independent, but coöperating in the collecting, exchanging and selling of news. In each case, furthermore, it was a matter of no difficulty in the outset, for any
journal, willing to incur its proportion of expense, to become a
member of one of these organizations ; but afterwards, as the
privilege of membership became valuable, the several organizations, of their own volition, and with a view to their own interests, imposed restrictions on membership.

But with all this the telegraph has no concern, and it is difficult to see how the Government could interfere with the existing order of things in respect to this matter, even if it had as
full control of the wires as the Postmaster-General claims that
it should exercise. The existing telegraph companies, having
in view the amount and regularity of the work to be performed,
and also the interests of the public, contract with the several

---

* At present, beside the "New York Associated Press," there are in existence
the "New England Associated Press;" the "New York State;" the "Western;"
the "Northwestern;" the "Kansas & Missouri;" the "Southern," and the
"California."

organizations of the "Associated Press" to forward their despatches at what may be termed exceedingly low "wholesale prices;" but if any other association or company, being free to organize, should apply for like privileges, there can be no question but that they would be granted. The grievance complained of, therefore, if it really exists, rests upon the "Associated Press," which, naturally enough, are unwilling to share advantages, derived from long establishment in business, with every new comer and rival, and not with the telegraph which conveys their messages, any more than with the railroad, the steamboat or the stage coach, which, in certain cases, takes the place of the telegraph in performing similar service.

As illustrating, furthermore, what the telegraph is, respectively, under a free and a Government system, attention is asked to the fact that if, at the present time, we were to compute all the news matter delivered by the telegraph to the "press," as separately transmitted to each paper, it would comprise an aggregate equal to all the despatches of every kind sent over all the telegraphs of the world, within a given period selected for comparison. When a calculation in respect to this matter was made some years ago, it was shown that for the year 1866 the whole number of messages transmitted in Continental Europe was 12,902,538, for which the gross receipts were $11,597,632.71; but that, during the same year, the total number of messages furnished to the newspapers of the United States (dividing the total of words by twenty, and computing separately for each paper), was 14,725,181, and the gross receipts for the same $521,509. And since this time the amount of "press" matter transmitted by the American telegraphs has greatly increased; the "Western Associated Press" alone taking an average of 10,000 words for each of the 365 nights of the year. As another illustration of the peculiarly American character of the "Associated Press," and of the remarkable results that have flowed from the facilities afforded to it by the telegraph under private management, reference may be made to the statement made before a committee of Congress, in April, 1870, by the President of the Western Union, "that he would undertake to produce an American journal, printed a thousand miles from the Atlantic coast, that should contain more *news* from all parts of the world in a single issue than could be gleaned from the London *Times* in a week." In a report from the H. R. Committee on Appropriations to accompany Mr. Palmer's bill in favor of the "Hubbard telegraph," December, 1872, the increase of "press" messages in Great Britain since the absorption of the telegraph by the Government is brought forward as an argument in favor of a change in the telegraphic service of the United States ; and yet in the same connection it is stated that the whole number of "news" words sent by the Government telegraph, a year after its establishment (or in 1870–'71), for the whole United Kingdom, was not quite 20,000 daily during the session of Parliament, and nearly 15,000 daily during the remainder of the year—a result, in comparison with what the "press" of the United States have for years required of the telegraph, almost too insignificant to be used as an illustration.

If the "Associated Press," therefore, is a monopoly, it is a monopoly in which nearly every reader of newspapers is an indirect participant and shareholder; and for whatever of benefit has resulted from the system, which finds no parallel in Europe, the people of the United States "are indebted to the Government for the one negative quality of letting the 'press' and the telegraph alone."

THE HUBBARD PROPOSITION.

The case of the Government having been thus considered, it remains but to examine the proposition of the so-called "Postal Telegraph," advocated by Mr. Hubbard. But in doing this a singular difficulty is experienced of finding out exactly what the "Hubbard proposition" really is ; for its authors, although professing as far back as 1869 to understand most clearly the nature of their recommendations to Congress, have caused at least five separate and different bills, or bills in the nature of amendments, to be reported—two in the course of a single month (December, 1872), and four in the course of a single year. In general, however, it may be said of them that, in common with the proposition of the Postmaster-General, the interference of the Government in a sphere of business that does not pertain in any degree to the functions or well-ordering of a Republican State, is the thing primarily sought for. But apart from this circumstauce, which alone ought to furnish a sufficient reason for uncompromising opposition on the part of all those who believe in holding the Federal Government strictly to its original basis, the simple, impartial statement of the proposal of Mr. Hubbard would seem of itself to constitute the most unanswerable argument against its endorsement and acceptance that could possibly be presented.

Mr. Hubbard says, in the outset, to the Government, if you will assume all the expenses of the service, other than what depend on the mere operating and maintaining of the wires— namely, offices and their equipments suitable and sufficient for operators, instruments and batteries at all the stations; all clerk, bookkeeper and messenger service; all fuel, lights, stamps, paper* and envelopes; allow us to use the various Post-office facilities we may require; relieve us from all State and local taxes; guarantee *ten* per cent. per annum on all the stock of the company, provided the receipts be sufficient, and give in addition a bonus of *one million* ten per cent. stock for what are pleasantly termed the expenses of "organizing and connecting wires," then the new company will, in turn, contract with the Government to transmit messages for the public at rates somewhat cheaper—"priority dispatches" excepted—than are charged at present. That relieved from such burdens, and endowed with such privileges, Mr. Hubbard and his associates could afford to make good his averment in respect to charges seems not improbable; but that the Western Union and other existing telegraph companies, if endowed with equal privileges, would be willing to guarantee equal or greater reductions in rates may also be taken for granted. Mr. Hubbard, therefore, would seem to be debarred in the outset from claiming that his proposed organization can offer to the Government any more favorable basis for negotiating for the establishment of cheaper rates than would be offered by the organizations already performing service. He, therefore, in reality, asks the Government to take a position which no free government ought ever to allow itself to be placed in—namely, that of deciding between

---

* At the present time the Western Union Company alone requires 500 reams of paper per month of a single description, to meet the consumption of the forms upon which the messages transmitted over its wires are written.

two private parties, representing equally private interests, which one it will favor and which it will crush. Nay, more, he calls upon the Government to go further, and place itself in opposition to those companies and organizations who, when the telegraph business was an experiment, undertook the risk, and extend its favor and bounty to other parties, who, now that success has been won, are willing to enter into the possession and enjoyment of other men's labor. If this be justice, it is of a quality more honored in the breach than in the observance.

It is intimated that the facilities asked of the Government, under Mr. Hubbard's proposition, are of a kind which will not entail much additional expenditure, and that the offices and clerks already required by the Post-office may, to a great extent, be made available for telegraphic purposes; but this plea is almost too specious to require serious consideration. The Government of the United States performs no service except at a much greater expense than would be incurred under similar circumstances by individuals, and all the instincts, precedents and predispositions of those who serve it are in a direction contrary to the practice of economy! If there is, therefore, as is constantly maintained, any real and true intent to put an end to the constantly increasing burden of national expenditures, there must be an inflexible determination on the part of those who control the Government to avoid every new occasion or pretext for expenditure.

Again, the bill of Mr. Hubbard contains a provision which, as has been already shown in discussing the Government proposition, frees the company chartered by it from just that responsibility to the public which it is indispensable should exist to ensure against indifference, breach of trust and neglect; inasmuch as, in making the company an agent of the United States, it gives them the same immunity from the payment of damages which is now possessed by the Post-office in the case of the non-delivery of letters intrusted to the mails. It also frees the company from all risk of defalcation and embezzlement, and transfers the same to the Government through a provision that the Post-office Department is to be the agent to whom, in the first instance, all payments for the transmission of messages are to be made by means of stamps.

It is also interesting to note that this proposed charter of the so-called Postal Telegraph Company, while professing to be in the interests of the great general public, and in opposition to everything like monopoly, in reality, but as it were covertly, provides for the creation of a monopoly of the most offensive and objectionable character ; inasmuch as it authorizes the putting aside of the ordinary messages of the public—whatever may be the pressure of their necessity—and the giving of priority of transmission to such other messages as may be registered and pay double. It seems clear that the effect of this would be to place the wires at all times at the exclusive disposition of those to whom immediate dispatch was an item of greater consideration than expense ; and if, as not unlikely, this should prove to be the case in respect to the majority of business and social messages, then the general result of this provision would be to raise the general average cost of telegraphic communication, and so completely neutralize and defeat the alleged object of the Hubbard proposition. It has, therefore, been not unaptly suggested that the title of the " Postal Telegraph " bill should be so amended as to read, "an act for the increasing of the rates of correspondence by the telegraph."

But a more objectionable feature of the proposed " Postal Telegraph" bill, and one which, whether its authors so intend it or not, gives to the whole scheme the aspect of a device for the direct pecuniary enrichment of those concerned, is the provision for the issue of stock, to the extent of one million of dollars, to defray the expenses of organization and the connection of the lines of the new company with the various postal stations. Now, as there are no provisions in the bill which require the contribution of any money as the basis of the issue of this stock, or which regulate its apportionment; and as the legitimate expenses for organization must be but trifling ; and as the creation of additional stock is expressly authorized to defray the expenses of all lines and wires purchased or constructed, the inference is unavoidable that the million of dollars in question is to be divided among the incorporators or other persons whose services in behalf of the charter may be considered as desirable. And as this special stock is to be entitled to receive dividends out of the receipts by the Government for the transmission of messages, at

the rate of ten per cent. per annum, it follows that its authorization by Congress would be equivalent to imposing a tax, in perpe-
tuity, of $100,000 per annum on the American people using the
telegraph, and all for the exclusive purpose of giving a bonus to
the incorporators named in the bill, as an inducement for them
to engage in a business in which they have now no investment,
and in the conduct of which no experience.

PREPAYMENT BY STAMPS.

It is to be observed that the bill of Mr. Hubbard, and also
that advocated by the Government, provide, as a new and essential feature, for the prepayment of all telegraphic messages ; and
that, too, as in the case of letters, through the agency of stamps.
At first thought these provisions strike one as likely to prove
most effective and desirable ; but a little consideration will reveal
the fallacy contained in them. Thus, a very large proportion of
the messages transmitted by telegraph are in the nature of questions, in respect to which the interest vests exclusively with the
inquirer. A, for example, living in New York, asks B, in Chicago, if he knows whether C is in his city ; if D is good for a
loan, or if E will grant an interview, or speak at a political meeting. If B should be required to pay for his answer, in which he
has little or no interest beyond that growing out of social relations, it is very probable that the question would not be put in
the first instance, and almost certain that the answer would not
be returned in the second. If A agrees to pay for B's answer when
received at the office in Chicago, the New York office must either
give him credit in Chicago or require a deposit in advance for the
unknown cost of B's message when received, and afterwards, by
some complicated system of accounts, establish a clearing between
the office in New York and the office in Chicago. The result
would probably be that a not inconsiderable part of the business
now intrusted to the wires would be done away with, or would
be found to involve an element of cost and trouble which has
not been taken into consideration. And so again in respect to
the use of stamps. In a country of limited extent, as England
or Belgium, where there is one rate per word for all distances,
stamps may be made available ; but in the United States, where,
in addition to the endless variation in the number of words,

messages of the same number of words are to pay differently for
different circuits, and differently by day and by night, the num-.
ber of stamps that would be required and the calculation and
adjustment made necessary, would be a matter of no little expense to the Government and perplexity to the citizen. And
as some indication of what this item of stamp expenditure is
likely to amount to, it may be stated, in the far more limited ·
sphere of the Internal Revenue, the whole number ordered for
that office for the year 1868 was 367,536,332.

RELATION OF THE VOLUME OF TELEGRAPHIC BUSINESS TO THE
AGGREGATE OF TELEGRAPHIC EXPENDITURES.

There is another fallacy involved in the idea of reduced telegraphic tariffs, which the advocates of the "Government" and
"Hubbard" propositions have alike endeavored to make popular, and that is, that the business of the telegraph follows in general the same law as the business of the Post-office ; and that
a reduction of the tariff on telegraph messages to one half, one
third, or, as Mr. Gratz Brown claimed in 1865, to one twentieth
of the present average rates, would be attended with such an
increase of business as to afford the maximum of profits in proportion to the investment.   If this be true, it further follows that
the Government or Mr. Hubbard, in proposing much lower rates
than are now charged, are not only perfectly sure of the basis
on which they propose to operate it, but also that the management of the existing companies is so short sighted and penurious
that it prefers to adopt the one policy which brings with it the
smallest ratio of profit with the minimum of satisfaction to the
public.   Now, that a reduction of rates in telegraphing tends to
stimulate business, and that, under very low tariffs, the increase
in the number of messages offered for transmission is something
enormous, cannot be disputed; but a careful examination of the
telegraphic statistics of different countries, which within a recent
period only have been collected and tabulated, brings to light
this fact, also, that in any large system of lines, after a certain
volume of business has been attained, an increase in the number
of messages is always followed by an increase of expenditures,
which, though not fully proportioned to the increase of business,
still approximates it closely.   That this, furthermore, must be

so, will appear evident, when it is remembered that the business of telegraphing is closely akin to the business of writing letters, and that *" if written letters were paid for by the word, increase of correspondence would not materially reduce their cost."* Thus, for example, in operating the telegraph, each message must be first booked and accounted for; then, in transmitting, it must be spelt out letter by letter, and so, to all intents and purposes, be rewritten, and then rewritten a third time by the operator who receives it. During the time of its transmission it monopolizes the use of one wire and the labor of the operators who work it, and afterwards of the clerk who records the despatch and the messenger who delivers it. On the other hand, in ordinary business, it need require no more time to sell a large bill of goods than a small one, or to record the sale and collect the payment in the one case than in the other; and, in like manner, a locomotive or a ship which can transport one hundred passengers, or one ton of mail bags, can generally, without any material increase of expense, perform double the work if found necessary. If there were, therefore, no statistical information whatever available concerning the peculiar work of the telegraph, it would be only a common sense inference that the benefit resulting from a great quantity of operations must be less in telegraphy than in almost any other industry.

But exact statistics on this subject are, as already stated, not wanting; and an examination of those of almost every country in Europe shows that the recent great increase in the business of the telegraph there experienced, which the advocates of the " Government " and " Hubbard " propositions like to dwell upon as the result to be especially sought for in the United States, has only been attained through the adoption of rates so utterly destructive of profit that only Governments which can readily resort to taxation to make up a deficit can afford, under such circumstances, to own and manage a telegraph. Thus, for example, a comparison of the telegraphic statistics of North Germany, Bavaria, Belgium, Holland and Denmark, for the years 1865 and 1870, affords the following striking and instructive results :

NORTH GERMANY.—Increase in the number of messages, 259 per cent.; increase of receipts, 76 per cent. ; increase of expenditures, 83 per cent.

BAVARIA.—Increase of messages, 63 per cent. ; increase of receipts, 17 per cent. ; increase of expenditures, 149 per cent.

BELGIUM.—Increase of messages, 252 per cent. ; increase of receipts, 79 per cent. ; increase of expenditures, 61 per cent.

HOLLAND.—Increase of messages, 142 per cent. ; increase of receipts, 17 per cent. ; increase of expenditures, 62 per cent.

DENMARK.—Increase of messages, 149 per cent. ; increase of receipts, 19 per cent. ; increase of expenditures, 38 per cent.

In like manner an examination of the statistics of the business of the Western Union Company also shows that, although 137,-191 miles of wire were operated and 12,444,000 messages sent in 1872, as compared with 85,291 miles and 5,879,000 messages in 1867, the net receipts of the Company from all sources for 1872 were only $165,803 in excess of those of 1867.

The public, therefore, can readily understand how it is that a majority of all the telegraph systems of the States of Europe, notwithstanding great economy and efficiency in management, continue to show an annual deficit. Neither ought it to be a matter of surprise that the most eminent of telegraph authorities in Europe have, as the result of their most recent investigations, entirely reversed the opinions which they originally regarded as unassailable. Thus, in his recent work, " Statistics of the Telegraph," first presented to the Statistical Society of London in June, 1872, Sir James Anderson says : " *Like every one else, I entertained the belief at one time that a reduced tariff was the key to success in private telegraph enterprise,*" and " *that this success was not realized in practice was disappointing in the extreme.*" Referring, also, to what are called in Europe " international telegrams," which correspond with the telegrams transmitted in this country between the States, he says : " *However much every one engaged in the control of telegraphic enterprise may desire to reduce the tariff and increase the correspondence, they should not forget that this increase, although certain, will decrease the revenue,*" and again, " *that a reduction of tariff leads to a diminution of the net product, even under the most favorable conditions.*"

And again, M. Jamar, Minister of Public Works in Belgium, in a recent report, reviewing the experience of the telegraph in that country under twenty years of Government control,* announces the conclusions arrived at as follows :

* *Annals of the Public Works of Belgium*, vol. xxviii.

" That in Belgium, notwithstanding the existence of the most favorable circumstances, *all reduction of tariff has resulted in a diminution of net product.*" Sir James Anderson and M. Jamar also agree that the results of the telegraphic experience of Europe establishes this further fact, that telegrams relating to commercial and business matters (which constitute the bulk of the telegraphic correspondence of the United States) follow in their movement " the variations of political or financial conditions," and are " only influenced in a secondary degree by the alterations of the tariff."

Now, if these conclusions be correct, and Sir James Anderson, of England, and M. Jamar, of Belgium, unite in saying that no data can be found to refute them, it therefore follows that the establishment, through the direct or indirect agency of the Federal Government, of a greatly reduced system of telegraphic tariffs, is something which is sure to have an adjunct in some form of additional Federal taxation—a taxation, moreover, which is not to be limited to and paid by the comparatively small number of people who use the telegraph, but is to be distributed over a population of which not one thirtieth part have any direct interest in the subject.

Finally, while there are very many precedents for a government extending its sphere of business and influence so far as to include the ownership of railroads, telegraphs and express agencies; and many also for the ordaining of how men shall live, what they shall wear, what church attend, and where they shall trade, there are few or none to be found where a government has entered into a partnership with private individuals for the carrying on of business, in which all the loss and responsibility is to accrue to the party of the first part, and all the pecuniary profit to the party of the second part; and in which a divided responsibility in the management is almost certain to result in unsatisfactory conclusions.

If we accept, also, the statement of its special advocates, the " Hubbard proposition" is, after all, but the " Government proposition" in disguise ; for the report made by the Select Committee of the House in 1870, in favor of the " Postal Telegraph," after demonstrating by a great array of fact and argument the impolicy and anti-Republican character of the

" Government scheme" for absorbing and working the telegraph, goes on to speak of the Hubbard proposition as follows : " The system is a step toward the governmental; it will introduce the telegraph into the post-offices, and if, after trial, the public good requires it, the lines can be purchased by the Government at an appraised value."

Furthermore, as it is represented alike by the advocates of the Government plan for absorbing the telegraph, and by the friends of the partnership or postal telegraph, that the Federal Government cannot have the facilities which it needs under the existing system, and that its demands for service have been treated most arrogantly, attention is asked to the following extract of a letter addressed by the President of the Western Union Telegraph Company to the Chairman of the House Committee on Appropriations—the particular subject matter being a difference of opinion between the Signal Service Bureau and the Western Union Company, in reference to the compensation to be awarded to the former for the performance of services :

" NEW YORK, *April* 12*th*, 1872.

" I beg to offer the following suggestion : That authority be given to the President of the United States, in the event of the failure of the Signal Office to secure, by negotiation, terms and conditions deemed reasonable for the transmission of the weather reports and the other services connected therewith, to appoint an arbitrator on behalf of the United States, to meet one appointed by the telegraph company; the two thus appointed to have authority to choose an umpire, in case of disagreement. The decision of the arbitrators to be binding for the fiscal year 1872–'73, and for that portion of the current year beyond the expiration of the present arrangement.

" I would be pleased to have this letter made a part of the record.

" I am, very respectfully, etc.,

" WILLIAM ORTON, *President.*

" Hon. JAMES A. GARFIELD,
    " *Chairman, etc., Washington, D. C.*"

NOTE.—Since the above was written, the advocates of the " Hubbard Proposition," apparently foreseeing that the public would not be likely to look with favor on the creation and distribution of the one million ten per cent. stock for the purpose of "organizing" and "connecting wires;" nor upon the system of "double paid priority messages," have caused (Dec. 19th, 1872) two new bills to be reported—one in the Senate and one in the House—in both of which the above provisions are omitted and the following new ones substituted :

First.—The capital of the "Postal Telegraph" Company is fixed at $20,000,000, to be paid up in cash as required ; but as a report from the Committee on Appropriations (H. R.) accompanying this bill states that the expenditures required to carry out the scheme of a "Government Telegraph," occupying substantially the same field as the "Postal Telegraph," would involve the necessity for appropriations or a bonded indebtedness estimated at least at "$75,000,000," it is difficult to resist the inference that the advocates of the "Postal Telegraph" have some other object primarily in view than the accommodation of the public.

Second.—The charge for the transmission of telegrams is to be one cent a word for each circuit through which it shall be transmitted; two hundred and fifty miles to constitute a circuit for all distances not exceeding five hundred miles ; and five hundred miles for all greater distances. From the receipts from the sale of telegraph stamps the Postmaster-General is required to deduct five cents for each telegram transmitted—irrespective of the amount paid for it—to defray the Government expenditures for doing everything except operating and maintaining the lines, and then pay over the remainder to the postal company as full compensation for their share of the work. Again, in all previous bills establishing the "Postal Telegraph," it is assumed that the stock of the company is to receive an annual interest of *ten per cent.,* and it is fair to suppose, although no rate of interest is mentioned in the new bills, that the expectant investors of capital under them still hold to such anticipation. But if this be so, it is difficult, looking at the scheme from a merely financial standpoint, to see why the Federal Government, which can obtain money in abundance at 6 per cent., and expects to borrow at no distant day at 4 or 4½ per cent., should, with the ostensible object of giving the public cheap telegraphic facilities, contract with a private company for the investment of capital, on conditions which are manifestly expected to afford, out of the tariff imposed on messages, and through the aid of Government facilities, a rate of interest of from four to six per cent. greater.

Third.—A telegraphic stamp of five cents is required to be affixed to every telegram not transmitted by the lines of the Postal Telegraph Company—Government messages, and messages transmitted on lines maintained solely for private use, excepted ; and that herein is to be found the " meat and marrow " of the new proposition will appear evident from the following considerations : Thus, in the bill representing the scheme of the Government, it is expressly provided (and in accordance with the Constitution) that all private or corporate telegraphic property taken by the Federal authorities shall be paid for on appraisement ; and in all the former bills establishing the " Postal Telegraph " it has been apparently assumed that all other companies might continue to operate their lines, provided they were able to do so, in competition with such rates as the Postal Telegraph Company, with a large share of its expenses assumed by the Government, might see fit to establish. But in the new bills the arbitrary tax of *five cents* imposed on each message transmitted by all other companies, and from which the messages of the Postal Company are to be exempt, creates an instrumentality which will effectually enable the Postal Company to crush out all other companies without making compensation, and virtually enables them to say to its rivals, " Unite with us, and put in your property on our terms, or wind up your affairs as speedily as possible, and leave it to us to administer upon your effects." If, however, there is yet anything of legal force in the old maxim, "*Quod facit per alium facit per se,*" the Federal Government, in authorizing such indirect confiscation of private property, could not escape being involved (in a moral liability, at least) for heavy damages ; but the proposition for destroying by Federal taxation private property under one ownership for the benefit of similar property under similar ownership is not thereby rendered any less extraordinary and despotic.

CONCLUSION.

In thus submitting the results of my investigations, I would take occasion to remark that the whole case has been so often and so fully argued and reviewed by committees of Congress, the press, and the special advocates of the several involved interests, that little of originality can attach to any new presentation. I have, therefore, aimed at nothing more than to present the main facts of the case in such a way as will facilitate their clear and easy comprehension. And when that comprehension is attained to by the people, there can be little doubt on which side the friends of a truly free Government and the opponents of official centralization and interference will make haste to array themselves.

I am, yours most respectfully,

DAVID A. WELLS.

APPENDIX A.

The following important correspondence between the Post-office Department and the President of the Western Union Telegraph Company, detailing the statistics of the business of the latter for the year 1872, was not included in the report of the Postmaster-General :

Executive Office,
WESTERN UNION TELEGRAPH COMPANY,
NEW YORK, *October* 19, 1872.

HON. J. A. J. CRESWELL,
    Postmaster-General, Washington, D. C.

SIR—Referring to your communication of date August 26, 1872, I now have to submit the following information, in reply to your inquiries.

On the first day of July, 1872, this Company controlled and operated 62,032 miles of line, and 137,190 miles of wire. Of this amount 1,212 miles of line and 2,742 miles of wire are in New Brunswick and Nova Scotia, and 512 miles of line, bearing one wire, in British Columbia; leaving 60,308 miles of line and 133,936 miles of wire in the United States. The number of offices operated on that day was 5,237.

During the year ending June 30, 1872, there were sent :

    10,271,935 paid messages.
      660,203 partially paid and free messages, and
    1,512,361 press messages.

The number of press messages is an estimate made by dividing the number of words sent for the press by thirty, which is taken as about the average number of words in ordinary commercial and social messages.

The number of messages stated does not include messages sent by and for railroad companies between stations on the line of the roads, nor service messages of the Telegraph Company. Of these two classes no record is kept. The use of one wire on many important railroad routes is almost wholly devoted to the transmission of railroad messages.

The gross receipts of the Company for the year ending June 30, 1872, were $8,457,095.77, and the gross expenses, exclusive of construction, were $5,666,863.16.

    I have the honor to be, with great respect,
        Your obedient servant,

    (Signed,)   WILLIAM ORTON,
                        President.

Executive Office,
WESTERN UNION TELEGRAPH COMPANY,
NEW YORK, *October* 28, 1872.

HON. J. W. MARSHALL,
Acting Postmaster-General,
Washington, D. C.

SIR—I have had the honor to receive your communication of date October 25th, inquiring as to what portion of the gross receipts of the company, during the last fiscal year, was on account of press dispatches, and what proportion of the gross expenses are charged to salaries and maintenance, respectively, and whether any part of said sum is on account of payments made for leases of lines of other companies.

In reply thereto, I have to say that the gross revenue was derived as follows:

For transmission of messages...............................		$7,040,803.53
" " press reports...........................		979,083.71
" " market reports		107,579.72
" " weather reports.......................		137,522.88
From all other sources......................................		192,105.93
Total receipts...............................		$8,457,095.77

The disbursements were as follows:

Paid other lines...	$160,514.74
Refunded and uncollectible.................................	59,881.01
Salaries..	3,058,363.22
Messengers..	293,908.30
Printing and Stationery.......................................	166,196.24
Rent, light and fuel..	328,999.48
Office furniture, fixtures and repairing.....................	116,345.62
Instruments and battery....................................	240,991.02
Claims for damages and law expenses...............	41,530.68
Taxes... ..	45,445.21
Repair and maintenance of lines.............................	930,005.17
Rent of lines leased.......................................	150,082.42
Miscellaneous...	74,600.05
	$5,666,863.10

It is probable that the receipts for press reports were slightly in excess of the amount stated, as the separation is made during the month by reinspection of the messages, and some press messages may be overlooked.

The receipts for market reports are not paid by the press.

Those "from other sources" include premium on gold received from the tolls accruing to the company on cable business, subsidies, commissions on money transfers, and dividends on stock held by the company.

The disbursement for messenger service is almost entirely for salaries, and the amount paid for repair and maintenance of lines includes the salaries of the repairers.

I am, very respectfully, etc.,

(Signed), WILLIAM ORTON,

President.

STATISTICS OF THE OPERATION OF GOVERNMENT TELEGRAPHS FOR 1870.

The following Table, copied from the *Journal of the Telegraph*, gives the results of the operation of the principal government telegraphs in Europe and Asia for 1870. The receipts and expenses of Great Britain and Ireland are for fourteen months. These figures show that the expenses exceeded the receipts by $5,220,135, and that the cost of transmitting the messages averaged 63 cents.

	Miles of Line.	Miles of Wire.	Number of Government Offices.	Number of Offices of Private Companies.	Total Number of Messages Sent.	Total Receipts for Messages.	Ordinary Working Expenses.	Extraordinary Expenses.	Total Expenditures.
North Germany	15,049	50,291	1,078	1,327	5,272,321	$1,621,501	$1,721,855	$36,215	$1,758,070
Bavaria	4,040	12,832	317	326	492,188	162,248	125,450	159,385	284,835
Belgium	2,696	8,788	217	228	1,592,079	310,938	287,700	18,030	305,730
Denmark	1,217	3,181	75	75	313,245	104,280	95,156	18,384	113,540
Spain	7,204	16,489	170	29	744,070	289,340	715,109		715,109
Austria	14,021	26,643	536	363	2,264,558	929,221	1,192,104	183,303	1,375,407
Hungary	5,908	17,426	246	241	1,289,155	438,665	467,747	250,074	717,821
Italy	10,514	30,906	600	463	1,813,320	945,234	812,448	142,954	955,402
Norway	3,831	6,606	95	47	364,009	161,565	139,586	87,154	226,740
Holland	1,856	6,297	119	115	1,356,812	256,861	347,677	57,894	405,571
Portugal	1,793	3,347	109	9	165,391	56,368	153,056		153,056
Roumania	2,061	2,713	58		423,341	213,025	296,829	14,000	310,829
Russia	26,987	53,649	491	213	2,301,679	2,736,200	1,902,102	349,736	2,251,838
Sweden	4,048	10,089	99	187	494,111	224,200	201,540	24,940	226,480
Switzerland	3,203	6,866	483	63	1,329,061	251,432	213,130	27,480	240,610
Turkey	15,827	26,381	348	45	457,993	1,010,184	874,217	100,971	975,188
Great Britain and Ireland	29,746	130,008	2,000	1,780	10,084,020	3,865,127	2,277,195	4,486,166	6,763,362
Indo-European	2,115	3,418	10		41,000	281,250	340,000		340,000
British India	14,939	24,538	197	537	512,648	599,713	1,224,587	331,312	1,555,899
Totals	167,055	439,468	7,248	6,048	31,311,001	$14,455,352	$13,387,488	$6,287,998	$19,675,487

APPENDIX C.

EXECUTIVE OFFICE,

𝖂𝖊𝖘𝖙𝖊𝖗𝖓 𝖀𝖓𝖎𝖔𝖓 𝕿𝖊𝖑𝖊𝖌𝖗𝖆𝖕𝖍 𝕮𝖔𝖒𝖕𝖆𝖓𝖞,

NEW YORK, *October* 15, 1872.

BRIG. GENERAL ALBERT J. MYER,

Chief Signal Officer, &c., &c., War Department,

Washington, D. C.

SIR—I have the honor to acknowledge the receipt of your communication of September 12, 1872. Absence from the city, and the unusual pressure of business preceding and incident to the annual meetings of the Stockholders and Directors of the Company, including the preparation of my Annual Report, have prevented an earlier reply.

My letter of August 28, 1872, presented the views of the Company concerning the arrangement made with the United States in May, 1871, and which expired June 30, 1872; it also sought to establish the justice of the claim of the Company for compensation for services rendered the Signal Office under that arrangement during the last nine months of the term.

A careful examination of the reply has failed to discover therein any indication that the claim is considered unjust or inconsistent with the original and supplementary agreements made with the representatives of the United States. It is inferred, therefore, that the accounts have been approved, and that the statement, " the office is authorized to direct the settlement of them," is intended to be understood that the office has directed them to be paid.

Much gratification has been derived from the perusal of the somewhat elaborate history of the first arrangement made between the Signal Office and the Company, which you have taken the trouble to give; and although the relation of events anterior to May, 1871, with the matters of account and claims for payment for services rendered by the Company from October 1, 1871, to July 1, 1872, is scarcely apparent, yet it is agreeable to the Managers of the Company to learn that the views of the Signal Office, heretofore expressed, concerning their action in tendering the free use of the Company's lines, and all other facilities at their disposal required to inaugurate the Weather Reports, at a time when there was no appropriation from which compensation could be made, are unchanged.

There is, however, a liability to draw an erroneous inference from the statement referring to this arrangement, which seems to attribute the action of the Company to its inability to fix in advance a proper rate of compensation for this service. It was represented to the Company that, before the Signal Office could make use of the Telegraph, instruments must be procured and other facilities provided, and expenses incurred which might exhaust the appropriation; it was, therefore, impossible to say what sum, or if any sum at all would be available for the payment of telegraphic service. It was the suggestion of the President of the Company that a preliminary service of four months be undertaken—not merely for the purpose of ascertaining the cost of such service, but because : first, the Chief Signal Officer expected to require all the funds at his disposal for the purchase of apparatus, and for other necessary expenses preliminary to the transmission of telegraphic reports ; and, secondly, the period of four months would expire with the Congress which would be in session during three months of the term, and which it was expected would be influenced by the results of the experiment to appropriate such a sum as "future negotiation" should show was necessary. It subsequently appeared that the Chief Signal Officer was correct in assuming that no part of the appropriation under his control, when the experimental term commenced, was available for the payment of telegraphic charges.

But the expectation of the Company that, during the period of four months for which it had stipulated to make no charge, some effort would be made by the Chief Signal Officer to negotiate an arrangement for the future was not realized. The Signal Office made no application to the Company for "future negotiation" on any basis during that term. "The public spirit which prompted the perfectly fair and liberal proposition made at that time on the part of the Company" was disappointed at its reception by the Signal Office, and the gratification which its more generous recognition has subsequently afforded is not quite complete, because of the fact that it comes in reply to the repeated applications of the Company for payment of claims for service rendered, the justice of which has not been denied, although the claims still remain unpaid.

It seems necessary at this point to state that, in order to relieve the President of the Company as far as possible from the merely clerical labor of preparing the papers necessary for the inauguration of the Weather Reports, the Chief Signal Officer kindly took that labor upon himself. As compensation for the service to be rendered during the experimental term was not expected, and the material stipulation was that made by the Company agreeing to make no claim for service, except for any balance of the appropriation which might remain after all other charges had been paid, the President did not hesitate to sign the memorandum prepared by the Chief Signal Officer, notwithstanding it contained what were deemed immaterial stipulations, which it was well known to all connected with the Telegraph could not be literally performed. If it was "the essential part of the understanding" of the Chief Signal Officer, in the preparation of the memorandum which he submitted to the President of the

Company for execution, after the use of the Company's wires had been tendered, that the experiment was merely to procure data "as a basis for future negotiation," it is to be regretted that the President of the Company did not then—as he does not now —so understand it. The Company did not intend to stipulate to inaugurate a new system of accounts; nor was it expected that the evidence which its records afford, and the opinions of its most experienced managers in addition thereto, would be wholly disregarded in any subsequent consideration of the value of the service rendered the Signal Office.

The experience of the first two months demonstrated to the managers of the Company that the service they had undertaken for the Signal Office was so burdensome and expensive, and so damaging in its effect upon other business, that no ordinary rate of compensation would enable them to continue it without serious loss. It occurred to them to suggest that possibly the compensation might be increased without cost to the United States by an arrangement which should give the Company all the telegraphic business of the several departments. Such an arrangement did not then, nor does it now, seem to be an improper one to suggest or to make. The ordinary business of the Government, at the rates then paid, afforded a profit to the Company. The Signal Reports would not afford a profit at the same rates, because of the more difficult and expensive character of the service. Besides, there was a manifest injustice in putting an onerous and profitless service upon this Company by one department of the Government while another was giving profitable business to our competitors. The justice and propriety of this view of the case was subsequently recognized fully, not only by the Chief Signal Officer, in respect to the business of his office, but by his professional adviser, the Honorable William Whiting. It was understood, as a part of the arrangement made in May, 1871, in the negotiation of which the Chief Signal Officer had the able assistance of Mr. Whiting, that the Signal Reports were to be given exclusively to this Company; and, also, that the telegraph business of all the departments was to be diverted to our lines, so far as this could be done, by representing to the officials of those departments the character and value of the services which the Company had then undertaken to render for the United States. This was all that was asked to be or that could be done in that direction in the absence of special authority.

The assumption that the action, or rather the non-action, of the Signal Office, upon the suggestion of the Company that a portion of the compensation for future service should be made by giving to it the ordinary business of the other departments, contributed to "the difficulties which made necessary the conferences terminating in the Spring of 1871" is entirely erroneous. Those difficulties resulted from other causes altogether, and those over which the Company had no control. The fact that no attempt was made to negotiate with the Company, during the experimental term, for a continuation of the service beyond that term, occasioned surprise; but an explanation was soon found in information which reached the Company that the influence of the Signal Office was being exerted upon Congress to procure the enactment of a proviso to the bill making appropriations for the Weather Reports, which indicated an expectation on the part of the Signal Office that the Company could be compelled to continue the service without negotiation, and to accept such compensation as the Signal Office should advise the Postmaster-General was sufficient. The fact that this proviso became a law seemed to establish the correctness of the information which had been received concerning it.

It thus appears that the first return received for "the public spirit which prompted the perfectly fair and liberal proposition made by the Company" to enable the Weather Reports to be inaugurated, was—not an inquiry to ascertain the views of the Company as to the cost of the service, as the basis of negotiation for its continuation, but the enactment of a law, upon *ex parte* representations, without notice to the Company, and without opportunity to be heard before Congress, which seemed to be designed to enable the Signal Office to compel the performance of the service in future upon such terms as it might see fit to impose.

The repeated efforts of the Company to ascertain the views of the Signal Office, as to service beyond the experimental term, were unsuccessful. The arrangement expired by limitation on the first of March. It was continued at the request of the Signal Office until the end of the session of Congress, March 3d, when it ceased—simply because no agreement had been made with the Company for continuing it.

The authority of the Postmaster-General to fix the telegraphic charges for Government messages, under the Act of Congress approved July 24, 1866, was not denied. The Company did not, however, admit the right of that officer to have control of our wires, to direct when and how circuits should be made up, and by what routes messages should be sent towards their destination; nor did it admit the right of any officer of the Government to say, in effect, that private citizens, holding no office under the Government, could be required to open their offices at unusual and inconvenient hours in the morning, and to keep them open at night until the permission of a Government official to close them had been given; yet the course of the Signal Office towards the Company seemed to imply that such authority over its wires, and offices, and employés, was conferred by the law of Congress, which was understood to have been enacted with the knowledge and approval, if not at the solicitation of the Chief Signal Officer.

The Company had performed, during four months, a new and difficult service without compensation. It had been ready during that time, as it has been at all times since, to negotiate with the representatives of the United States for any service desired by any Department of the Government, and for this particular service to accept a less average rate of compensation than is paid for other telegraphic business. But justice to the stockholders, and the self-respect of the managers of the Company, alike required that an apparent attempt to place the control of the Company's property and business in the hands of officials of the Government should be resisted promptly and firmly. It was under such circumstances, and for such reasons alone, that the managers of the Company were reluctantly constrained to discontinue the transmission of the Weather Reports.

Subsequently, negotiations were opened with the Company by the Chief Signal Officer, assisted by the Honorable William Whiting. These negotiations resulted in an agreement between the United States and the Company for the transmission of the Weather Reports for one year from May 24, 1871.

The Company was represented in this negotiation by its President, and Mr. George B. Prescott, its Electrician. It was their understanding that the service of the Company was to be performed according to a certain schedule of circuits, and in the words of a numerical cipher, both of which were then submitted and made the basis of the agreement.

The right of the United States to require the performance by the Company of the peculiar service desired by the Signal Office, at rates of compensation to be fixed by the Postmaster-General, was not admitted. The compensation was fixed by agreement; and, although it was deemed inadequate by the representatives of the Company, it was accepted—partly because of their desire to contribute to the success of a scheme which it was believed would prove of benefit to the public, and partly because of representations that the appropriation would not justify larger compensation. The compensation agreed upon was for the transmission of the words of a certain cipher over particular circuits, both of which were submitted. It was not, however, expected by the representatives of the Company that both the cipher and the circuits were to be adhered to inflexibly. On the other hand, it was not expected that changes would be made which would increase the cost of the service to the Company.

In December, 1871, the Company was notified that an entirely new cipher would be put in operation on the first day of the new year. A very slight examination of the proposed cipher satisfied the Managers of the Company that its use would greatly increase the difficulties, and consequently the cost of the service, and therefore they objected to its introduction as a violation of the agreement. But, notwithstanding the objections of the Company, the new cipher went into operation on January 1, 1872. The working of the new cipher was carefully watched, and the result justified fully the apprehensions which the Managers of the Company had previously expressed concerning it. The time of the occupation of the Company's wires was materially increased, while, at the same time, at the rate agreed upon per word, the compensation was materially diminished.

An examination of the reports transmitted upon the New York and Lake City, the New York and Milwaukee, and New York and Portland circuits, from the sixth to the fourteenth of January, inclusive, developed the following facts: The average daily occupation of these three circuits with Weather Reports was thirteen hours and fifty-four minutes. Before the new cipher was introduced the average time was ten hours and thirty-eight minutes, and the average number of words transmitted in that time was 7,876, or at the rate of 12.3 words per minute. But with the new cipher there were transmitted in thirteen hours and fifty-four minutes but 5,370 words, being at the rate of 6.4 words per minute. Thus, for the increased occupation of our wires, owing to the difficulties of transmitting this ingeniously constructed cipher, we would receive at the contract rate per word more than thirty per cent. less compensation.

Subsequently, the position of the Company in this regard was sustained by the opinion of the Honorable William Whiting, who recommended that the rate per circuit for Signal Service messages be increased from two to three cents per word. In his communication on this subject he says :

" This conclusion is founded upon the test of the practical " use of the cipher now adopted, which shows that it is more ex- " pensive than the one originally adopted—and as the new cipher was " introduced on the first of January last, I shall also recommend " that the increased rate shall be applied from and after that date."

Although this opinion bears date May 9, 1872, neither the compensation at the rate named therein, nor any compensation whatever, has been received by the Company for the period during which the new cipher has been in operation, nor for the three months next preceding.*

The change from two to three cents per word is spoken of as an increase of fifty per cent., and without explanation the impression may be conveyed that such an increase was asked and allowed. As a matter of fact, however, there was no increase of compensation by the change from two cents to three cents per word, for the reason that it required a longer time to transmit the less number of words of the new cipher. The minimum number of words in the original cipher transmitted daily over any of the circuits was 44. At two cents per word the Company would receive 88 cents. The minimum of the new cipher was 31 words. At three cents per word the daily product would be 93 cents. This shows an apparent increase of only $5\frac{6}{10}$ per cent.; yet the wires were occupied an average of from five to eight per cent. longer each day in transmitting 31 words of the new cipher than 44 of the old. The use of the new cipher increased considerably the number of service messages required to correct errors resulting from its inartistic construction, and these were sent without compensation, as stipulated in the agreement. The Managers of the Company do not desire to enter again upon a discussion of the subject of the rates. The illustration submitted, showing the time a particular circuit was occupied, and the compensation payable therefor, loses whatever force it may appear to have in the presence of the following statement of facts :

The signal service business for the month of January, 1872, at

* See Note, page 93.

the rate of two cents per word for each circuit, would pay the Company $86,926 in a year. If the same service were charged at the rates established by the Postmaster-General for other Government messages—that is to say, one cent per word for each circuit of 250 miles, it would amount to $195,275; while, at the average rates charged the public, the same service would amount to $445,321.

A majority of the gross receipts of the Company is from general business at average rates.

It has been repeatedly demonstrated that it costs the Company seventy per cent. of its gross receipts to carry on the business. If Signal Office business costs only the average of all other business it would yield the average profits. But Signal Office Reports have paid less than half the average rate, and cost more than the average to transmit; precisely how much more has not been stated, for the reason that it is not possible to ascertain. These reports monopolized not merely wires and circuits, but at times the whole system of circuits over large portions of territory. In the question of the cost there is involved not only the actual expense for specific service, but the damage resulting from other business being delayed. For every operator employed in sending and receiving Signal Reports it sometimes happened that two would be idle, because their wires were taken to make the special circuits. When the President of one of the most important Railroad Companies in the country will state the cost each of carrying a limited number of passengers by special train, three times a day, such trains to have priority over all others, the service to begin at the same hour each day and to continue daily for a year, then the managers of this Company will undertake to show that the cost of a precisely similar service by the Telegraph is certainly greater than sending ordinary messages in the usual way.

On page 135 of the Annual Report of the Chief Signal Officer to the Secretary of War for the fiscal year ended June 30, 1871, is a table which exhibits the rates then charged by all the Telegraph Companies from Washington to 65 of the most important telegraph stations in the United States, and also a comparison between the rates charged the public and those fixed by the Postmaster-General on Government business for single messages and for messages of 100 words. The comparison is as follows:

Average rate paid by the public per message, $2.29. The same message, at Government rate, $1.25. For 100 words, rate paid by the public, $13.98. By the Government, $4.14.

Concerning this exhibit the Chief Signal Officer remarks: "Cal-culations made from the above table show an average saving to the United States, beyond what had been paid previously in the case of the shorter messages classified as above, of 45 per cent., and in the longer messages, of 70 per cent., which rate increases in favor of the United States when the number of words exceeds 100."

That this conclusion is justified by the exhibit is not ques-

6

tioned. But something more appears to be proven than is contained in the statement quoted. If the cost of ordinary Telegraphic business is 70 per cent. of the gross receipts at the average rates paid by private citizens, it follows that a part at least of the "saving to the United States," which resulted from the reduction of 45 per cent. in the rates for Government messages made by the Postmaster-General, was at the expense of the Telegraph Companies, who performed the service for the United States at rates below the average cost.

It seems proper to remark, in this connection, that although the table referred to in the report of the Chief Signal Officer fairly exhibits the advantages which the Government derives over individuals in the use of the Telegraph, it conveys an erroneous impression of the average rates actually paid. If Washington sends the same number of messages to each of the 65 stations named in the table, then the average charge per message would be ascertained by adding together the 65 separate rates and dividing the sum by the number of stations. For example : The charge from Washington to New York is given as 49 cents. From Washington to San Diego, California, $8.51. The average of these charges is, therefore, $4.50; but it is probable that of every 100 messages from Washington there will be ninety-nine destined to New York to one for San Diego. On this basis the average, instead of $4.50, would be but 57 cents.

But the substitution of the new cipher was not the only embarrassment from which the Company suffered in connection with Signal Office business.

While the negotiations were in progress between the representatives of the Signal Office and of the Company, in the Spring of 1871, it was represented by the Chief Signal Officer that, in addition to all the other facilities required, it was necessary that he should have at his disposal special circuits between Washington and New York, Washington and Chicago, and Washington and New Orleans. The wires for these circuits were to be connected with the Signal Office at 7.45 A. M., 4.45 P. M., and 11.45 P. M., daily, and at such other times as the Signal Office should call for them. These circuits were in addition to the scheduled circuits upon which the regular tri-daily Weather Reports were to be transmitted. It was represented that it was necessary for the Chief Signal Officer to be able to communicate directly and promptly with the Observer Sergeants at the three cities named, during the time the regular reports were being received at the Signal Office, and without interrupting them or otherwise interfering with their transmission. Desiring to provide every facility required for the efficient transaction of this business, the Company consented to supply these special circuits.

The new arrangement had been in force but a short time, however, when it was ascertained that these special circuits were being put to other uses than the correction of errors in reports and other matters of importance directly connected with their transmission. It was found that they were being taken for purposes of display, during the most crowded hours of the day, when they were most useful to the public, and, therefore, most valuable to the Company. Nor were the improper uses of the Company's wires confined to those composing the three special circuits. Other and equally important circuits, including those connecting the Atlantic and Pacific coasts, were sometimes taken by the Signal Office, without notice to or permission of the Company, to give exhibitions to invited guests, and to promote the convenience or gratify the whims of its attachés.

The following are copies of some of the messages—reams of which are now in the Company's possession—sent from and exchanged with the Signal Office over circuits provided by the Company with the understanding that they were to be used only in emergencies, and for the transmission of business of special importance. The cost of this service, computed at ordinary rates, would amount to thousands of dollars:

CONVERSATION BETWEEN THE SIGNAL OFFICE AT WASHINGTON, NEW YORK, BOSTON AND CHICAGO, August 7th, 1871.

Signal Office to Boston.—The Secretary of War asks, " What is the weather and " thermometer ? Is Observer about there ? Tell him yourself, if not."

Boston to Signal Office.—" Weather hazy—pleasant—East. Don't know about " thermometer."

Signal Office to Boston.—" Thanks of the Secretary of War. O. K."

(SIGNAL OFFICE CALLS NEW YORK.)

Signal Office to New York.—" What wires are you working to Chicago ?"

New York to Signal Office.—" We are working three wires to Chicago."

Signal Office to New York.—" Can you stay on here for a few minutes?"

New York to Signal Office.—" Very busy, but will do it. Jump in at end of " message."

(SIGNAL OFFICE CALLS CHICAGO.)

Signal Office to Chicago.—" Is S. or G. there ?"

Chicago to Signal Office.—" Who do you want ?"

Signal Office to Chicago.—" Is G. or S. there ?"

Chicago to Signal Office.—" Yes, wait a minute. I'll get them."

Signal Office to Chicago.—" Good morning. The Secretary of War is here again. " Are you working through to San Francisco ? Can you put West on for a " minute ?"

Chicago to Signal Office.—" West O. K., can put it on here, but it will be slow " work. I can repeat it quicker than you can work through, and make it appear as " though you were working direct. Won't that do ?"

Signal Office to Chicago.—" He has nothing important to say. Only wanted to " see if wires would work. He has been trying the Franklin lines, but there is not " much show for them."

Chicago to Signal Office.—" I'll put it on if you think best; but this is the very " worst time of day for our business."

Signal Office to Chicago.—" Let it go till some other day."

Chicago to Signal Office.—"Suppose you arrange for to-morrow morning, say "10.30, Washington time, then I will have every thing ready. I am short of "wires and crowded with business now."

Signal Office to Chicago.—"O. K. Will let you know. 12.30."

———

SIGNAL OFFICE, WASHINGTON, WITH SAN FRANCISCO AND INTERMEDIATE STATIONS, 10 A. M., August 9th, 1871.

Signal Office to Chicago.—"Is Mr. Swain in the office?"

Chicago to Signal Office.—"Yes."

Signal Office to Chicago.—"The Secretary of War wants to see how soon we "can get San Francisco. Please connect the wires through."

Chicago to Signal Office.—"I will put you in communication with San Francisco "now. Wait a moment."

(The wires were connected through, and San Francisco answered the call at 10.12.)

Signal Office to San Francisco.—"Good morning. The Secretary of War is here. "Please give him the state of the weather and thermometer at San Francisco. Is "Carusi about?"

San Francisco to Signal Office.—"Good morning, Mr. Secretary. It is cloudy. "No wind. Thermometer 54. Mr. Carusi is not in the office, but we can have "him here in five minutes."

Signal Office to San Francisco.—"Please call Observer." (The Signal Office here made some unintelligible signals.)

Chicago to Signal Office.—"Who are you calling?"

Signal Office to Chicago.—"Is Cheyenne and Corinne here?"

Chicago to Signal Office.—"Yes."

Corinne to Chicago.—"Do you want us?"

Chicago to Corinne.—"Yes. Washington is here, and wants you. Answer "him."

Signal Office to Corinne. "Please give the Secretary of War the state of the "weather."

Corinne to Signal Office.—"Little hazy. Thermometer 75."

Signal Office to Corinne.—"O. K."

(SIGNAL OFFICE CALLS CHEYENNE, AND IS IMMEDIATELY ANSWERED.)

Signal Office to Cheyenne.—"What is state of the weather?"

Cheyenne to Signal Office.—"Very cloudy and windy. Looks like rain."

(SIGNAL OFFICE CALLS SAN FRANCISCO.)

Signal Office to San Francisco.—"Has Carusi come?"

San Francisco to Signal Office.—"He will be here in a minute. Boy gone after "him. Lillis sends compliments to the Secretary."

Signal Office to San Francisco.—"The Secretary of War sends compliments. "Weather broiling hot here."

San Francisco to Signal Office.—"Here is Carusi."

Signal Office to Observer, San Francisco.—"How far is your office from the Tele-"graph Office?'   "(Signed),   GEN. MYER."

San Francisco to Signal Office.—"It is one square from the office."

Signal Office to Observer, San Francisco.—"Have you a barometer reading ready, " or would you have to make one?"

Signal Office to Managers and Operators at Stations between Washington and San Francisco.—"The Secretary of War tenders his thanks and congratulations to all "managers and operators for their success in working this morning. 10.50 A. M. " The wires worked nicely. *Two* minutes only were occupied in obtaining direct " communication between Washington and San Francisco."

CONVERSATION BETWEEN SIGNAL OFFICE AND CINCINNATI, at 3.20 P. M., September 6, 1871.

Signal Office to Cincinnati.—"Good afternoon. Do you know an operator "named B. F. H——, now at Council Bluffs, said to have worked in your " office?"

Cincinnati to Signal Office.—"Wait a minute. Good afternoon. I had a man "here named H——. He was not much as an operator. Very steady man. "Don't remember initials. Don't find his name now on my books. He afterwards " went to Omaha. Our manager there can tell more about his ability than I can."

Signal Office to Cincinnati.—"Can you conveniently find out for me his quali- "fications, habits, character, pedigree, &c.? Maybe Mr. Bliss would know. " Would like to know where he came from."

Cincinnati to Signal Office.—"His initials are H. H. H——. I will inquire "and notify you."

CONVERSATION BETWEEN SIGNAL OFFICE AND CHICAGO, September 16th, 1871, 8.40 P. M.

(SIGNAL OFFICE CALLS CHICAGO.)

Signal Office to Chicago.—"Is it S. or G., or is Maynard there?"

Chicago to Signal Office.—"It is G. What can I do for the Government to-day?"

Signal Office to Chicago.—"Good morning. Valuable service, as usual. In "explanation of loss of 49 and 50 we have had report: 'Can't raise; generally at' " night.' Wanted to know whether that meant: 'Can't raise some office,' or "something else. Do you know about it? Is there a chance to tighten screws " on North-Western?"

Chicago to Signal Office.—"O. K. I believe that has reference to office through " which the midnight reports from the North are expected to be passed. The "record book very frequently, and I think generally, reads at night. Can't raise "Fort Howard. We were told by Green Bay, I think it was, that he would not " sit up for signals without an order from his superintendent, Mr. Robertson. I "inferred, from the style of his language, that they were a kind of self-governing " people in Green Bay, and concluded that the service was not organized in that " direction."

Signal Office to Chicago.—"They report Fort Howard has a wire run into his "house and gets extra salary for doing the signal business. Wish you would " keep watch of them, and if there is any reason why the wire is not in order, and "signals don't come. post me. Meanwhile I'll pay my respects to them through "the Superintendent. Has the Observer supplied you with carbon paper "enough?"

Chicago to Signal Office.—"Yes, he has, thank you. We will do as you desire."

Signal Office to Chicago.—" Please take this message:

" *From* SIGNAL OFFICE, WASHINGTON, 16, *to* SERGEANT A. BRUNER, MILWAUKEE.
" Is Lieutenant Adams inspecting your station? Answer.

"(Signed),   II. W. HOWGATE."

CONVERSATION BETWEEN SIGNAL OFFICE AND INDIAN-APOLIS, 10 A. M., October 9th, 1871.

Signal Office to Indianapolis.—" Have you got any more signals?"

Indianapolis to Signal Office.—" I have tried every possible way to get Keokuk, "Davenport or Milwaukee signals, but so far no show."

Signal Office to Indianapolis.—" Much obliged. Will you be in office this P. M."?

Indianapolis to Signal Office.—" Yes, all day."

Signal Office to Indianapolis.—" Will you please let me know, say about two "o'clock, what is the situation at Chicago—whether prospect of getting afternoon "signals through regularly? If not, want to try to get other route. Can you get, "probably, a wire to Omaha, if Chicago wires are not all right?"

Indianapolis to Signal Office.—" Probably may get one round Ko. Will try to get "an opening somewhere before afternoon signals. The situation at Chicago at "present is rather gloomy. Thirty squares are destroyed."

Signal Office to Indianapolis.—" All right, all right. Can you give me the situa-"tion at Chicago now? The Secretary of War wants to know."

Indianapolis to Signal Office.—" The latest from Chicago is a message from Mr. "Wilson, Superintendent at Chicago, to Mr. Orton, New York, in which he says "thirty squares, the entire business portion of Chicago, has been destroyed. The "fire is still raging. This message came from Galena direct from Chicago."

Signal Office to Indianapolis.—" Much obliged. Let me know if there is any "change there, please."

Indianapolis to Signal Office.—" Will post you of any further information."

CONVERSATION BETWEEN SIGNAL OFFICE AND CINCINNATI, 10 A. M., October 17th, 1871.

Signal Office to Cincinnati.—" Say, Ham, get two signals, 47 and 70."

Cincinnati to Signal Office.—" Wait a minute."

Signal Office to Cincinnati.—" Find them."

Cincinnati to Signal Office.—" Here are 47 and 70.

Signal Office to Cincinnati.—" Please repeat them."

Cincinnati to Signal Office.—"0 3 2 7 0
0 8   8
0 6 1 7 1
2 0 0 0 0
0 0 9 4 7
0 9 6 4 6
1 0 1 7 2
5 3 0 0 0."

Signal Office to Cincinnati.—"Thank you. It is awful cold; eight degrees below "zero. Please rush these Government."

Signal Office, Washington, D. C., October 17th.—"Observer, Keokuk. Repeat "temperature, this morning's report, quick.

"H. W. HOWGATE,

" *A. S. O. & Asst.*"

Signal Office, Washington, D. C., October 17th.—"Observer, Corinne. Repeat "temperature, this morning's report, quick.

"H. W. Howgate,

"*A. S. O. & Asst.*"

CONVERSATION BETWEEN SIGNAL OFFICE AND AUGUSTA,

Ga., 10 A. M., Oct. 31st, 1871.

Signal Office to Augusta.—"Can I see G. a minute?"

Augusta to Signal Office.—"Go ahead."

Signal Office to Augusta.—"Good morning. How do you receive reports 27, "28 and 55 from New Orleans? Are they generally in before you send yours on "coast circuit?

Augusta to Signal Office.—"No. They come about the same time, when we "start, and that is a little ahead of schedule time. We always try to get ours and "coast South first, so they can send them West. 72 is generally late; the rest "pretty prompt."

Signal Office to Augusta.—"Think of changing schedules so as to have you send "those four reports on coast circuit, to save time here and at C. Can you do it "as well as not? Probably it will put your sending time back about five minutes."

Augusta to Signal Office.—"Do you mean that it will make it earlier or later?"

Signal Office to Augusta.—"Later."

Augusta to Signal Office.—"Yes. We can do it easy enough then. See no reason "why it couldn't be done. We get half an hour before you do on coast."

Signal Office to Augusta.—"All right. Is there anything new that way about "signals—anything want tightening?"

Augusta to Signal Office.—"No. The new Observer sticks to his office very "closely, and seems to attend to his business."

CONVERSATION BETWEEN SIGNAL OFFICE AND CHICAGO,

at 3 o'clock P. M., November 1, 1871.

Signal Office to Chicago.—"Is Sholes there?"

Chicago to Signal Office.—"Here is York or Swain."

Signal Office to Chicago.—"Wanted to speak with Sholes a minute, if he is in."

Chicago to Signal Office.—"No. Here is York, though."

Signal Office to Chicago.—"When will S. be in?"

Chicago to Signal Office.—"He ought to be here now. Time for his return."

Signal Office to Chicago.—"Tell him want to see him. Who is Superintendent of "Portland (Oregon)?"

Chicago to Signal Office.—"Half minute. Asking San Francisco now. San "Francisco says it is C. Plummer. Here Sholes comes."

Signal Office to Chicago.—"Sholes, do you remember the matter we were "speaking of eve I left S. D.?"

Chicago to Signal Office.—"Good afternoon. Yes; presume you mean regarding "situation in Washington?"

Signal Office to Chicago.—"How does the man feel about it now? How much "will he take?"

Chicago to Signal Office.—"Where would he be located?"

Signal Office to Chicago.—" Here. Some telegraphing—some clerking—with me. "You know about what situation is worth here, and you also know what Chicago is "now. We offer any (lost about ten words here). Don't know how much can offer. "Want find out what will cost, then get authority. Don't remember what he got "there."

Chicago to Signal Office.—" How soon would you want him? Can you wait few "days for a letter?"

Signal Office to Chicago.—" Want him soon as possible. If case hopeful, will "you write particulars how much he got there?"

Chicago to Signal Office.—" He can't decide to-day. He gets 115. He will "write you if you can wait few days for a letter."

Signal Office to Chicago.—" Tell him to do so. I will also write. Good after-"noon. Thank you."

———

CONVERSATION BETWEEN SIGNAL OFFICE AND PHILA-DELPHIA, 1.07 P. M., Nov. 9th, 1871.

Signal Office to Philadelphia.—" Is Robinson there?"

Philadelphia to Signal Office.—" Robinson is out of town. G. is here."

Signal Office to Philadelphia.—" I wish to see him a minute."

Philadelphia to Signal Office.—" In half a minute. He is very busy with Pitts-"burgh. Will he here in a minute."

Signal Office to Philadelphia.—" Do you know anything about the small-pox "business—any way to get vaccine matter reliably good?"

Philadelphia to Signal Office.—" Disease don't seem to decrease much. Think "you could get it from any reliable physician here."

Signal Office to Philadelphia.—" I supposed so. Wish you would ask G. or R. "if they know such a man, and can get me some conveniently. I don't know any "one to send to for it."

Philadelphia to Signal Office.—" G. says, ' Don't know of any one just now. Will "let you know soon. Will inquire.'"

Signal Office to Philadelphia.—" Much obliged."

Philadelphia to Signal Office.—" Not at all."

———

CONVERSATION BETWEEN SIGNAL OFFICE AND CHICAGO, November 6th, 1871, 10.11 A. M.

Signal Office to Chicago.—" Is Sholes there?"

Chicago to Signal Office.—" Yes."

Signal Office to Chicago.—" At key?"

Chicago to Signal Office.—" No."

Signal Office to Chicago.—" Please ask him here."

Chicago to Signal Office.—" Good morning. Your letter was received yesterday. "He expressed himself as much obliged for first choice, but under the circum-"stances, enlistment, &c., there is hardly inducement enough. With very little "extra hours' work every night can make it 130 here. Hope it has not incon-"venienced you or your plans."

Signal Office to Chicago.—" Good morning. Received no inconvenience. Sorry "can't do better. Have to come to it gradually, you see. Glad, however, he is "doing so well."

Chicago to Signal Office.—"Tell him I am all right for the present. Are you "coming out this way again soon?"

Signal Office to Chicago.—"Can't tell when. Hope to be able to do so before "long."

Chicago to Signal Office.—All right. Will see you when you come. It's likely "that I shall be in Washington this winter on a visit. Will see you then."

Signal Office to Chicago.—"Hope so. Good morning."

CONVERSATION BETWEEN SIGNAL OFFICE AND CHICAGO, November 18, 1871, 11.19 A. M.

Signal Office to Chicago.—"Please ask Chief if he can tell me the nature and "extent of the storm near Omaha."

Chicago to Signal Office.—"Good morning. Mr. M. will do so in a minute. Had "a very severe wind and snow storm west of here last night. Our masts at the "Missouri River blown down. All lines down between Council Bluffs and Omaha. "Don't know how far west the storm extended. We are sending messengers from "Council Bluffs to Omaha. May have some signal reports after awhile."

Signal Office to Chicago.—"Has the storm passed away, or is it moving east?"

Chicago to Signal Office.—"It is moving east. Cautionary signals are up here. "It is raining at Bluffs now."

Signal Office to Chicago.—"Thanks. Martin R—— applies for a place. Want "a first class man to enlist at 120 dollars. Can you send such a man to me?"

Chicago to Signal Office.—"R—— not first class; would probably do, however. "If he wishes to go I'll arrange to relieve him. Know of no one now that can be "spared. Are you in a hurry?"

Signal Office to Chicago.—"No. Want none but reliable men."

Chicago to Signal Office.—"He is all right, but I don't consider him first class "operator."

Signal Office to Chicago.—"All right."

CONVERSATION BETWEEN SIGNAL OFFICE AND BALTIMORE, November 21st, 1871, 2.30 P. M.

Signal Office to Baltimore—"Is W. there?"

Baltimore to Signal Office.—"No, sir. A. W. is here."

Signal Office to Baltimore.—"Can I see him a minute?"

Baltimore to Signal Office.—"Yes; go ahead."

Signal Office to A. W., Baltimore.—"Good morning. Can you tell me who is the "best oculist in Baltimore? Friend wants to find one there."

Baltimore to Signal Office.—"Yes. Dr. Reuling has the reputation of being the "best here. His office is on North Charles street, between Mulberry and Saratoga 'streets. He has performed some wonderful cures."

Signal Office to Baltimore.—"Much obliged. All right."

SIGNAL OFFICE, WASHINGTON, WITH CINCINNATI, 1.35 P. M., February 14th, 1872.

Signal Office to Cincinnati.—"Give us Chicago a minute."

(CHICAGO WIRE CONNECTED.)

Signal Office to Chicago.—" Can I see one of your chiefs a miuute ?"

Chicago to Signal Office.—"Yes."

Signal Office to Chicago.—" Good afternoon. You know McC——, at the "Supply Department. His daughter here would like to know if he is at home. "Understands he was going to Wisconsin."

Chicago to Signal Office.—"Will see. Can't get the office now. Can find out "and send you a message soon. Operator there has gone to dinner."

Signal Office to Chicago.—" Please do. If away, do they know when he will "return? How do you get my signals?"

Chicago to Signal Office.—" Very well now. Bad day to-day, or was this morn-"ing. Heavy wind broke wires. I'll let you know as soon as I can get that off."

Signal Office to Chicago.—" Mrs. Mack arranging to go home when she finds that "he is there. O. K."

SIGNAL OFFICE WITH CINCINNATI, 11.85 A. M., February 15th, 1872.

Signal Office to Cincinnati.—" Can you send a message to Chicago and get "answer right away?"

Cincinnati to Signal Office.—" Yes."

Signal Office to Cincinnati.—" Take this."

" *From* SIGNAL OFFICE, WASHINGTON, 15th,
     " *To* J. K. McCONAUGHEY, SUPPLY DEPARTMENT, CHICAGO.
"Your wife leaves at 7.45 this evening *via* Wheeling and Columbus. Can you " meet her on the road? I am waiting answer.
                " (Signed),   GEO. C. MAYNARD."

" Chicago should be able to get answer at once, if he is at office. If you work " direct to the Supply Department, send there."

Cincinnati to Signal Office, at 12.20 P. M.—" I requested Chicago to get quick "answer to you. Said he would. I'll ask him again."

Signal Office to Cincinnati.—" Please do."

Feb. 19th, 1872, at 6.15 P. M.

(SIGNAL OFFICE TOOK THE CIRCUIT WITH CINCINNATI.)

Signal Office to Cincinnati.—" Is Horton in ?"

Cincinnati to Signal Office.—" Yes."

Signal Office to Cincinnati.—" Good evening. Received your letter this evening. "Talked the matter up with Chief. It will probably be O. K. now. You need not " say so, but likely one of the trio will come; but your man."

Cincinnati to Signal Office.—" Was afraid they had been trying to oust him. He " is really very capable, and was ' propery ' *division labor* here. There would be no " trouble, but fact is," &c.

CONVERSATION BETWEEN SIGNAL OFFICE AND BALTIMORE, February 28th, 1872, 12 P. M.

Signal Office to Baltimore.—" Can I see Wolf a minute?" *To Wolf.*—" Do you "know at what time in afternoon and evening trains leave Baltimore for Wash-"ington ?"

Baltimore to Signal Office.—" To G. C. M. There is one leaves at 2 P. M., one " at 3.50 P. M., one at 4.40 P. M., one at 8.30 P. M.; and one about 9.30 P. M."

Signal Office to Baltimore.—" Thanks. That's trains enough. May drop in on " you to-morrow."

Baltimore to Signal Office.—" Do. Will be glad to see you."

It will be noted that the occupation of the wires which these conversations illustrate was at other times than the regular hours named in the schedules for making up the special circuits; and it can hardly fail to excite surprise that the Signal Office should interrupt and suspend the business of the public on the great commercial lines of the country during the most active hours of the day with such trifling matters. The propriety of exhibiting the working of the wires to the Honorable Secretary of War is not questioned; yet it would have pleased the Company better to have received an intimation that it would be agreeable to him to accept a courtesy from it than to learn afterwards that it had been extended without the knowledge of its officers. But the propriety of taking the wires for the purpose of inquiring the times of departure of trains, for negotiating the enlistment of Observer Sergeants, for the purchase of vaccine matter, or any of the various other purposes not directly connected with Commerce and Agriculture, is not apparent, even if the Company was to be compensated for their use. But when it is understood that the Company was not deemed entitled to compensation for such occupation of its wires, and that no complete record was kept whereby it would be possible to ascertain the extent to which it was carried on, it will not excite surprise that the Company became anxious to be relieved of so grievous a burden.

Another serious difficulty arose from the issuing of orders from the Signal Office to the Company's employés. When the arrangement with the Signal Office was made, it was understood that all changes or modifications of the service should be promulgated to the employés of the Company through its officers, but in several instances this course was not adopted, the Signal Office making such changes without notice to or the consent of the Company. Thus, in August, 1871, reports from Portland, Boston, New York and Baltimore were sent to New Orleans from Augusta without the knowledge of the Company's officers, and in September other changes were made in the transmission of reports over the southern circuit.

In October arrangements were made with the Company for holding offices open for the reception of Storm Signal Reports. On the 20th of December orders were sent by the Signal Office to several of these offices, notifying them of the discontinuance of the reports for the winter, but no notice of such action was sent to the Executive Office of the Company, and the fact was only incidentally learned through the offices which had been instructed. In order to prevent the confusion and derangement of business, resulting from the issuing of instructions by the Signal Office over the wires to the employés of the Company, it became necessary to give notice that all orders relating to the working of the

Company's lines which did not come from the proper officers of the Company would be disregarded.

Notwithstanding the frequent complaints and urgent protests of the Company these abuses were not remedied. It became neces·sary, therefore, for the protection of the Company's interests, that some decided action should be taken; and accordingly, after full consideration of the subject by the Executive Committee, notice was given to the Honorable Secretary of War, by letter, dated March 4, 1872, of a desire to terminate the arrangement at the expiration of the year for which it had been made; but, at the request of the Signal Office, the service was continued until the end of the fiscal year, June 30, 1872. During the interval the Company was invited to send representatives to meet those of the Signal Office at Washington, on the second day of May, 1872, for conference upon the matters pending between the United States and the Telegraph Companies. Pursuant to this invitation, the representatives of the Company attended at the Signal Office on that day, and being invited to submit a proposition for continuing the transmission of Weather Reports, they submitted the following :

" To transmit the Weather Reports for the year succeeding May 24th, 1872, substantially on the basis fixed by the Postmaster-General for the transmission of telegraphic communications other than Signal Service Messages and Reports—that is to say, one cent per word for each circuit, or unit of distance of 250 miles, or fractional part thereof, through which it shall be transmitted—the distance to be computed by adding the distances from one station to another, where messages are dropped or received on the route between the initial and terminal stations of each working circuit, and in addition thereto one fourth of one cent per word for each drop at such intermediate stations; all words to be counted, and no communication to be at a rate less than twenty-five cents on each circuit."

It will be seen that this was an offer to transmit the Weather Reports over special circuits at fixed times, for the compensation established by the Postmaster-General for other Government business, except for the extra service required to take copies of the reports at intermediate stations on the circuits over which they were transmitted.

In the ordinary transmission of messages two operators are required—one to send, the other to receive. The time of two operators engaged at intermediate stations, in taking what are technically called " drop " copies, is worth to the Company precisely the same as if they were engaged in sending and receiving messages in the ordinary way. But, as in the case of the Weather Reports, the operators connected therewith were all on the same wire in any circuit, it was deemed equitable to treat four drops, requiring four operators, as equivalent to the cost of ordinary transmission on a circuit of 250 miles, and it was there·fore proposed to charge, in addition to the one cent per word for each 250 miles, one fourth of one cent per word for each drop at the intermediate stations.

This proposition was declined by the representatives of the Signal Office, and no offer was made then or subsequently to the Company for the continuance of the service. But the Congress then in session enacted a provision to the appropriation for continuing the Weather Reports during the next fiscal year, for subjecting to severe penalties any Telegraph Company which should neglect or refuse to perform any telegraphic service for the United States required by any officer thereof, at a rate of compensation fixed by the Postmaster-General. The Company was informed that this provision was drafted and submitted to the Committee on Appropriations by the representatives of the Signal Office, and its enactment urged by them.

At an interview between the representatives of the Signal Office and of the Company, after the adjournment of Congress, and before the expiration of the fiscal year, the former distinctly declined to negotiate for continuing the service, alleging as a reason that they had the right to require its performance. This right was not admitted by the Company, and the service terminated.

The foregoing statements, together with those made in previous communications, contain all that is material concerning the relations of the Signal Office and of this Company in connection with the transmission of the Weather Reports, except the discussion of the subject before the Committee on Appropriations of the House of Representatives. As the official record of the proceedings before the Committee has been published, it is not deemed necessary to make further reference thereto in this connection.

It is gratifying to the Company to know that the Signal Office was able to make satisfactory arrangements for the transmission of the Weather Reports by the lines of other Telegraph Companies—whereby this Company has been relieved from burdens which it was unable to bear—without inconvenience to the Signal Office, and without depriving the public of the valuable results of its operations.

I have the honor to be, very respectfully,

Your obedient servant,

(Signed),   WILLIAM ORTON,

PRESIDENT.

NOTE.—The bills of the Company for transmitting the Weather Reports for the ten months ending July 31, 1872, amounting to $102,391.51, were paid October 28th, 1872, by order of the Honorable Secretary of War.

APPENDIX D. *

REMONSTRANCE OF THE WESTERN UNION TELEGRAPH COMP'Y
AGAINST THE POSTAL TELEGRAPH BILL.
(Senate Bill, No. 341.)

EXECUTIVE OFFICE,

Western Union Telegraph Co.,
NEW YORK, *February* 13, 1872.

To the Honorable,
The Senate of the United States.

THE WESTERN UNION TELEGRAPH COMPANY hereby respectfully re-monstrates against the passage of Senate Bill No. 341, entitled, " A Bill to Connect the Telegraph with the Postal Service, and to Re-duce the Rates of Correspondence by Telegraph," reported by the Senate Committee on Post-offices and Post-roads (Report No. 20), January 22d, 1872.

The following are some of the objections which we urge to the bill :

First.—Although the Report truly states that " the Western Union Telegraph Company performs nine tenths of the telegraph business, and fairly represents the telegraph system of the country," this Company has not been applied to by your Committee for any information either concerning its own business or in relation to telegraphy generally ; nor has it been offered an opportunity to be heard upon the subject before the Committee. On a single occasion, two years ago, the President of this Company was, on his own application, accorded a hearing before the Committee, limited to fifteen minutes.

Under these circumstances the Managers of this Company have been much surprised at the publication, in a Senate document, of statements concerning this Company, which are erroneous in fact, or in the inferences to be established, and which are used to justify the very extraordinary measures embraced in this bill.

This Company is not prepared to admit that the Senate of the United States is the proper tribunal before which to try the corpo-rations created by the States, either for alleged undue expansion of capital, unreasonable charges, or inadequate facilities ; but we claim that, whether the measure reported by the Committee on Post-offices and Post-roads is based upon charges against this Com-pany, or upon alleged considerations of public policy, the dictates of justice and the practice of the Senate alike require an inquiry into the facts, and a careful investigation of the interests to be effected, before adopting legislation so important in its conse-quences. Representing, as this Company does in a large degree, the telegraph property, the telegraph experience, and the telegraph progress of the country, we claim that, in any proposed legislation affecting telegraph property and business so vitally as the provisions of this bill, we are entitled to a hearing, both as to the necessity alleged to exist for Congressional action, and the effect of such action upon the private property involved.

We protest against the assumption by the Committee of the Senate, without proof and without having been heard in our defence, that the business of the Western Union Telegraph Company is conducted in disregard of the rights of the public to such an extent as to render it necessary for Congress to intervene. We are not advised that any person has applied to the Senate for the redress of any grievance alleged against this Company. Its Managers are believed to possess the confidence of the public, and are earnestly striving to meet their wants by extending their lines into new territory, and by enlarging telegraphic facilities as rapidly as the growth of business demands. The telegraphic facilities of the United States have been increased within less than six years past by the construction of thirty thousand miles of line and seventy thousand miles of wire, and the opening of more than three thousand new stations. Of this development the WESTERN UNION COMPANY has provided more than half, and has expended therefor about five million dollars, in addition to the contributions of Railway Companies included in its system, which amount to two and a half million dollars more. Probably, the gross expenditure for new telegraphic property by all the companies in the country, including railways, has amounted to nearly or quite twelve millions of dollars within these six years. During this period the average charge for messages has been reduced one half, and work has been in progress for some time by this Company preparatory to further reductions, which will be made at an early day.

There have been paid in dividends to stockholders in telegraph companies, during the period of this development, about five millions of dollars, or an average of less than one million a year. This would be ten per cent.—the rate contemplated by this bill— on a capital of ten millions, which is less than the sum invested during the same time in extending and improving the telegraph system, which previously represented more lines and larger revenues than those for which Great Britain recently paid more than thirty million dollars in gold. That the capital invested in telegraphs in the United States is not now, and has not of late been receiving adequate compensation, is well known to all who are acquainted with the facts. The investment has been made, however, in the confident expectation of a suitable return as the country progressed in population and wealth. This Company has considered the ordinary risks incident to competing enterprises, where success depends on the patronage of the public, but they have wholly overlooked the possibility of danger from the Government, or of an attempt by Congress either to take their property or interfere with their business without just compensation, or to create a competing Company, and then to confer upon that company the right of exclusive use of the vast facilities provided for the postal service at the public expense.

Private enterprise has already established the telegraph throughout every State in the Union, and in all the Territories but one (Arizona). The value of the services it has rendered, without charge, in the interest of science, and to sufferers by fire, and flood, and pestilence, is far beyond that of all the pecuniary contributions it has received. Millions of acres of the public domain have been granted to railway corporations, while the telegraph has received no grants of land except whereon to plant its poles.

While the deficiency—nearly $25,000,000—in the revenues of the Post-office Department within the last five years has been defrayed by taxation upon the people, the extensions of the telegraph within the same period have been made by means of private capital, furnished by private citizens. This bill attacks the results of this enterprise, and, if it becomes a law, will be fatal to them.

Second.—This bill creates a corporation and confers upon the corporators special privileges and extraordinary powers. *Upon what principle and for what reason the particular persons named in this bill are proposed to be made the recipients of a franchise never granted by Congress before, and of immense pecuniary value, in the event that they shall be enabled, under cover of its provisions, to grasp the telegraph property of the corporations created by the States, and now engaged in the business, we are not informed.* They are authorized to issue one million dollars of its stock " for expenses of organization," and as there is nothing in the bill to prevent the distribution of this stock among the corporators, we assume that to be their expectation. The bill contains no provision requiring the contribution of any money as the basis for the issue of such stock. This stock is entitled to receive dividends at the rate of ten per cent. per annum, so that Congress is, in effect, imposing a tax of one hundred thousand dollars a year, to be levied either upon the Post-offices or the senders of messages, to give a bonus to the beneficiaries under this bill, as an inducement to engage in a business in which they have now no investment, and in the conduct of which they have had no experience. If it be the policy of the Government to give so large a bonus to encourage investments in telegraphic enterprises, we submit that justice requires that companies now engaged in the business, and whose property is at hazard, shall at least be permitted to compete for the gift.

Third.—The bill provides that certain expenses, heretofore borne by telegraph companies, such as rent, lights, fuel, messenger and clerical services, and also for stamps, shall hereafter be borne by the Post-office Department—the inference being that the necessary labor can be performed without increasing either the number of officials or the expenses of the Department, and that it is on account of the saving thus effected that the telegraphic service can be performed by the corporation created by the bill at rates which all past experience in this country has found to be unprofitable. The fact that this illusive feature has escaped the scrutiny of the Committee on Post-offices and Post-roads is another evidence of the injustice of acting on the bill without subjecting its provisions to the criticisms of interested and competent experts. The bill provides for a class of messages (section 2) termed "registered telegrams," "which shall have priority of transmission," and on which double rates may be charged. On examining the Report of the Committee, to ascertain the reason for conferring a privilege of such immense value, we find no reference made on the subject.

This Company remonstrate against a scheme which gives a million dollars to create a new monopoly, under the pretence of checking an existing one, and which, under the plea of effecting " a greater reduction of rates than was obtained in Great Britain," covertly authorizes putting aside the ordinary messages of the public, whatever the pressure of their necessities, and giving up the wires to priority messages at double rates—the effect of which must inevitably be to establish the priority rates for messages requiring immediate despatch. The priority rates under this bill are higher than the present average rate.

We remonstrate against the passage of a bill which proposes to hire out the Government Post-offices, furnished, and warmed, and lighted, and the services of Government *employés* to private parties, unless to the highest and most responsible bidder. Especially do we protest against being excluded from such competition, and being put on the defensive by those whose investments in the business will be made, if made at all, after they have realized from the gratuities which the bill proposes to confer.

Fourth.—The bill, in effect, exempts the property and business of the Company which it creates from State and municipal taxation. It also makes the Company the agent of the United States ; so that the public would be as completely without redress, in case of neglect to forward and deliver messages, as they now are for the loss of registered letters and other valuables entrusted to the mails; at the same time all the risks of defalcations by postmasters and clerks, of theft or counterfeiting of stamps, are thrown upon the Post-office Department.

The Western Union Telegraph Company does not desire that the Government shall purchase their property. It has confidence in the future growth of the country in population, commerce and wealth. In the benefits of that growth the telegraph must largely participate. It relies upon the future for a just return for the great expenditure it has already made, and is still making, to enlarge and improve its service. If, however, this Company fails to meet the just expectations of the public, it is suggested that the true remedy is to require the surrender of its property, under the conditions of the law of 1866. But, until a state of things exists which makes interference by the Government necessary for the protection of public interests, this Company asks to be permitted to control and conduct its own business without Congressional intervention.

We remonstrate against the passage of this bill, because it would depreciate the value of the Company's property for the benefit of private parties. It cannot be that Congress would enact a law, the necessary and direct effect of which would be to depreciate the value of private property which they have the right to purchase, with a view to diminish the compensation to be paid therefor.

When this Company accepted the provisions of the Act of 1866, it was upon the assumption that a compact was thereby entered into between the Government and the Company—(1) that we were not to be interfered with by Congress until the expiration of five years ; and (2) that thereafter we were only to be liable to be dispossessed of our property at a valuation to be fixed by arbitrators in whose appointment we should have an equal voice. This Company submits to the Senate whether the enactment of such a law as that reported by the Committee would not be a violation of the compact into which we entered, relying upon the good faith of Congress. Under that compact we are to-day transmitting messages for every department of the Government, giving them priority over all other business, at rates fixed by the Postmaster-General, which do not pay us for the cost of the service. Is it . unreasonable in us to ask, as we now do, either that the compact be performed on the part of the Government or that this Company be released from its obligations ?

Common justice requires that if Congress is to establish a competing enterprise, in which the Government is to be the active and only responsible partner, it shall leave this Company untrammelled by the restraints of a compact whose reciprocal conditions it wholly disregards.

The owners of telegraph property would be justified in petitioning Congress for relief from many of the burdens it is obliged to bear ; but this Company asks nothing except a thorough investigation of the subject, at which they shall be permitted to answer any charges affecting their administration, and that they be allowed also an equitable participation in whatever privileges are offered by Congress with a view to making cheaper telegraphy possible.

The Western Union Telegraph Company relies upon Congress to protect their property from a scheme which, while it pretends to promise desirable reforms, and provides a princely bonus ostensibly to secure them, makes no provision either for compensation to the owners for private property virtually destroyed, nor for securing to the public any benefits promised them. We are unable to regard it otherwise than as a scheme to enrich its promoters at the expense of the public treasury, and of the private interests which it seeks to supplant.

WILLIAM ORTON,
HORACE F. CLARK,
E. D. MORGAN,
MOSES TAYLOR,
ALONZO B. CORNELL,
AUGUSTUS SCHELL,

Committee of the Board of Directors of the Western Union Telegraph Company.

PROCEEDINGS

OF

THE COMMITTEE ON APPROPRIATIONS

IN THE MATTER OF

THE POSTAL TELEGRAPH.

POSTAL TELEGRAPH.

WASHINGTON, D. C., 17th *Dec.*, 1872.

The Committee on Appropriations held an evening session in order to give a hearing to the representatives of the various Telegraph Companies of the country, on the proposed postal telegraph system. The following proceedings took place:

REMARKS OF MR. THURSTON.

Mr. THURSTON, President of the Pacific and Atlantic Telegraph Company, stated that under the Act of 1866 his Company recognized its obligation to sell its line to the Government at whatever price might be fixed by the arbitrators provided for in that law. He was prepared to show the cost of the line to the Company—its real actual cost, with unwatered stock. But he had not come before the Committee to make any statement himself, but rather to hear what other gentlemen had to say. He was prepared, however, to answer any questions of the Committee. As to the Hubbard bill, his Company had great objection to it, and looked upon it as a decided wrong for the Government to create a monopoly for the purpose of wiping out private enterprise. If the Government itself should assume the telegraph business, as he supposed it had a constitutional and legal right to do under the Act of 1866, his Company had nothing to oppose to it. But the Hubbard bill he regarded as unjust and unfair. His Company was perfectly willing for the Government to use its lines on the terms of the Hubbard bill, and would be very well satisfied to be guaranteed six per cent. on its capital instead of ten per cent. The proposition in the Hubbard bill that the Government should furnish office room, stationery, receiving and delivering clerks, messengers, &c., would save half the current expenses of Telegraph Companies. The rates in the Hubbard bill were presumed to be less than those now charged, and under which his Company was making no profits. He was sure that all the Telegraph Companies would be willing to assent to the terms of the Hubbard bill, and let the Postmaster General fix the rates for messages if the Government would guarantee them 10 per cent. on their capital. His own Company would be well satisfied with six per cent.

Mr. HALE.—You would adopt the same rates as those proposed in the Hubbard bill, and ask no higher guarantee than 6 per cent. ?

Mr. THURSTON.—We would.

The CHAIRMAN.—What do you mean when you speak of 6 per cent. on your capital?

Mr. THURSTON.—I mean six per cent. on the whole cost of our line, with no watered stock.

The CHAIRMAN.—Please state to the Committee the extent of your lines, and what was their cost.

Mr. THURSTON.—Our lines run northwest to St. Paul; south to New Orleans; east to New York, Philadelphia and Baltimore; and west to St. Louis. They run up and down the Mississippi river from St. Louis to St. Paul, branching at Dubuque to Chicago, and extending from Chicago to Pittsburgh, whence they branch to the three principal eastern cities that I have named. They also extend from Pittsburg to Cincinnati, and run down to New Orleans by way of Louisville, Nashville and Memphis. In round numbers we have 5,000 miles of line and about 10,000 miles of wire. It has cost us $1,982,000, and that amount of stock has been issued. That amount, as near as I can figure it, is as small a sum as such an extent of line can be built for. Our stock has been all sold for cash, at par; and it has netted us that sum, less commissions and expenses in placing it. Our materials were all bought at the lowest market price for cash. The labor has been done in the same manner, and the line has cost us $1,982,000. It is possible that, under other circumstances, a line might be built for less.

The CHAIRMAN.—When was your line built?

Mr. THURSTON.—Our line has been built from 1866 up to the present time.

The CHAIRMAN.—Is it costing less now than at first?

Mr. THURSTON.—No, sir; about the same. Wire is much higher now.

The CHAIRMAN.—What rate per mile does it cost you?

Mr. THURSTON.—The whole 5,000 miles of line have cost us an average of $400 a mile, or $200 a wire. That includes all the expenses. It includes the purchase of rights of way. We paid in one case $165,000 for one right of way. It includes all travelling expenses incident to procuring rights of way, and all the expenses of a Company in existence for six years, during which time we have been steadily constructing lines. We have not been building any for the last year.

The CHAIRMAN.—How was it that you had to buy rights of way? Do you not go upon lines that are declared post routes by Congress?

Mr. THURSTON.—Generally we do; but in all cases we had to fight our way, and we found it cheaper to purchase certain privileges from railroad companies than to go through lawsuits. I came to Washington a few days ago for the purpose of consulting the Attorney General on the rates to be fixed by the

Government for the transmission of its messages. He claimed the right to fix those prices under the law of 1866. I asked Mr. Whiting, who represented the Attorney General at the time, if the Government considered that law a contract. He said, " Yes, most certainly, it was accepted on the part of your Company." I said, " I want to ask you one question: Does the Government propose to carry out its part of the contract ?" He said, " Certainly." I said, " Well, at the present time, our hands being tied, we are at great expense in constructing our lines from Memphis to New Orleans, our right of way being contested by the New Orleans and Jackson Railroad Company on their road. They have sued us, cut down our poles, and refused to carry our materials, and have charged us with being common trespassers. I wish the Government of the United States then to carry out its part of the contract and compel that Company to give us right of way and proper transportation under that Act." He declined to do it, or to express any opinion on the subject. I mention this to show that that is all the benefit we have derived under the Act of 1866, whereas, on the other hand, we have been doing the signal service business for a long time at rates that are absolutely a loss to us of one half. We found it cheaper to buy rights of way.

Mr. HALE.—You say that you have not been extending your lines for the last year. Why is that?

Mr. THURSTON.—On a very simple principle of good business. We have no money, and we never run in debt.

Mr. HALE.—You extended your line to the point that you found it profitable to do so?

Mr. THURSTON.—No, sir. We could extend our line further and make it profitable. The fact is, a telegraph line must reach out continually into new territory if it is to continue to do business. You cannot run a telegraph line with any profit upon isolated roads. You must have it so as to accommodate all customers. The business of a telegraph line is somewhat like the business of a large grocery or dry goods house ; it has its regular customers. A very small amount of its business is derived from transient customers. Its principal business is from regular customers—men with whom we have to keep an account, and to whom we render bills at the end of the month. The transient business, the mere message of the man who may come in to-day to send a message, and whom we may not see again for a month, amounts to nothing. Therefore, it is necessary for us to have as large a connection as possible with the business centres of the country. This line of ours was constructed on that principle. We reach all the direct centres of trade with as little expense as possible. It was got up at the close of 1865 with a view of making a competing line with the

Western Union Telegraph Company, which was at that time a monopoly. The stock of our line was taken principally by merchants, not so much for profit as for the purpose of getting up cheap telegraphing. The stock has not been on the market.

Mr. HALE.—You do not propose now to extend your lines further, but have arrived at about the extent you desire?

Mr. THURSTON.—If this question of Governmental telegraphing was not pending we should probably extend our lines much further—that is, we should fill in the territory better.

Mr. PALMER.—You spoke of the signal service business. Are you doing any portion of it now?

Mr. THURSTON.—Yes, a large portion of it.

Mr. PALMER.—At what rates?

Mr. THURSTON.—We are getting a rate of three cents per word on a given circuit, as designated by the signal officers, which circuit is in contradistinction to the circuit as designated by the Postmaster General.

Mr. PALMER.—Can you tell what the average length of a circuit is?

Mr. THURSTON.—No, sir; it varies very much.

Mr. PALMER.—It is the same, substantially, as it has been for a year or two?

Mr. THURSTON.—No, sir; one circuit is from Cincinnati to New Orleans, for which we get thirty cents a message from the signal service, and for which we charge the public $1.50 per message, and do not make money at that.

The CHAIRMAN.—Please state to the Committee the amount of real estate, offices and the like, held by your Company. You have stated the cost of the line, and I suppose that includes real estate?

Mr. THURSTON.—I meant the cost of the line and equipment. We own no real estate.

The CHAIRMAN.—Did you include the offices in your statement?

Mr. THURSTON.—I include the equipment of the offices. We rent the offices.

The CHAIRMAN.—Your statement of about $2,000,000 in round numbers is the total cost of all that you own as a Company?

Mr. THURSTON.—Yes.

The CHAIRMAN.—What is the average number of wires along your lines?

Mr. THURSTON.—From New York to Philadelphia we have five wires; from Philadelphia to Pittsburg we have three wires; from Baltimore to Pittsburg, two; from Pittsburg to Cincinnati, three; from Cincinnati to Chicago, two; from Cincinnati to New Orleans, two; from St. Louis to St. Paul, two; from St.

Louis, by way of Terre Haute to a point on the Chicago line, two. It is a two wire line with the exception of about 150 miles.

Mr. HALE.—How do your rates compare with the rates of the Western Union Telegraph Company between the same places?

Mr. THURSTON.—They are the same at present.

Mr. HALE.—How long has that been the case?

Mr. THURSTON.—Since the first of May.

Mr. HALE.—How were they before?

Mr. THURSTON.—They were the same between the same places.

Mr. HALE.—Why did you say since the first of May?

Mr. THURSTON.—Because up to that time they were not precisely the same. There was a little variation in the rates up to the first of May. At that time there was an advance of rates. Previously to that the rates varied now and then.

Mr. HALE.—Since the first of May your Company and the Western Union Company have had the same rates?

Mr. THURSTON.—Yes, sir. The rates that we have now are the rates which the Company which I represent established when we first commenced business ; they are about half the rates which the Western Union Company charged before then. After our line was of sufficient length that they found it able to inter fere with their business, they reduced the rates which we had established fully one half. That competition went on for three years, and, of course, no money was made by the Companies. It was a losing business. By an agreement between the two Companies the rates were advanced on the first of May last ; but we only agreed to put them back to the point at which we first started.

The CHAIRMAN.—Are your rates the same now ?

Mr. THURSTON.—Yes.

The CHAIRMAN.—Is there any other relation between the two Companies besides the one you have mentioned—such as ownership ?

Mr. THURSTON.—No, sir.

The CHAIRMAN.—No combination in work ?

Mr. THURSTON.—No, sir.

The CHAIRMAN.—Are you in combination with any other telegraph line ?

Mr. THURSTON.—No further than the mere interchange of messages. Messages are interchanged between us and the Franklin Company, the Atlantic and Pacific Company, and the Great Western Company. We simply exchange messages one with the other, when we take them for points in one another's line. There is no combination existing, in the full sense of the word.

Mr. NIBLACK.—What is the proper name of your Company?
Mr. THURSTON.—The Pacific and Atlantic Telegraph Company.

The CHAIRMAN.—Has the question ever been raised in your Company as to the right of the United States under the Act of 1866? Have you ever contested it with the Government or denied it in any way?

Mr. THURSTON.—No, sir. We do not pretend to contest it or deny it under our acceptance of that Act.

The CHAIRMAN.—Have you ever refused to send any message for the Government?

Mr. THURSTON.—No, sir. We have protested against the compensation, and my protest is now on file in the signal offices, showing distinctly that we are doing the work at one half its cost to the Company. I propose at the proper time to make application to the proper authorities for recompense for the money that we have lost in doing the service for the Government. I stated the matter very fully in my protest on file in the signal office.

The CHAIRMAN.—When?

Mr. THURSTON.—Some time last summer.

The CHAIRMAN.—Does the mode adopted by the signal offices of sending its messages interfere with your business any more than any other ordinary form of messages?

Mr. THURSTON.—Yes.

The CHAIRMAN.—In what way?

Mr. THURSTON.—We have certain hours at which signal messages are supposed to be handed us, at which time we are expected to transmit them without delay, giving them preference over all other business. Until those messages are handed in we cannot fully handle our wires, nor undertake to send long messages, because we would have to interrupt them when the signal messages come in. The result is that the wires lie comparatively idle, waiting for the signal messages. Of course there are a few messages sent in the meantime in regard to handling the wires, or such office business as is needed; but effectually and practically the wires are at the service of the United States for one hour's time. When that hour expires the orders are to go on with the regular business of the office; but during that hour's time the wires are kept virtually at the service of the signal office.

The CHAIRMAN.—Is the peculiar arrangement of circuits and dropping messages a matter of disadvantage to you?

Mr. THURSTON.—Yes, sir.

The CHAIRMAN.—In what way?

Mr. THURSTON.—The circuits are purely arbitrary and are not circuits of the Company. The signal service makes our circuit for us from New Orleans to Cincinnati whether our Superintendent makes it so or not, and we must send its messages over all the circuit ; then the messages have to be dropped, and for these drops we get no compensation. For instance, we send a regular commercial message from Cincinnati to New Orleans, and we receive for it $1.50 ; the signal service sends its messages between the same points, and we receive for it only 80 cents—but that message is also dropped at Louisville, Nashville and Memphis. There are one, two, three, four messages delivered for 30 cents. But the signal service says : " No, this " goes the whole length of the wire; it is heard at each office as " it passes through ; it goes through those offices anyway, and " the dropping of it is no extra expense to the Company." If that message, which goes from Cincinnati to New Orleans was sent primarily from Cincinnati to Louisville, it would be a message, and would be paid for at the rate of 80 cents ; the manipulation in sending it from Cincinnati would be the same, and the labor of receiving it at Louisville would be precisely the same. But the signal service says that it is no trouble to have the message dropped at Louisville, and yet the operator has to be on hand there, and has to go through the same manipulations in receiving that dropped message as if it had been sent primarily, and only from Cincinnati to Louisville. The result is that a signal service message sent from Cincinnati to New Orleans employs four offices, and requires the same services to be performed as four commercial ˙messages would require, and yet the signal service pays for only one message, and pays for that only 20 per cent. of that which a commercial message would pay.

The CHAIRMAN.—The operators would be at the intermediate offices anyhow, would they not?

Mr. THURSTON.—They might not be. It is not likely that some of them would be at their offices at 12 o'clock at night. It would not be necessary.

The CHAIRMAN.—What do you estimate the present value of your lines at?

Mr. THURSTON.—We estimate their present value commercially. We have gone through six years' hard work, toil and struggle, getting up our line, disposing of our stock, acquiring facilities, and sustaining the establishment of our line against the Western Union Telegraph Company, which attempted to crush us out. Our stockholders have been without any income all this time; they have established a business at a loss, or at the loss of interest on capital, and they look to it, the same as any other business man would, to repay them in the future. When a business has been established—a rolling mill, a foundry, or a manufactory—the value of it is not precisely what its owner has paid for it in dollars or cents, but what it is worth to him as a future means of subsistence and profit. Therefore, when we estimate what our lines are worth, we do not estimate them at what they may have cost us, but as to what they are worth in the future as a means of earning money for the stockholders—what they would be worth to sell to anybody else to-morrow. A man who had spent some time in establishing a large manufactory might say, "This only cost me $100,000, but really it is worth $200,000, and I do not want to sell it for less." That is the view we take. While we only spent $2,000,000 on our line, and spent it very niggardly and very economically, we do not feel disposed to dispose of our property at an undervaluation. We consider our line worth $3,000,000.

Mr. HALE.—Is your stock in the market?

Mr. THURSTON.—No, sir; it is not in the general market.

The CHAIRMAN.—What would you say is the cost to your Company per word for doing associated press work?

Mr. THURSTON.—I am not prepared to answer that question at present.

The CHAIRMAN.—Is it your opinion that you are doing that work for less than cost?

Mr. THURSTON.—I do not presume we are.

The CHAIRMAN.—You have stated that you are doing the work of the signal service at less than cost.

Mr. THURSTON.—Yes, and I am prepared to show it very clearly from my letters on file at the signal office.

The CHAIRMAN.—How does the rate which the signal service pays you compare with the rate which the associated press pays you?

Mr. THURSTON.—I cannot compare the rates, because we send the associated press reports in a different manner and in a different form. We send a great deal of specials. Our associated press business is not like the associated press business of the Western Union Company.

The CHAIRMAN.—What are those rates? I suppose your rates were on the same basis as the Western Union Company.

Mr. THURSTON.—Very nearly on the same basis. The understanding between the Western Union Telegraph Company and ourselves is, that neither Company shall make a change of rates without the concurrence of the other Company—that is, in regard to our regular business; but in regard to these press rates we may change them as we see proper.

The CHAIRMAN.—Can you remember readily what those rates are?

Mr. THURSTON.—Not readily. A short time ago—a week or so since—a proposition was before me for sending despatches from Washington City to Cincinnati, and, I think, Chicago, and

4½ and 5 cents a word was the price to be paid. That was for specials.

The CHAIRMAN.—How many drops were included in that?

Mr. THURSTON.—One at Pittsburg and one at Cincinnati.

The CHAIRMAN.—If you can furnish us a statement on those points as to the rates charged the associated press by your Company—the rate per word, the distance sent, and the number of duplicates or drops—we should be very glad you would do so, the object being to ascertain and make a fair comparison between press work and signal service work.

Mr. THURSTON.—I am going back to Pittsburg to-morrow and will transmit the information in a letter.

Mr. PALMER.—What press associations do you work for?

Mr. THURSTON.—We transmit for the American Press Association.

Mr. PALMER.—Where does it collect its news?

Mr. THURSTON.—In New York City, and Cincinnati and Chicago.

Mr. PALMER.—Where does it make its headquarters?

Mr. THURSTON.—The president of it resides in Philadelphia.

REMARKS OF MR. BROWN.

Mr. JAMES W. BROWN, President of the Franklin Telegraph Company, stated that the managers and stockholders of that Company regarded the Hubbard bill with great disfavor. They thought that some of its provisions were striking at the very life of the Franklin Telegraph Company. That Company was organized about six years ago. During that six years it had been running in sharp competition with the Western Union Telegraph Company, over what he believed was well known as "the worst burned district" in the United States. In other words, the tariff had been lower in proportion to the length of wires than in any other part of the country. For six or seven years they had been losing, or at least, not making any money, and had accumulated quite a debt. Last year was the first year that the Franklin Telegraph Company had managed to make any profit. Last year the Company had saved from its earnings about $2,000, and this year it expected to save a much larger sum. Now that it appeared that there was the slightest probability of Congress passing the Hubbard bill, the Company felt very much concerned about it. The Company felt that the profitable business which it had been doing last year and this year was not so much owing to its present management as it was owing to its increase of business through its extension of wires and opening of new lines, which had become feeders to the Franklin line. The Franklin Company had gradually built up its business, and it now felt a great deal of concern in seeing that any steps were being taken to destroy its business. It felt that it had been gradually educating the public up to the telegraph business, and that, if the Hubbard bill should pass, the Company was going to lose its reward. He, therefore, came here in the name of the Franklin Telegraph Company's stockholders, to protest, if he could use the word, against any corporation being organized to enter into competition with existing Telegraph Companies under the very favorable terms proposed in the Hubbard bill. On looking over that bill he discovered that the tariff rates would not be materially reduced from those which the Franklin Telegraph Company was now charging. For instance, the rate between New York and Boston would be twenty-five cents under the Hubbard bill, and the Franklin Telegraph Company was now charging only thirty cents. That was a circuit of 250 miles. For two circuits of 500 miles the rate under the Hubbard bill would be forty cents, and the Franklin Telegraph Company was doing that service—from Boston to Washington—for fifty cents; therefore, there was not much difference between the rates, while, on the other hand, the Company to be organized under the Hubbard bill was to be furnished by the Government with office room, stationery, clerks and messengers, and was to import its material free of duty—and for all those advantages it would only pay to the United States the sum of five cents on every telegram transmitted. It cost the Franklin Telegraph Company over six cents a message for delivering its messages in Boston and New York, where, owing to the large amount of business done, the work was done cheaper than at smaller stations; so that, if the Government should only receive five cents on each message delivered, it would be giving a bonus to the Company.

Mr. PALMER.—What do you mean when you speak of delivering and receiving clerks?

Mr. BROWN.—When a message comes in to the counter there is a man there to receive it, who is called the receiving clerk. That message has to be taken and numbered, and, after it is numbered, it goes to the operator. That is what we call receiving messages. When a message is to be delivered it is sent from the operator to a clerk, and passes through two or three hands before it reaches the message boy, who receives two cents for delivering it. The delivery only costs us six cents in the average; while, for the five cents which the Government is to receive under the Hubbard bill on each message, the Government is not only to deliver but to receive the message, to furnish the office with fuel and stationery, and to make the telegraph property free of tax. These bills must be paid by some one, and must, of course, fall on the Government. Our people feel that if such advantages are to be given to any corporation, those corporations which have educated the public up to the present point, and which have labored as they have done, should have them in preference to a Company which has not yet got a mile of wire or a telegraph office. Our Company is of opinion that if its property is to pass out of its hands it shall not pass into the hands of any new Company on the basis of an appraisement by four or five men, but that if the Government is going to interest itself in telegraphing, it should go into it as a business on its own account. If the business is to be done by the people at all, it should be done by the people thoroughly, and for the people, and by the agents of the people.

The CHAIRMAN.—What would your Company say if it was offered the privileges of this bill?

Mr. BROWN.—I think our people would accept it and be glad to do so.

The CHAIRMAN.—You think you would make as much money under it as you do now?

Mr. BROWN.—That is a subject to which I have not given much thought, but I think we could. My idea is that if a man has a telegraph message to send, and can send it for five cents cheaper from the Post-office than he can send it from an office next door, he will send it to the Post-office rather than send it next door and pay five cents more. But if our line alone had this position, of course the competing companies would immediately place their tariff on the same basis, and then the difficulty would come up again.

The CHAIRMAN.—Has your Company done any work for the Government?

Mr. BROWN.—Yes, sir; we do a good deal of department work and a part of the signal service business.

The CHAIRMAN.—What is your experience as to the signal service business?

Mr. BROWN.—We have tried to do our best. We believe that the business has been done satisfactorily to the signal office, and it has been entirely satisfactory to us.

The CHAIRMAN.—You receive what you think is a reasonable compensation for the work?

Mr. BROWN.—Yes, sir; we are satisfied. We are in "the burned district," where we are accustomed to low rates.

The CHAIRMAN.—Has any question ever been raised by your Company as to its obligation to perform work for the Government?

Mr. BROWN.—I think the matter may have been spoken of. When we accepted the Act of 1866 we did it with a full understanding of what we were about, and we were entirely satisfied to take upon ourselves such burdens as the United States might impose.

The CHAIRMAN.—You regarded the franchises which the Government gave you under that Act as pretty valuable to your Company?

Mr. BROWN.—So far we have not had occasion to find them of much value.

The CHAIRMAN.—Would you be glad to be relieved from the obligations of that Act?

Mr. BROWN.—No, sir; we do not care anything about them.

The CHAIRMAN.—You prefer to hold to its benefits and bear its burdens?

Mr. BROWN.—We do not complain of any burdens.

The CHAIRMAN.—What does your Company say to the plan of the Postmaster General for the postal telegraph?

Mr. BROWN.—The idea of some of our leading men is, that if the Government chooses to go into this business we have no objection. We hold our telegraph property the same as we might hold ten bales of cotton; if we get what we think a fair equivalent for it the Government can have it.

The CHAIRMAN.—What do you think would be a fair price for your property?

Mr. BROWN.—I think about $500,000.

The CHAIRMAN.—What is the basis of your estimate?

Mr. BROWN.—The cost of our property.

Mr. PALMER.—How many miles of line have you?

Mr. BROWN.—We have two routes from Boston to New York—two distinct routes—and we have one route from New York to Washington. That, of course, you see, doubles the distances from New York to Boston. We have six wires between Boston and New York, seven between New York and Philadelphia, and four between Philadelphia and Washington.

Mr. PALMER.—How many miles of wire in all?

Mr. BROWN.—3,000.

Mr. PALMER.—What is the length of the signal service circuits on your line?

Mr. BROWN.—That I cannot answer. I am not sufficiently familiar with the subject. I do not know the length of circuits on other lines.

Mr. HALE.—When you say you have 3,000 miles of wire you count your duplicates and triplicates, you do not mean 3,000 miles of route?

Mr. BROWN.—Oh, no; of wire.

Mr. HALE.—How many miles of route have you?

Mr. BROWN.—750 miles, in round numbers; from Boston to New York two routes, and from Washington to New York one route.

Mr. HALE.—How do your rates compare with the Western Union Company's rates for private despatches?

Mr. BROWN.—They are always the same. I believe that is the rule all over the country. Wherever the Western Union lines run our rates are always the same.

Mr. HALE.—You are not extending your lines?

Mr. BROWN.—We are not extending our route. We are oc·casionally putting on new wires. We put on two wires between New York and Philadelphia last spring to accommodate our business.

Mr. HALE (to Mr. Thurston).—Did you mean 5,000 miles of route or 5,000 miles of wire as the extension of your line?

Mr. THURSTON.—5,000 miles of route and 10,000 miles of wire.

Mr. BROWN.—In the matter of rates it is perhaps well understood that no sooner does one Company drop its rates than the other Company immediately conforms to them, otherwise it would soon lose its business. Therefore, whenever the Western Union Company lowers its rates it is immediately followed by the opposition Company.

REMARKS OF MR. SWEET.

Mr. E. D. L. SWEET, executive manager of the Atlantic and Pacific Telegraph Company, stated that the executive officers of the Atlantic and Pacific Telegraph Company and its stockholders were, so far as expression had been given, of the opinion that the telegraph business of the country can be satisfactorily done by companies operating under private corporations, and that while the Atlantic and Pacific Telegraph Company might be glad to avail itself of such legislation as would enable Telegraph Companies to do business at less than present rates, it is opposed to the plans now under consideration by that Committee, and desires permission to state its objections more at length in writing.

The CHAIRMAN.—Are the signal service circuits long on your line?

Mr. SWEET.—Yes, sir; we have no signal service circuit that is less than 1,200 miles long. The shortest we have is between New York and Milwaukee, which is (the way the line runs) over 1,200 miles.

Mr. HALE.—How many miles of route has your Company?

Mr. SWEET.—Our line runs from New York to San Fran·cisco. That is substantially the route, but it is done in some parts by connections. We own 7,000 miles of wire and, I think, about 2,600 miles of route, extending from New York to Saratoga, and Albany and Syracuse, and there dividing into two routes, one by way of Oswego, and one by way of Auburn to Clyde. That is one route. From Buffalo there are two routes to Chicago by way of Detroit and Sandusky, extending down to Cincinnati, then across the State of Iowa and to Ogden. That is the extent of the line that we own. At Ogden we connect, by contract, with the Central Pacific Telegraph Company, and their lines are known as the Central Pacific Division of our Company, but they are not included in the statement made to the Postmaster General as to the extent of our wires.

The CHAIRMAN.—Have you given the Postmaster General the estimated cost of your lines?

Mr. SWEET.—No, sir; nor am I prepared to give it to-night.

The CHAIRMAN.—Please to put it in your written statement.

Mr. SWEET.—I will submit the matter to our Executive Committee.

The CHAIRMAN.—You will also please to state your rates for messages.

Mr. SWEET.—Our rates are the same as those of the Western Union Telegraph Company, and always have been so.

The CHAIRMAN.—Please say to your Company that the committee would be glad to know the cost of your line, and such other facts as you have heard given here to-night by the representatives of other telegraph companies.

Mr. SWEET.—I shall do so. My reason for coming here to-night was, that I might make a memorandum of all the points of inquiry.

The CHAIRMAN.—I would like to say to all the gentlemen who have been heard to night, that the committee may find it necessary to propound some inquiries not yet made. If so, we will notify them by letter.

Mr. ORTON, President of the Western Union Telegraph Company, said:

As I was unable to be present when the hearing commenced this evening, I am only informed, by what I have heard during the last ten minutes, as to the course of the proceedings to night, and I therefore rise to inquire whether the committee desire to examine the representatives of the Western Union Company on the subject now under consideration.

The CHAIRMAN.—The simple facts of the case are: that, by resolution of the House, of December 4th, so much of the President's Message and of the Report of the Postmaster General as relates to the subject of the postal telegraph was referred to this committee. By a similar resolution last year the same subject was also referred to this committee; and under that resolution at last session some progress was made in a general inquiry, first about the relations of the Telegraph Companies to the signal service, and second, upon the general question of a bill known as

the Hubbard bill. That bill is still in the hands of this com·
mittee, as it has been presented and modified ; and additional
facts and suggestions and recommendations of the President
and of the Postmaster General have also come to the commit·
tee; and on the whole subject the committee has desired to
know whether any of those Telegraph Companies have anything
new to offer.

Mr. NIBLACK.—Permit me to state my view of the question.
By the message of the President, calling attention to the Report
of the Postmaster General, we are asked to take measures to·
wards establishing a postal telegraph operated by the Govern·
ment. From another source the Hubbard bill is urged upon
us. Others again have appeared before us at different times
and urged that Congress should not interfere with the subject
at all. These three views of the case are now before us for our
consideration.

The CHAIRMAN.—Precisely.

Mr. NIBLACK.—These, I suppose, are the points to which we
desire gentlemen to direct their attention.

The CHAIRMAN.—In addition to what has been so well stated
by Mr. Niblack, this committee desires to represent the aspira·
tions of the American people on this subject, as far as it knows
what they are, and also to secure to the Government whatever
is just and right. The telegraph public is now represented ·in
this room. The question is, shall the Government do nothing ?
shall it take the lines and carry on the business itself? or shall it
allow a third party, as suggested in the Hubbard bill, to do the
business ? These are the questions we have to pass upon.

Mr. NIBLACK.—We have heard more on the subject of the
Hubbard plan than on any other.

Mr. PALMER.—As I understand it the several presidents of
the telegraph lines have sent requests to be heard ; and, so far as
I am concerned, I am perfectly. willing that they shall speak in
their own way on the subject.

The CHAIRMAN.—Certainly. The meeting is called for the
sake of hearing what the Telegraph Companies have to say on
this whole subject, and we have this evening heard from all but
the Western Union Telegraph Company. The field is your
own, Mr. Orton.

REMARKS OF MR. ORTON.

Mr. ORTON.—I regret, Mr. Chairman, that, owing to the
fatigues of the journey here, and to a day and night of extraor·
dinary work before leaving New York, I am in no condition at
this time to do justice to the subject; but with the permission of
the committee I will submit a few suggestions which occur to me

on reading the report of the Postmaster General, which I hold in my hand.

I believe that the Western Union Telegraph Company is the only Company mentioned by the Postmaster General in his report, although reference is made incidentally to other companies ; and, as I conceive that the allusions to the Western Union Company are not entirely just, and do not represent the facts, either so far as they concern that Company or so far as they relate to the telegraph business generally in this country or in Europe, I desire to occupy a little time in the consideration of this report.

The first point to which I will invite the attention of the committee is the reference of the Postmaster General to the rates established in 1871 for signal service messages ; and I will say at the outset that I have no desire to enter on a re-discussion of the question. But, in order that this brief review of the report may touch all the topics, I will merely say in this connection that the Postmaster General has misunderstood the position of the Western Union Telegraph Company concerning the signal service business. He says ; " The Western Union Company " contended, first, that the signal service messages, which, to be " effective, require simultaneous transmission through special " circuits at certain times, were not covered by the second sec- " tion of the Act approved July 24th, 1866."

When I had the honor to appear before the committee at the last session of Congress I endeavored to explain that the Company with which I am connected claimed no right to scrutinize the messages of any person representing himself to be an agent or officer of the United States, and that the objection which we made to the claim of the Postmaster General in that regard was, that, after having exercised the authority which the law expressly confers upon him to fix the rates on Government messages, we understood that he claimed something more—namely : to direct by what route a message should be transmitted from the initial to the terminal station, and what intermediate stations on that route should be included in it ; and also at what hours of the day the offices of the Company should be open for the reception of such messages, in order that a continuous circuit might be made up to be worked synchronously across the continent, including the intermediate stations, and the messages transmitted over that circuit, and dropped at the intermediate stations and delivered at the terminal stations simultaneously. We claimed that the Act of 1866 did not confer such authority on the Posmaster General. We claimed, furthermore, that the rates to be fixed by that officer under the law of 1866 are uniform rates ; that, having fixed a rate on Government business of one cent per word on each circuit of 250 miles (under which, for illustration, the tariff on a Government message from Washington to Chicago, being four circuits, would be four cents a word), it was not competent for him to say that another class of Government business between Washington and Chicago, sent by a more circuitous route, and involving more labor on the part of the Company, should be sent for *three* cents a word ; and yet this difference was involved in the claim of the Postmaster General. For example : under the general order, a message from the Secretary of War to General Sheridan, whose headquarters are at Chicago, delivered to us here, entitled to priority, but transmitted within the discretion of the Company by whatever routes and wires would best perform the service, pays *four* cents a word. We are entitled to receive four cents a word for that ; but under the order concerning the signal service business it became necessary to send the message by way of New York, including in the circuit a large number of stations which are not in it as ordinarily worked with Chicago ; and for that service the rate fixed was *three* cents a word. Now, we submit very respectfully, Mr. Chairman, that the law which authorizes the Postmaster General to fix rates, necessarily and inevitably requires the fixing of a uniform rate for the like service, and that a message from Washington to Chicago must have a uniform price for it ; that if the Government requires a message to be transmitted between Washington and Chicago in an unusual manner, in order that other service than that which is usual in connection with the message may be performed in connection therewith, for such extraordinary service we claim that extraordinary compensation is due. This is briefly the view of The Western Union Telegraph Company on that point.

The report of the Postmaster General speaks of the liberality of Congress towards the telegraph as follows :

" When through the liberality of Congress the first telegraph " line had been constructed, and the partial success of the inven" tion demonstrated.——"

I do not desire to detract in the smallest degree from whatever merit is due to Congress on account of its liberality toward the telegraph ; but it seems proper to call the attention of the committee to the fact, that $30,000 was contributed to enable Professor Morse to make an experiment with the telegraph, and that the line which was built with that appropriation, after having been operated for a time by the Government, was found to be an expense—that it was not self-sustaining, and the Government gave it away simply to stop that expense. That appropriation is the only one that I remember to have been made by Congress for the benefit of the telegraphs of the United States, with the single exception of that made in 1861, when Congress authorized a contract to be made with any party who would give adequate security to construct and maintain a telegraph line between the Missouri River and the Pacific Ocean, the free use of which should be given to the United States for 10 years, in consideration of $40,000 a year. Such a contract was made, the line was constructed, and has been in operation ever since. The contract price promised by the United States has been fully paid and the contract has expired; but I claim that the Government simply paid for service which was richly worth the cost. But, if it was not, there is one other fact in that connection which is entitled to mention. Since 1862 the telegraph has paid into the Federal Treasury over a million and a half of dollars for taxes.

Mr. NIBLACK.—Do you mean all the Companies, or your Company only?

Mr. ORTON.—I mean all the Companies, since the internal revenue laws went into operation, which was in 1862. Therefore, if we consider that the $40,000 a year was a contribution by the United States for which it received no equivalent, still, while it was paying that out with one hand with the other it was taking in three times as much.

The telegraph, therefore, it is but fair to say, stands before the people of the United States as the product of private enterprise, and is not the debtor of the Government for a single dollar. Congress has given hundreds of millions for other enterprises—hundreds of millions in bonds and lands to railways, and, so far as I know, not a single Telegraph Company in the United States is to-day the recipient, directly or indirectly, of one single dollar of benefit conferred by the Federal Government. We make no complaint of that. It has been a favorite investment with but few people. It has paid less during the last six years, while I have been actively connected with it, to the owners of the property, on whatever basis the estimate is made, than any other active public investment in the United States. Whether the estimate be made on the basis of the cost of the lines, on the market value of the stock, or on any other basis—the telegraph business in the United States during the last six years has paid less on the average than investments in other corporations.

Reference is made, in the Postmaster General's report, to a possible rivalry between the business of the post-office and the telegraph in this country. Without reading from the report of the Postmaster General, and certainly without desiring to do him any injustice, I think I am justified in saying that his report contemplates a state of things under which the telegraph might become the competitor of the mails, and the revenues of the post-office might suffer from such competition. That is the inference which I draw from certain general statements in the report. Now, I can only express an opinion on that point, and

I shall not undertake to refer to statistics in support of it; but it is my opinion that the telegraph contributes far more to the development of the postal service than it draws from it as a re-sult of its competition. That is to say, between any two cities of the United States the increase in the correspondence by mail will be in a larger ratio than the increase in the correspondence by telegraph, whatever that increase may be. While I shall not undertake to support the opinion by data, I will state, as the result of my investigation of the subject, that the telegraph, in-stead of being the rival of the postal service—a something which is going to interfere with it or detract from its revenues—is a constant stimulant to increase the correspondence by mail, and therefore to increase the postal revenues. Let me remark, in this connection, that notwithstanding the fact that the wires of the Western Union Telegraph Company are absolutely idle for at least six hours in the twenty-four, we probably pay a very much larger sum for postage every year than any other private cor-poration in the United States. With our offices, and wires, and men, and all the necessary appliances for conducting the busi-ness, without apparently any increase of cost, we still pay large sums annually for postage, simply because there is a department of correspondence which it is impossible for the telegraph to do. For example : It cannot audit its own accounts. I do not mean to say that it is physically impossible to do so by tele-graph, but that the expense of doing it with accuracy would be vastly greater than it is to do it by mail.

Mr. NIBLACK.—You mean in the transaction of official busi-ness between the offices?

Mr. ORTON.—Yes, sir. It is very difficult for the telegraph to be accurate in the transmission of figures. I read again from the report:

" The natural policy of private Companies is to extend facili-" ties slowly, and only to profitable points; to let their business " augment gradually, and to reap larger profits from a small " number of messages, while a Government system, managed in " the interests of the people, pursues exactly the opposite " course."

I suppose that it is entirely correct to say that it is the natural policy of men engaged in every department of business so to conduct it as to make the largest legitimate profit. The tele-graph, however, has not been behind the development of the country in population, in scarcely any section. It has kept pace with the railways all over the country, and there are hun-dreds, if not thousands of miles of telegraph in operation to-day where there are no railways, and where, I think, the mails only run two or three times a week. The telegraph is being rapidly developed in Northern Texas, the Indian Territory, Kansas,

Colorado, Montana, California, Northern Michigan, and other sections of the country, where I think the mails are not run every day. It is not too much to say that the telegraph has fairly kept pace with the growth of the country ; but, if it has not, I still am of opinion that it would be unjust to charge it with any special selfishness. Investments are made in telegraph property for the sole purpose of making profit. We make no pretense to being a philanthropic or benevolent institution. We only claim that, having received no benefits from Congress other than that general protection of the laws to which all citizens are entitled, we are not liable to any special charges, even if we do not keep up with the general expectation in the provision of facilities. I quote again :

"Meanwhile, the immediate defects and abuses of the tele-"graph call loudly for reform."

If there is anybody, Mr. Chairman, who alleges before this committee, or before Congress, or before any department of the Government, abuses concerning the conduct of its business by the Company with which I am connected, I shall esteem it a favor to be informed of the fact. But I submit, unless allegations are made, which, not being denied, do call for reform, whether it is just for the head of an executive department of the Government to charge citizens engaged in a lawful enterprise, by the investment of their own capital, with " defects and abuses," without supporting that charge by something which, undenied, would be acccepted as evidence of the fact.

I do not admit that the question of the value of telegraph property is, under present circumstances, an entirely proper subject for consideration by this committee, and for this reason: Under the law of 1866 the Federal Government has the right to purchase all the lines and property of the Companies which have accepted the provisions of that Act, at an *appraised value*, to be ascertained by five competent disinterested persons, two of whom shall be selected by the Postmaster General of the United States, two by the Company interested, and one by the four so previously selected. Now, while the general question of what it might cost the United States to acquire all the telegraph lines may be a proper subject for consideration, I conceive that anything which looks like anticipating the award of that jury, in the selection of which the Companies have an equal voice, is unfair ; and I therefore except to that portion of the report of the Postmaster General which discusses this question of the value of the telegraph lines of the United States.

I desire to have the attention of the committee especially to what I am about to read. The report states as follows:

"The majority of lines in this country have been built very "cheaply, their entire cost, including patents, being probably

" much less than $10,000,000. In fact, the poles have been
" erected in many cases entirely without cost to the Telegraph
" Companies by the railroads along whose tracks they are built."
* * * (I fail to see how that affects the question of their value.)
" The cost of a new system, equal in extent to the present,
" would, at the above rates, be $11,880,000."

Now, I submit whether these general charges of defects of
administration, this prejudicing of the condition of the property,
and this fixing of its value, is a fair proceeding on the part of
an executive officer of the United States towards Companies
whose obligation to part with their property is coupled with
their right to be represented on the jury that is to settle the
question of its value. No reason for the opinions here expressed,
and to which I have just referred, is given in the report—no
satisfactory reason—but I find in the appendix a detailed estimate by Mr. Charles T. Chester, of New York; and I would be
glad to know whether the statement which I have just quoted
from the report as to the probable cost of duplicating the present telegraph system of the United States, is based upon this
estimate, on page 169 of the Postmaster General's report. Has
the committee any information on that subject?

THE CHAIRMAN.—I presume the committee has no information on that subject. The Chairman has not. Perhaps the
Postmaster General may.

The POSTMASTER GENERAL.—That result is gathered in part
from that report of Chester's, in part from other information, and
also in part from the reports of Mr. Orton himself. It is not
confined to Mr. Chester's statement or to any other statement.

Mr. ORTON.—If my reports have been as widely misapprehend-
ed as the report of Mr. Chester has been, I can begin to comprehend how such a statement as that came to be made. The committee will pardon me for calling attention again to the fact that
there are two statements made in the report: first, that all the
telegraph property in the United States probably cost " *much
less*" than $10,000,000; and secondly, that it can be reproduced
for $11,880,000. The only witness whom the Postmaster
General brings forward to support this statement is Mr. Charles
T. Chester, of New York, whose estimate is found on page 169
of the report. The principal item in that estimate is 175,000
miles of wire, and you will note particularly that it says " *duty
free.*" Now, the duty on telegraph wire is over 60 per cent.;
and more than half of the 20,000 miles of wire which the Western Union Company erected in the year 1872 it was obliged to
import, and to pay thereon duty at the rate of about 68 per cent.,
less 10 per cent. since the 1st of July last, I think. In this estimate, then, this principal item, representing more than $6,000,000,
is for wire *duty free.* Now, the committee will bear in mind

that this is the witness who, presumptively, is put upon the stand, if not to prove the statement of the Postmaster General, at least to justify its being made; and I know it will surprise the committee, as it surprised me, on examining Mr. Chester's estimate in detail, and on footing it up (notwithstanding that its principal item, representing more than $6,000,000, is for wire duty free) to find that the total is eighteen and one quarter millions of dollars. Let me repeat: The Postmaster General alleges that all the telegraph property in the United States cost less than $10,000,000, and that it can be all reproduced for $11,880,000, and he puts upon the stand a witness whose estimate takes $6,000,000 worth of wire at 60 per cent. less than it costs, and that witness testifies that it would cost *eighteen and one quarter millions of dollars!*

Mr. HALE.—He says it can be put up for about 25 per cent. below that estimate.

Mr. ORTON.—Would not that 25 per cent. be fully offset by the 60 per cent. on the wire? That is what the rest of us would have to pay.

Now, Mr. Chairman, I propose to inquire concerning the competency of Mr. Charles T. Chester to be a Government witness in this trial, on an indictment by the Postmaster General, of the Telegraph Companies of the United States for not having spent more of their own money in the development of a businesss that has brought less average return than any other public investment in the country within the last six years.

Was there no one actively connected with the telegraph business; no unprejudiced person in the United States, having knowledge of the facts, of whom inquiry might have been made and whose testimony would have been entitled to weight?

Mr. Charles T. Chester never constructed but one telegraph line, and that was built in the City of New York within the last three years. It is the Fire Alarm Telegraph of that city. And we have had the curiosity to investigate Mr. Charles T. Chester's Fire Alarm Telegraph, and have obtained from the Fire Department an inventory of the property which he put into it, and from the Comptroller of the City the bill which he presented to the city for it.

He erected 625 miles of wire, and his bill for it, on file to-day in the office of the Comptroller of the City of New York, is $850,000. Now, at the rate that Mr. Charles T. Chester, who offers to build a line (which the Postmaster General says can be built for $11,880,000) for eighteen and a quarter million dollars, if you will let him import his wire free of duty—at the rate which Mr. Charles T. Chester charges the City of New York, the telegraph lines in the United States would amount to $238,-000,000! There were eighty miles of poles. If we make the calculation on the basis of the miles of poles the result would be nearly $800,000,000 ! · But if his bill for $850,000 were to be audited on the basis of his estimate of eighteen and a quarter millions, for a system of telegraph equal to that now in operation in the United States, the Comptroller would pay him but $65,000 !

Mr. SARGENT.—Is there not some difference in the number of instruments and their character, between the Fire Alarm Telegraph and the ordinary business telegraph, which would account for some difference in the cost?

Mr. ORTON.—Yes, sir; I think there is. As a general thing it costs very much less in proportion to equip that sort of telegraph than it does to equip a regular telegraph for commercial business.

Perhaps, Mr. Chairman, as a specimen brick, this is a little better, clearer, and more decided a specimen than we shall be able to produce as we go through with the other estimates and exhibits in this report, and yet, without a single exception, on analyzing them, the result will be substantially the same.

But I acquit the Postmaster General of an intention to do the telegraph business of the United States so great an injustice as he has undoubtedly done it. This is not his work. The young gentleman who has been permitted to use the dignity of a high officer to shield himself while making an assault on private citizens and on private enterprises is the same who appeared before this committee at the last session of Congress as the volunteer advocate of the Government side of this question.

I say I acquit the Postmaster General of an intention to do so great an injustice as has been done, not only to the Companies, but, as I submit very respectfully, to himself and to his great office. But I do ask that, in the further consideration of this question, by whatever department of the Government, some regard be paid to the fact : that there are connected with the telegraph business in the United States gentlemen who have been engaged in it almost since its commencement; gentlemen of ripe experience, of high character, and whose opinions and whose statements of fact are certainly entitled to as much weight as the guesses of this clerk, who has been permitted in an official document to assail private citizens and private enterprises in the name of the Postmaster General.

Let me say a word on the question of value. The telegraph and railroad companies in the United States have invested, *during the last six years*, more cash in the production of telegraph property than the gross sum named in the Postmaster General's report as the cost of all the lines in the country.

The CHAIRMAN.—Do you mean by that that more cash capital has been invested in the actual structure?

Mr. ORTON.—Yes, sir.

The CHAIRMAN.—You exclude stock operations?

Mr. ORTON.—I exclude stock operations. I mean exactly what I say : More cash has been invested in the production of telegraph property—not stock—but poles, wires, instruments, apparatus, buildings, patents, etc., than the Postmaster General's report states to be the cost of all the telegraph property in the country.

Now, the question which becomes necessary for this committee to consider at the outset is the expediency of the Government of the United States embarking in the telegraph business.

The population of the United States is now about 40 millions. The number of messages sent by all the telegraph lines in the country in a year is less than 20 millions. This fact, therefore, appears : that of every two persons in the United States, one of them, once in a year, has occasion to send a telegraph message at the average cost of sixty-two cents, or thirty-one cents for each person. Of the 40 millions probably 39 millions never send a message at all, yet each one of them must have, in every one of the 365 days in the year, food, and clothing, and shelter. By what right does the Government, organized for the common benefit, and maintained at the common expense, propose to tax the whole people of the United States for the convenience of so small a percentage of the population? Is it not a strange and anomalous condition of things that Congress sits considering an attack upon private parties and property by a department of the Government which seeks to inaugurate proceedings for the acquisition of their property, and for embarking in the telegraph business at the public expense, to promote the convenience of a mere handful of people, not one of whom comes here to complain, or to ask for any relief, while thousands and tens of thousands are either homeless or suffering for lack of food, fuel or clothing, and for whose comfort the Government makes no provision whatever?

I trust, Mr. Chairman, that this committee will believe me entirely sincere when I say that neither on this nor on any former occasion have I intended to be wanting in that respect which is due to the members of the committee and to the officers of every department of the Government of the United States. Six years ago we entered, as we supposed, into a compact with the United States, either that we were to be permitted to go on and conduct our business without Governmental interference, or that the Government would take our property at the appraisement of a jury in whose selection we should have an equal voice, and that we should then be permitted to withdraw our capital and invest it in other enterprises. Scarcely was the ink dry on the signature that gave validity to that act before schemes were introduced into Congress, and have been pressed at every session since, which have rendered it necessary for the officers and representatives of the telegraph to be in attendance on Congress, under circumstances of great personal inconvenience, at very considerable expense, and to the neglect and injury of the business with which they are connected. If, therefore, I have sometimes exhibited impatience, it is, first, because I am compelled always to be in a hurry; and, secondly, because I have felt, as I feel now, that we have been the injured party and not the aggressor; that we have endeavored to keep in good faith the compact into which we entered on the invitation of Congress; and yet we are obliged to come here at every session to defend our property, our business, and our management from unprovoked assaults by parties whose interests or whose prejudices tempt them to suppress or distort the facts, or who for lack of knowledge and experience seem unable to comprehend them.

Let me ask, on behalf of the property which I represent, and of the interests with which I am connected, that some definite action be taken on this subject at this session. It is due to all the interests involved, as well as to the honor and good faith of the United States, that something shall be settled. I stated a few moments ago that the Company with which I am connected had erected, during the year 1872, 20,000 miles of wire. The indications are that we shall be required to erect, during the year 1873, at least 25,000 miles of wire, notwithstanding the fact that we are now engaged in equipping our lines with an apparatus which we have demonstrated to our entire satisfaction is capable of doubling the capacity of every wire we have. Is it unfair, Mr. Chairman, in anticipation of such an investment, involving probably an expense of a million of dollars on the part of the Western Union Company, and perhaps another million by railroad companies, in connection with which lines will be constructed, that we should ask Congress to take some action by which we can judge whether every time we make an investment in this business we put it at hazard. Is the million of dollars which we shall probably invest during the next year to be put at hazard? Do the United States contemplate proceeding for its confiscation? At all events, are we not entitled to notice as to what the Government does contemplate, in order that we may elect whether to incur the risk of investing these large sums annually, or whether we will retain and distribute them among our stockholders. I submit that between man and man this would be only fair—that common sense of justice which is called "fair play." The citizen of the United States is certainly entitled to ask this from the Government of the United States. We ask nothing more. We admit our obligation to deliver our property to the Government under the provisions of

the Act of 1866 whenever Congress shall direct the appointment of appraisers, and shall appropriate the funds where-
with to pay their award. But we object to this apparent
attempt to create a public opinion in advance of the appraisement, which is to operate on the appraisers to the
prejudice of our rights. It is not necessary to discuss the
question now, whether we are entitled, under that Act, to
the simple cost of the poles and wires, or whether we are
entitled to something more. The value is to be decided by arbitration, in accordance with the terms of the Act, to which we have
agreed, and the arbitrators are the judges. We certainly shall
not agree to any attempt to ascertain first what the appraisement will be, in order that if it is a good bargain you may
accept it, or, if it is a bad one, you may decline it. We agree
to abide by the result of arbitration as provided in the Act, and
I hope that before Congress adjourns some action will be taken
which shall be an indication to the holders of shares in the
various Telegraph Companies of the United States, whether it
will be prudent for them to continue to hold such property, and
to the managers of the Companies whether it will be prudent for
them to continue to invest a portion of their earnings in the
extension of the property, or what it will be necessary for them
to do to meet whatever shall appear to be or shall be declared to
be the determination of the Government in that respect.

THE HUBBARD BILL.

I am quite unequal to the discussion of the details of the bill
of Mr. Hubbard. I now speak of the bill as I last saw it. If
the committee have allowed any modifications of it I have not
been apprized of them. But the bill, as I last saw it, is a scheme
for the incorporation by Congress of a Company authorized to
engage in the telegraph business in all the States and Territories,
conditioned that the rates at which messages shall be sent by
this Company shall be the rates named in the bill, which rates
are apparently considerably less than the present average rates.
But there is a provision in the bill authorizing "priority messages" at double rates. But, Mr. Chairman, every message is a
priority message. That is what the telegraph is for. And
you will appreciate, I think, the force of that on learning the
following facts: It is now three years since, throughout the
territory east of the Missouri River, messages could be filed at
any telegraph office at any time during the day for transmission
at the convenience of the Company, and for delivery on the
following morning at half the tariff rates. That provision has
been in operation three years. It is thoroughly well known to
all people who have occasion to use the telegraph; and, although
the rates from New York, Boston, Philadelphia, Baltimore and

Washington to Texas, Western Arkansas and Kansas, are
$3 to $3.50 for a single message, with a few hours difference of
time, and without any inconvenience to the customer as to the
filing of the message at half these rates, the fact is that at this
time, after three years of use, but eleven per cent. of the telegraph business is done under this provision of half rates.

The CHAIRMAN.—Is that arrangement made by all the other
Companies as well as yours?

Mr. ORTON.—Yes, sir; all of them. Mr. Thurston, President
of the Pacific and Atlantic Company, I suppose (as I did not
file a caveat) is entitled to a patent on that scheme. I think, if
he was entirely frank, he would admit that he knew we were
going to do it; but he did it first, because it took us a great
while to work up the details before putting it in operation, and
so he started it on his lines before we did on ours. But it has
been in operation on all the lines of all the Companies during
the last three years. It did not at first include any territory
west of the Mississippi river.

Mr. THURSTON.—I wish to disclaim the credit of being so
much smarter than the President of the Western Union Telegraph Company, and I am happy to concede to him the com-
pliment of having originated the proposition of sending these
night despatches at half rates. It was the principle on which
our line was first created that that should form a feature of it
when the line was sufficiently extended to do so; and we had
it in contemplation, it seems, at the same time as the Western
Union people, without each other knowing it.

The CHAIRMAN.—Is the fact that you have such an arrangement so generally known to your customers that the eleven
per cent. represents the voluntary choice of the people; or is it
true that a considerable portion of your customers do not know
of the existence of that half rate?

Mr. ORTON.—When we inaugurated this scheme we considered that the people who sent and received messages every
day were the people whom it was to our interest to notify
first. The half rate message blank is printed in red ink.
These blanks were distributed, as other message blanks are
distributed, freely among the customers of the telegraph. A
small advertisement, of a size suitable to be enclosed in the envelope in which messages are delivered to our customers, printed
also in red, was printed to the extent of many millions, and was
supplied to the various offices of the Company, and a copy was
placed in the envelope with every message delivered for several
months. We argued that in the course of three months, if an
advertisement went out with every message delivered, we should
probably, during that period, reach the great majority of those
who patronize the telegraph. In addition to that cards were

provided and directed to be suspended in the telegraph offices. The blanks themselves are exposed there. And still more recently I directed an advertisement to be printed prominently on the envelopes used for enclosing messages to be delivered. We have taken the utmost pains to inform the public of the fact, and we believe the public is well informed of it. Certainly that is the case among those who are most in the habit of using the telegraph.

The CHAIRMAN.—Does this half fare arrangement apply to all your rates?

Mr. ORTON.—Yes, sir; to every office east of the Missouri River, including Kansas, Missouri, Arkansas, Louisiana and nearly all of Texas.

The CHAIRMAN.—Between here and New York, and between here and Boston, and between Boston and New York?

Mr. ORTON.—Yes, sir. We do not include in it the Pacific coast, for the reason that the line is so long and the difference in time is three hours. The great difficulty in maintaining that line, its liability to interruptions and the certainty that day and night business would get confused, has induced us to withhold putting it into operation on the Pacific coast. We intend, however, in lieu of that, to reduce the rates between the Atlantic and Pacific coasts at an early day—to still further reduce them. They are only about one half now what they were six years ago.

Now let me return to the Hubbard bill. I spoke of one of the provisions of that bill, being the authority to charge double the rates' named therein for messages entitled to priority, and I expressed the opinion that every message was a priority message; and I appealed to the fact that eighty-nine per cent. of the business of the Western Union Telegraph Company is priority business, or what would be priority business under the provisions of this bill. Therefore, taking the present day rates and night rates, and striking the average, the priority rate under Mr. Hubbard's bill is higher on the average than the present average rate. The bill, when I last saw it, provided for an issue of $1,000,000 of stock, without any other consideration than the vague expression " for expenses of organization." It contained no stipulation or guarantee on the part of the corporators that any single thing promised on the part of the corporation to be created by the bill should be performed. It is a stupendous job; an attempt to get the sanction of Congress to a scheme to enable stock to be floated, one million dollars of which could be divided among the corporators, without the obligation to account for a single dollar of it. When that has been done it is a good enough thing for its beneficiaries, if they never erect a pole or string a mile of wire; and I predict that if that bill shall become a law the Company created by it will never build a thousand miles of telegraph line. And yet it may be a splendid thing for its promoters. It will do the public no good, and do the Government no good; on the contrary, if this scheme should fail, would it not have discredited Governmental connection with the telegraph; would it not postpone the time (if that time is ever to come) when the Government shall control the business?

The CHAIRMAN.—Please to explain precisely what you mean when you say that the corporators may make a good thing of it without their erecting a pole or building a mile of line?

Mr. ORTON.—When this bill becomes a law, I assume that the first thing to be done under it is to organize the corporation; the next thing inevitably is to sell some of the stock, for until the proceeds of the sale of the stock are on hand they certainly will have nothing with which to buy lines that are already built or to build new ones. Suppose they sell $1.000,-000 of stock, and no more—they have a right to distribute that among the corporators, and are under no obligation to account to anybody for it. I assume that no moral question is involved in connection with taking that which Congress freely gives. I certainly raise no such question. If Congress gives the authority to twenty or thirty gentlemen to collect $1,000.000 from the public, and to distribute it among themselves, that is about the highest right to property I know of. But Congress exacts nothing from them in return, imposes no obligation on them then and thereafter to do anything. But suppose they should get $2,000,000 of stock and divide the $1,000,000, and then faithfully and judiciously expend the other million, and the scheme fails. They have burrowed a hole in the Post-office, interfered with and interrupted the postal service, vexed and harrassed the customers of the telegraph, who have been many times caught sending messages by the Government line to points not reached by it, disgusted the public generally; and certainly it seems to me that the people will not be in a very evangelical frame of mind towards Governmental connection with the telegraph, with such a specimen of the results before them.

But suppose it goes on and does better, what then? The Government has created a monopoly of which it can never be rid except by purchase. There may be no obligation on the part of the Government to buy the existing lines; there certainly would be an obligation on the part of the Government to buy that line. I submit that every share of stock subscribed to the corporation created by this Act would be so subscribed on the inducements held out by the Government of the United States, either that that Company is to make ten per cent on its capital, with an added million for expenses of organization, or, failing in that, the United States is to buy the property.

Now, I read in the public prints that the Secretary of the Treasury has recently been before a committee of Congress, asking for legislation to enable him to pay a larger commission than is now allowed by law for the negotiation of bonds of the United States at a lower rate of interest than is paid on the greater part of the public debt. This bill is a scheme to enable a private corporation, after its corporators have made $1,000,000, to make ten per cent on all the balance of their investment, with the one million included. What is the propriety of such a partnership, with such a *quasi* guarantee of such a rate of interest, on the part of the United States, which certainly is abundantly able to go into market and borrow money at half that rate of interest? What is the necessity for the Government to set up partners in the business who do not own a rod of telegraph in the United States, and who never did an hour's work at the telegraph business in their lives—what is the propriety of the Government setting up such parties in opposition to the capital and experience which, for more than twenty years, have been developing a telegraph system which, notwithstanding the disparaging statements made concerning it in the report of the Postmaster General, compares favorably with any telegraph system on the globe?

Now, a word on the subject of rates. More than sixty per cent. of the cost of conducting the telegraph business is paid for labor, yet we are obliged constantly to meet statements and arguments based upon the rates paid in Europe.

THE CHAIRMAN.—Does that refer to the running expenses, or to the building expenses as well?

Mr. ORTON.—It refers to conducting the business. Sixty per cent. of the whole cost is for labor.

Mr. NIBLACK.—What do you include in the word " labor "— do you include operators?

Mr. ORTON.—I include the wages of operators, of course. It is a work of men and of hands, not of steam engines—a work of individuals, the expense of which increases almost in the direct ratio of the increased volume of business. It is all very well to say that if you have an immense mass of it it can be done more cheaply. Ask the stenographer there who is reporting these proceedings how much cheaper he can work if he has the work of four men put upon him at once. There is a limit to human capacity. If correspondence were all paid for by the written word, would the price of it be any cheaper if the volume was largely increased? And yet every word of every message is written out in detail by the fingers of the telegraph operator. No matter how you may increase the speed of transmission, or cheapen some of the processes, every single message is the product of the labor of human fingers. Now, I

understand it to have been the settled policy of every administration for more than forty years to secure a higher rate of
wages for labor in the United States than is paid in any other
country ; and especially has it been the policy of the United
States to protect its laboring citizens from competition with the
product of the cheaper labor of continental Europe. In view of
this fact, and of that which I have already stated—that more
than sixty per cent. of the current expenses of conducting telegraph business is paid directly in wages—is it fair to ask that
private capital and enterprise shall perform in this country a
service which is so largely the product in detail of labor, at rates
corresponding with a similar service in other countries? I believe it is susceptible of simple demonstration that, considering
the difference in cost of labor and of material in Europe and in
the United States, telegraphing in the United States is decidedly
cheaper than in any country in Europe—I was going to say
than the average, but I say in any country in Europe. If you
will consider the difference simply in the wages paid to the employés, and the difference in the cost of materials, you will
find that telegraphing is cheaper in the United States than
in any country in Europe.

But that is not all : A day's work by the employés of the
Government is limited by law to eight hours, while the employés of the telegraph are required to work at least ten, and in
many cases twelve hours. I assume it will not be claimed that
the same persons in the employ of the Government would do
any more work in the same time than if in the service of private parties ; or that the former could hire telegraph operatives
at lower rates of wages than are now paid. It follows, therefore, that, on the basis of eight hours as a day's work, the present
annual expenditure to operate the telegraph would yield a product twenty per cent. less than the present, or that to maintain
the present product would require an increase of force and of
expenditure twenty-five per cent. greater than the present.
Surely, the Government would not discriminate against operatives and mechanics in the telegraphic department of its business, and require them to work from two to four hours more a
day than is now required of Government clerks, mechanics and
laborers.

In the report of the Postmaster General reference is made
to the Government Telegraph of Great Britain, and considerable space is devoted to the consideration of the question of a uniform rate. Now, sir, I admit that, if it were
practicable to remove the 40,000,000 of people of the United
States into the territory comprised in the States of New England
and New York, it would be entirely practicable to establish a
uniform rate. But see how unjust it is to compare this country

with Great Britain or France, each having a population approximating to our own, settled on an area but little larger than New England, while our population is spread over an area equal almost to the continent of Europe. Ten to fifteen miles of telegraph must be constructed and kept in repair in the United States to reach the same number of persons as in Great Britain or France are reached by one mile ; and when you consider that it costs on an average eight dollars per mile of wire per annum to keep constructed lines in repair, you will see what a difference there is in favor of those countries of denser population. Permit me to remark, further, in connection with the English telegraph, which is represented to be a success (and I believe it to be a success so far as its adminstration is concerned), that I think very erroneous views are entertained concerning the result of its operations financially. Whatever it may become hereafter, the British telegraph has cost the British Government more money every month since it has been in operation under the Government than it has received in revenue from such operations. Now, I am aware that an exhibit has been made showing a profit. I have examined that exhibit carefully ; and find that the apparent profit resulting from the operation of the British telegraph is obtained by charging an arbitrary sum to capital account. There is no evidence yet to satisfy me that the British telegraph is self-sustaining to-day. And yet it ought to be self-sustaining, and I have no doubt that it will ultimately become self-sustaining. Very much has been said concerning the enormous increase in the volume of business since the English Government took the telegraph and established a uniform rate. Let me make a statement in that connection. There are no more messages sent in Great Britain to-day, in proportion to the number of miles of wire and the number of stations and of employés, than there were before the Government took the lines from private hands and established a uniform rate. This is a very important fact, because there is involved in it the very essence of the law governing the development of the telegraph business.

The CHAIRMAN.—Is that the statistical rule on which telegraph companies consider growth to be gauged?

Mr. ORTON.—I am now about to state what I consider to be the rule. It is, that the increase in the volume of telegraph business is more directly proportioned to the increase of facilities than it is to any question of rates whatever ; and I would make, without the slightest hesitation, a wager covering the cost of the experiment, that if, say, between four cities, the experiment should be tried, in the one case, of reducing the rate one half, and, in the other case, of doubling the facilities without any reduction of the rates, the double volume of business will come quicker on the doubled facilities than on the reduced rates. Now, that is my opinion, and I would be glad to hear the views of the other gentlemen present, with whom I have not conferred.

Mr. THURSTON.—I fully confirm the opinion of the President of the Western Union Telegraph Company. We have found it so on our lines. And to-day we find, as the result of our business, that, with what has been called increased rates, over those that existed up to the 1st of May, the want of facilities alone prevents our business increasing ; and we are now increasing our facilities in order to increase our business.

Mr. SWEET.—Mr. Orton asked me that question to-day on the train, and I have been turning the thing over in my mind. I believe his statement to be substantially correct, so far as my experience goes.

The CHAIRMAN.—Does that indicate to your mind that the demand is for greater facilities rather than for cheaper rates?

Mr. SWEET.—For greater and more rapid facilities. The experience of night rates will demonstrate that. The question is not one of cheap rates ; it is upon the question of facilities, and of the rapidity with which messages are transmitted and delivered, that the increase of business depends.

The POSTMASTER GENERAL (to Mr. Thurston).—You say that your business increases if you increase facilities, notwithstanding that the prices may be also increased. Suppose your prices were lowered, would not the business be increased by that ?

Mr. THURSTON.—My experience in telegraph business brings it down to a very small point. It is, that no man sends a telegraph message for the mere pleasure of telegraphing. He merely sends it in order to gain time, or to make the profit which he expects to gain by economizing time, by forestalling the market, or something else ; and the question with him is not so much the cost of a message as the speed with which it is delivered. So, if you take a line between two large cities, with only one wire, and if you make the price of messages as low as you possibly can, the public will not be accommodated, and the business will not increase; but, if you put up more wires, and increase the facilities for telegraphing, you increase the business.

The POSTMASTER GENERAL.—That increase of business is obtained by multiplying the wires.

Mr. THURSTON.—Yes. By increasing the facilities and keeping the rates at the same price.

The POSTMASTER GENERAL.—Then it is unlike the postal business, and unlike the telegraph business in other countries.

Mr. THURSTON.—Take a large city like Pittsburg, where I reside, which is a manufacturing city, and take a factory there employing 400 people, and you will find that it is only one out of the four hundred that ever uses the telegraph ; the other

899 do not send a message in a year; but the one sends fifty or a hundred messages in a day; and we must use him as a merchant would use a customer—we must give him the facilities that he wants. The question with him is not one of price, but one as to how the service is performed.

The POSTMASTER GENERAL.—That would be the question with a great many more people if they had facilities, and if the telegraph was cheap enough to be within their reach.

The CHAIRMAN.—Mr. Brown, what is your opinion upon the point?

Mr. BROWN.—My impression is that the experience in some parts of the country has been that reducing the rates has very vastly increased the business, as in the West, for instance. I learned from Mr. Orton that putting the rate down to ten cents between Chicago and Milwaukee increased the business very vastly; but my impression has been that when a man pays 25 or 30 cents for a segar he does not care very much whether he pays five cents more or less for a telegraph message.

Mr. PALMER (to Mr. Orton).—If cheapening rates does not increase the volume of business why do you cheapen rates?

Mr. ORTON.—Have I been understood as saying that cheapening the rates did not increase the volume of business?

Mr. PALMER.—I thought that the tendency of your argument was to show that it was the increase of facilities rather than the reduction of prices that brought an increase of business.

Mr. ORTON.—Both of them tend undoubtedly to increase the business, but I believe that the development of the telegraph depends more upon the provision of increased facilities than on the reduction of rates—assuming, of course, that the rates are not exorbitant and prohibitary, but taking the average rates as they are to-day in the United States. And now let me support this: The tariff between New York and Cincinnati six years ago was $1.85 a message. Under the active competition inaugurated by the Company of which Mr. Thurston is the president, the rates were reduced to $1.50, $1.25, $1.00 and finally to 60 cents. At that rate the lines were operated for two years. The rates to intermediate places were reduced correspondingly, the rate between New York and Pittsburg being 25 cents. On the 1st of May last, by previous agreement, the rate between New York and Cincinnati was advanced from 60 cents to one dollar, and between New York and Pittsburg from 25 to 50 cents. Within the year preceding the Western Union Telegraph Company had very considerably increased its facilities between New York, Pittsburg and Cincinnati. The increase in the volume of business between the stations on that route, during the months of May, June and July of the present year, after an advance of from forty to one hundred per cent., was greater than the increase in the corresponding months in the previous years.

The CHAIRMAN.—Had there been an increase in the facilities?
Mr. ORTON.—Yes, I stated that as part of my preliminary
statement.
The CHAIRMAN.—What was the percentage of the increased
facilities?
Mr. ORTON.—I cannot answer that very well. The facilities
between two such cities as New York and Cincinnati do not depend upon the number of wires on any one route, although that
route may be the one mainly used for the business between
those two stations. It is the general increase of facilities East
and West on the lines that are available between the two sections.
I do not mean to say that the way to get a larger increase
of business next year than we have had heretofore is to make
a further increase in the tariff; I presume I shall not be misunderstood in that regard. I merely bring this illustration in
support of the opinion which I expressed as to the law governing the development of the telegraph business—first that it is a
question of facilities, and that, until ample facilities are provided
for the existing volume of business, there is certainly no great
inducement to make a reduction of rates. It costs a good deal
of money to provide those additional facilities. The Western
Union Telegraph Company has erected within the last two
years a wire of unusual size in this country—number six gauge—
between New York and Chicago. It is now completing one
between New York and Cincinnati of the same gauge, and has
ordered another of the same gauge between Pittsburg and
Chicago.
The CHAIRMAN.—Is there any other relation to the size
except strength?
Mr. ORTON.—The question of strength does not enter into the
case at all. The distance, telegraphically, between two stations
depends upon the size of the conductor, and it is possible to
bring New York and San Francisco telegraphically within the
same distance as New York and Boston, if you make the conductor large enough. On these larger conductors we are intro-
ducing Stearn's duplex system. We not only provide an
additional wire, but we equip it at once with an apparatus
which gives it double power. We bring Cincinnati and New
York nearer together telegraphically, and we make each wire
equal to two.
If I am not wearying the patience of the committee, I would
make a statement or two further in this connection. It will cost
for the wire which we contemplate erecting between New York
and St. Louis this spring at least $100,000—for one additional
wire. Suppose, for illustration, that there were but one wire
between New York and St. Louis, and that it had been until
recently capable of transmitting the volume of business required

to be transmitted between those two cities; but the inevitable growth, resulting partly from the use of the telegraph, and partly from the increase of population, and the development of business, carries the development of telegraph business ten per cent. beyond the capacity of that wire, it then becomes necessary to duplicate the entire investment, less the cost of the poles. Now, on this point let make a remark concerning the most unfortunate errors which the Postmaster General has permitted an uninformed person to put upon him and upon the country with official sanction. He states that the cost for additional wires is $30 per mile. Now, the smallest gauge of wire we use—No. 9 —weighs 340 lbs. to the mile, and it is worth to-day in the port of New York 10½ cents per pound. It requires very little knowledge of arithmetic to show that the cost there, before you have considered very far the question of making a telegraph, is about $36 a mile. And then, when it comes to transporting the wire an average of at least a thousand miles over the United States, hundreds of miles on the backs of pack horses to the place where it is to be erected, together with the insulators, cross-arms, tools and other requisite appliances for erecting it, I must confess my surprise at the declaration of the Postmaster General in an official document that additional wires can be erected in the United States at a cost of $30 a mile.

The CHAIRMAN.—I have just made a little figuring here from your statement. I understand you to say that the Western Union Telegraph Company would probably erect next year 25,000 additional miles of wire, at a cost of about a million of dollars; that would be forty dollars a mile, which is not very far from the estimate of the Postmaster General.

The POSTMASTER GENERAL.—With the duty off it is less than thirty dollars a mile.

The CHAIRMAN (to Mr. Orton).—Did I misunderstand you?

Mr. ORTON—You did not misunderstand me. I was not trying to be exact when I spoke of the cost as being a million of dollars, and I had in my mind only the expenditure which the Western Union Company would make. In the erection of 25,000 miles of new telegraph wire, it is probable that from one third to one-half of the total cost would be contributed by railroad companies. We are building a good deal of line every year at the cost of our Company of only the wire, insulators and instruments; the poles being provided and all the labor performed, except that of a competent foreman, by the railroad companies. Yet such lines, when completed, are as exclusively ours for use in transmitting messages for the public as if we had made the entire investment necessary to create them. In return for the contribution of the railroad companies we perform service for them on other lines. While, therefore, the addition of 25,000 miles of wire might not be entered as costing the Western Union Company in cash invested at the time more than $40 to $50 a mile, the total cost might be twice as much, the balance being contributed by railroad companies, or charged to profit and loss. The addition of a single wire may, and frequently does, involve the necessity of the reconstruction of the entire line, including the provision of new poles of larger carrying capacity. In that case the cost to the Western Union Company of the additional wire only would be charged to construction, the other expenses being put to profit and loss account, although the value of the whole line has been increased far beyond that of the additional wire. But when the additional wire has been erected as many operators are required to operate it as if it were the only wire on that route. It takes just as many operators to operate a second wire as it did for the first wire, and it will transmit as much matter as the first one did, so that the expense, in connection with the increased volume of business, keeps proportional with the increased volume; while every time the increase reaches a certain figure we must duplicate the investment—perhaps not absolutely, but we must make a very large addition to that investment.

Suppose that when the traffic of a railroad reached certain figures it became necessary to lay down a new track, and to provide a separate equipment for that track, and a separate staff for each department of its operations, you will see in a moment that a very large increase in business might become a great misfortune. So it has been found by our friends, who have sought the favor of the public in competition with the Western Union Telegraph Company by reducing their rates, that that was the short and sure road to destruction. And we are also quite satisfied with the result of that experience, since the difference in our own revenues by the larger rates enables us to provide the additional wires, which, being provided, constitute the ability of the stronger Company always to compete successfully with the weaker.

A single remark more. If it were true that all the telegraphs in the country could be reproduced for ten or eleven millions of dollars, would not that fact alone afford ample protection to the people of the United States from any very severe oppression on the part of Telegraph Companies? Is there any danger to the people of the United States from companies whose property can be duplicated for so small a sum of money? But, whether it is ten millions or fifty millions, or whatever the sum may be, there is no business of like general importance that can be established on so comparatively small a capital. A single wire between New York and Washington governs the tariff on 40 wires. If the line which Mr. Thurston's Company is, I believe, now work-

138

ing into Washington—a line of one wire—should elect to-morrow
to reduce the rate between New York and Washington one
half, it would be necessary for the Western Union Company
to follow in that reduction ; for, although, if we did not follow,
the public would be obliged still to give the majority of the
business to us at the higher rate, Mr. Thurston would inevitably
get all that he could possibly do by that line, and the fact that
he was willing to do all he could at that rate would undoubtedly
enable him to get the capital necessary to put up additional
wires ; and so, step by step, the difference between the two
would disappear, and unless we came down to the same rate we
should ultimately lose our business.

The POSTMASTER GENERAL.—I have one or two general remarks to make in reply to Mr. Orton. In my presentation of
the question with regard to the postal telegraph I am certain of
one thing—that I have not had a particle of feeling for or against
any Company. I have been looking solely to the public
interest. I have made no statement with a view to injure any
Company or to blast its prospects in the future, or to interfere
with any just compensation that may be awarded to it for its
property. On the contrary, I have made my statement only
after repeated solicitations from people of all grades of society,
some rich, some poor, some men in business and some in social
life, some from the East and some from the West; and that, too,
after Congress itself had inaugurated and carried out two or
three laborious and able investigations of the subject.

The distinguished President of the Western Union Telegraph
Company, who seems to be so exceedingly full of information
on the subject, has taken it upon himself to deal somewhat face-
tiously with the report of the Postmaster General, and rather to
express himself in terms of commiseration for the weakness
therein displayed. He has been especially severe upon the instrument that I have seen proper to use. Now, I admit that I
have had very few advantages in preparing this statement. I
have not had one dollar of public money at my disposal except
that which I can use by the assignment of a single clerk in the
department to gather information. I have availed myself of the
services of Mr. Lines, and I think that, so far as his private character is concerned, it will compare favorably with that of any
gentleman present—I was going to say with that of Mr. Orton
himself, but I wish to avoid the appearance of anything offensive. But Mr. Orton has seen proper to designate many of my
statements as the mere vaporings of an ignoramus, who has been
permitted to shield himself behind the dignity of a high officer.
Now, in the first place, I say to this committee that, so far as the
dignity of my office is concerned, I do not look to Mr. Orton, or
to any other man on the face of the earth, to protect it, or

to shield it, or to guide me how I shall treat it. In the discharge of my official duties I shall simply exercise my proper discretion fearlessly towards Mr. Orton individually, or towards him as President of the Western Union Telegraph Company. But I desired to present all the facts that may apply to this subject in all its lights, and at the same time I desired not only to be just to the people but to be fair and more than just—to be liberal to the members of those corporations who have heretofore enlisted in this business, and whose capital has been invested in the various lines. At the same time I wish to be understood that mere temper in this thing will not guide my action, as I am sure it will not guide yours. All that we seek to get at is the truth. To do that we want to ascertain exactly where we stand, precisely how much property these gentlemen have, exactly how much money they have invested; and when that is ascertained, the public mind will be prepared to say whether the Government will purchase these lines or not.

Now, we have listened to a two hours' oration from Mr. Orton, and we have not had from him a solitary word going to show what the expenditures of the Western Union Telegraph Company have been, nothing but a mere general declaration, which would not be regarded in a court of justice as worth a button. I appeal to any gentleman here, who is in the habit of trying cases, if he would for a moment dream of allowing a witness to retire from a witness stand after giving his own general opinions and declarations, and studiously concealing every fact. What I have asked for in this report is simply this, not that my statements should be taken as facts: I have presented them as the nearest approximation to facts which the means at my command enabled me to make, and I ask the committee to consider the statements which I have been enabled to present to them—statements all made in good faith—and then to do what I think prudent men ought always to do before engaging in any great work (and especially gentlemen like yourselves, acting in a representative capacity, as members of the American Congress), that is, simply to appoint a commission of the best men that we can designate in the land, with ample power to ascertain precisely how many miles of wire these gentlemen have, how many poles they have, how many batteries they have, how much property they have, precisely what amounts they have expended, and then, in the language of the Act of 1866, to determine what the Companies are entitled to for their lines, property and effects. That is the agreement which they have made. That is all that I have asked for. I do not ask you to take my statement, and to insist on taking the property of any telegraph Company; but I have asked you to appoint this commission, and in connection with it to appoint the appraisers,

throwing around them such guards as you may deem proper
and right for the protection of the people ; and when those
reports are made to you, with the facts reduced to figures as
accurately as the investigations of the ablest and most impartial
gentlemen we can obtain can arrive at, then I want this committee and Congress to determine whether the time has come
when the American people shall stand on this question on precisely the same platform with every civilized people in the
world ; and I believe that every nation in Europe to-day, that
has a telegraph at all, has put it under the charge of its Government. Even Canada, where that step has not yet been taken,
has marched forward to the establishment of a uniform rate of
compensation, applying to the whole extent of that country
which is next to our own in extent on the North American continent. And the directors of the Montreal Company have
already declared that on their uniform rate of 25 cents a message
they have had at least an increase of business amounting to
25 per cent. in the aggregate.

I have only asked the committee to avail themselves of all
proper means of investigation to arrive at the facts as accurately
as possible, and then to decide the question. I am not willing
to take Mr. Orton's mere generalities, and to allow him to make
his statement, without making the most careful scrutiny into his
detailed statement of facts.

Mr. NIBLACK.—Is it not true, also, that every Government that
has taken charge of the telegraph business has also taken charge
of the railroads, with the exception of Great Britain ?

The POSTMASTER GENERAL.—Canada has not.

Mr. ORTON.—Canada has not the Government telegraph.

The POSTMASTER GENERAL.—No, it has not the Governmental telegraph, but Canada has but one telegraph line, and
that is managed on the most liberal principles.

Mr. SWEET.—Canada has two telegraph companies.

The POSTMASTER GENERAL.—I am not as well informed on
that point as the gentleman, but in these estimates I have put
them on the basis of Government expenditure. You will
observe that I make an estimate on what these lines will cost
the Government to duplicate them. Of course that means with
all the advantages which the Government possesses. The
Government can run lines along mail routes. It would have no
duty to pay on the necessary importations. It would have all
those advantages and also the advantages of management.
These are the arguments that I urge why Government should
avail itself of this great work in behalf of the interests of the
people.

Mr. R. B. LINES said that, as to Mr. Chester's estimate,
it was to be borne in mind that it was made on the figures

given by Mr. Orton in his report some years since, and that Mr. Chester stated in his letter that wire was the most expensive item in the cost of telegraph lines, owing to the enormous increase in the cost of coal and labor in England, which rendered wire more than thirty per cent. higher now than it was six months since. Mr. Chester's estimate was on the basis of the wire being duty free, which would reduce the cost some two million dollars.

Mr. ORTON said he made no point as to the question of duty on wire beyond what he had done, but he should like Mr. Lines to explain how, in the body of the report, he had committed the honorable Postmaster General to a statement of $11,880,000 as the cost of duplicating the present lines of telegraph, when the only estimate submitted in support of that statement made the cost eighteen and a quarter millions.

The POSTMASTER GENERAL interposed, and said he would object to Mr. Lines giving any detailed information until some detailed information was given by the Western Union Telegraph Company, and he wanted it *under oath !*

Mr. ORTON replied that he had had no intimation, either from the Postmaster General or from the committee that any information was desired which had not been furnished by the Western Union Telegraph Company. He had responded with the utmost alacrity to every request made from the Post-office Department for information concerning the operations of the Western Union Telegraph Company, and with great particularity of detail, and yet he had not found in the report of the Postmaster General a single item of the statistics which he had furnished to him.

Mr. LINES remarked that the statistics furnished by Mr. Orton were all included in the report of the Postmaster General, together with statistics from all the other Companies. Mr. Lines proceeded to quote from the annual report of the Western Union Telegraph Company for 1869, and also from the report made to the House of Representatives by Hon. C. C. Washburne, of Wisconsin, in order to prove that the estimate in the Postmaster General's report was not at all below the figures furnished by Mr. Orton himself.

Mr. ORTON remarked that Hon. D. A. Wells had prepared at his request a report on the telegraph in this country and in Europe, which report had just been put in the hands of the printers, and he asked permission to file a copy of it with the committee.

The CHAIRMAN.—We shall be very glad to have it.

(Adjourned.)

* See Note, page 142.

NOTE.—Perhaps an apology is due to the public for having provoked a Cabinet Minister to temporarily forget the proprieties of the occasion by the exposure of errors which he had incorporated into an important official document. Respect for the Committee and for the office of Postmaster General of the United States restrained me at the time from making answer to the reflection upon my veracity implied by the demand for information "under oath." Neither by virtue of his office, nor by any authority conferred upon him by Congress, has the Postmaster General the right to require me to furnish information concerning the business under my charge; yet what he did ask for was completely and correctly furnished. And I submit whether it would not have been more decorous to have published with his report the information furnished concerning the operations of the Western Union Company, exposing the errors, if any were found, than—after suppressing my statements, and without attempting to reply to my exposure of his errors—to insinuate that which he did not directly charge. Doubtless, an air of solemnity would have been contributed to the propositions of Euclid if his demonstrations had been supplemented by an affidavit in support of their correctness. But it is not probable that the oath would have been accepted as conclusive if the demonstration had failed to convince.

W. O.

[*From the* JOURNAL OF THE TELEGRAPH.]

THE POSTMASTER-GENERAL'S REPORT.

In our last issue we reviewed, at some length, that portion of the Postmaster-General's Report relating to the telegraph, our criticisms being more particularly directed to the erroneous statements contained therein. It has been our aim to discuss the questions involved in the Governmental acquisition of the telegraph in a fair and candid spirit, and with such intelligence as the long experience and familiarity with the business of telegraphing enables us to employ. We have not imputed to the Postmaster-General any improper motives in the presentation to Congress of his singularly inaccurate and indefensible statements relating to the telegraph. The subject is too vast and complicated to be understood by a merely superficial examination, such as a Cabinet Officer, burdened with the cares and responsibilities of an important department, is able to devote to it. A business involving the employment of a capital of over sixty millions of dollars, of ten thousand skilled laborers, of six thousand separate places where it is transacted, and an annual expenditure of over seven millions of dollars, cannot be comprehended or grasped in all its details, except by a long and careful study of the subject by persons qualified by study and experience for the office. The mere fact that the Postmaster-General estimates the value of such a business at less than one sixth of the capital represented in it—a capital which, for the most part, has a market value of over 80 per cent. of its par value—shows not only that his estimate of its value is not shared by that portion of the public who have money to invest, but clearly indicates that he has not given the subject the careful and intelligent consideration which is due to it. Regarding the cost of the lines the Postmaster-General says:

" The majority of lines in this country have been built very cheaply. Their entire cost, including patents, being probably much less than $10,000,000. *In fact, the poles have been erected in many cases entirely without cost to the telegraph companies, by the railroads along whose tracks they are built.*"

Suppose the railroad companies had not only "erected" the poles, but furnished them, as well as the wires thereon, how would this affect the question of cost? In other words, what bearing has the question of who pays for a thing upon the cost of production?

A most striking commentary on the above statement of cost

is presented in the Postmaster-General's Report, in the only estimate for constructing a similar extent of lines furnished by him,
*which gives the cost at eighteen and a quarter millions of dollars,
providing the wire is imported free of duty.* When it is considered
that wire is one of the principal items of cost, and that the
duties on it amount to sixty-eight per cent., it will be perceived
that the Postmaster-General's statement of cost is more than
doubled by the only authority he brings forward to establish it.
Supposing, however, that it could be shown that the cost of
building a system of telegraphs, equal to those now in operation
in the United States, would not exceed twenty-five or thirty
millions of dollars, would this fact prove that the Government
could acquire them, or would have a right to acquire them at
that sum?

Section 3 of the Act of Congress, approved July 24, 1866,
upon which the Postmaster-General relies for obtaining possession
of the telegraphs now in operation in this country, provides as
follows:

"That the United States may, at any time after the expiration of five years
from the date of the passage of this Act, for postal, military, or other purposes,
purchase all the telegraph lines, property and effects of any or all of said companies, at an *appraised value,* to be ascertained by five competent, disinterested
persons, two of whom shall be selected by the Postmaster-General of the United
States, two by the company interested, and one by the four so previously selected."

Now, what is the meaning of the word *value* as applied to the
telegraph? Does it mean the cost merely of the poles, wire,
machinery, patents and other property, or does it include also
its business, good will, ability to earn money, etc.? The Postmaster-General assumes that it means simply the former, and
says:

"It may be proper to state that one of the companies has advanced the theory
that the Government should purchase not only its telegraph lines, property and
effects, but also the good will of its business, based on present and prospective
profits. As it is difficult to see how mere good will can be brought before the
appraisers, under the law as it stands, it is, perhaps, unnecessary for me to discuss
at much length the merits of this claim."

If the Postmaster-General's definition of value, namely, that
it is synonymous with cost, is correct, we are sadly in need of a
new dictionary, for all of those hitherto published give an entirely different meaning to the word. Webster's definition of
value is as follows:

"*The property or properties of a thing which render it useful; or the degree of,
such property or properties; worth; utility; importance; rate or estimated worth;
price deemed or accepted as equivalent to the utility of anything; amount obtained
in exchange for a thing.*"

It will be perceived that Webster, in no instance, makes the
value of a thing depend upon its *cost,* and we must confess our
surprise that a gentleman of Mr. Creswell's well known ability
could fall into so conspicuous an error. To illustrate the abso-

lute dissimilarity of the two words, and the entire absence of any necessary relation between them, let us consider the *cost* and *value* of an important invention. Take, for example, Stearns' Duplex Telegraph, the cost of which to the inventor was inconsiderable, but which is already earning the Western Union Company the interest on a million dollars per annum, and the value of which is almost inestimable. Or, on the other hand, take the Morse patent, whose cost to the company was very great, but which, having expired, is now without any value whatever.

It seems scarcely necessary to further discuss the question of the dissimilarity between the cost and value of a thing, as it must be apparent to every reflective mind, but we will produce one more practical illustration, on account of its direct bearing upon the case in point.

Mr. Frank Ives Scudamore, the Director-General of the Post-office Telegraphs in England, in his testimony before the Select Committee on the Electric Telegraph Bill, says:

"The sum that is charged by the companies for the construction of works generally includes a very large expenditure from first to last in getting up their plant of all kinds; it includes the cost of their leasehold property, and it includes the cost of their patents, which is very considerable in each year, and it also includes the preliminary expenses in getting bills before Parliament; it includes expense of every kind; it is not simply the manufacture of the mere posts and wires."

Question by Mr. GOSCHEN:

"Would you be able to put in a statement and analyze the two and a half millions of the companies? You are going to buy the assets of the companies, and some of those assets represent property—that is to say, posts and wires and instruments—assets which exist at this moment; another portion of it represents no value present at all; that is to say, a certain amount which has been spent on Parliamentary proceedings, patents which have expired, and so forth. Would you be able to show what amount is to be placed in each of those two classes?"

Answer by Mr. SCUDAMORE:

"I should be very glad, indeed, if you would not ask me to put in any statement of my views as to the *value* of their property?"

Question by Mr. GOSCHEN:

"I do not mean the *value;* I mean the *cost.* The capital accounts of the various companies will show what they have done with their capital, and it would enable the Committee to see what the public are actually buying."

Answer by Mr. SCUDAMORE:

"I am quite sure of that; *it would enable the committee to see what they would buy, as far as the expenditure of the companies is concerned; but that is not the only sum involved in buying the trade of a company. For instance, if I may take a very low case as an illustration, if you buy a public house you buy something more than the building, and the pots, and barrels and beer engines; you buy the trade which the man has acquired."*

The above quotation from Mr. Scudamore's testimony shows the view which the British Government took of their obliga-

* *Special Report from the Select Committee on the Electric Telegraph Bill; together with the Minutes of Evidence taken before them. Ordered by the House of Commons to be printed, 16th July, 1868. Page 152.*

tions to the telegraph companies whose property they proposed to acquire, and which they did acquire by paying for it a sum equal to twenty years' profit. Mr. Creswell says, in his recent report, that the profit of the telegraph companies in the United States for 1872, was $3,500,000, and if the statement is correct the lines are worth, on the basis of the purchase of the English lines, $70,000,000.

"But," says Mr. Creswell, " the manner in which the British Government recently acquired the telegraphs cannot bo cited as a precedent for the United States. There was no such previous agreement between Her Majesty's Government and the companies of the United Kingdom as is contained in our Act of 1866."

The above sentence is a most remarkable one, emanating as it does from a high officer of the Government, and taken in connection with the depreciatory manner in which the telegraph property of the country is alluded to. Let us analyze it and see what it actually means. It is not pretended that the British Government paid too much for the property which they purchased, and which was seven times as much as Mr. Creswell estimates a similar property to be worth here, but simply that there was no such agreement between the British Government and the telegraph companies as exists by virtue of the acceptance by the companies in the United States of the Act of 1866. Are we to infer by this that, if the British Government had possessed such a right as the Act of 1866 gives to our Government, it would have paid the telegraph companies less than their property is worth ? Or are we to infer that our Government is less fair in its dealings with its own citizens than the British Government is with its subjects? Either the one conclusion or the other must inevitably. be drawn from the premises laid down. We are unwilling however to believe that our Government is disposed to treat its citizens in so unfair a manner, or that Mr. Creswell would knowingly recommend it. On the contrary, we incline to believe that this view of the case was conceived by some assistant of the Postmaster-General, whose desire to acquire the property for the department at a cheap rate overcame his discretion or notions of equity.

But admitting, for the purpose of illustration, the improbable hypothesis that our Government is capable of taking advantage of a legal right to force a portion of its own citizens to sacrifice a large and important property, regardless of all questions of justice or equity involved in the case, we deny that the United States has acquired any such right over the property of the telegraph companies which accepted the conditions prescribed in the Act of July 24th, 1866. This Act, so far as it relates to the acquisition of the property, simply provides that the United States may purchase it at an appraised value, to be ascertained by five competent disinterested persons.

Now, according to Webster's definition of value, the value of the telegraphs cannot be less than the market price, because that can always be "obtained in exchange for them;" nor can it be less than "the price deemed equivalent to their worth, utility, importance or usefulness;" and the British Government, the only Government which has ever purchased an extensive tele-graph system, wholly constructed by private enterprise, has already established the precedent that the value of the lines and property of a telegraph company is equal to the sum of twenty years' net profits, which would make the value of the telegraphs in the United States at least $70,000,000. This sum, however, is but the commencement of the amount which the Government will be obliged to expend in the event of its going into the busi-ness of telegraphing.

If the Postmaster-General's estimate of the increase in the telegraphic correspondence of the country, under the proposed average reduction of the tariff to 33⅓ cents per message, is cor-, rect, and the number of messages annually transmitted is in-creased from 15,000,000 to 30,000,000, the satisfactory perform-ance of this increased traffic will require a proportionate increase in facilities, and, while these, in a great measure, may be supplied by the introduction of the duplex apparatus, there would still exist the necessity for the expenditure of a vast sum of money in the construction of additional lines.

The transmission of telegrams is totally unlike the trans-mission of letters; an increase in the number of letters is easily and readily provided for by the purchase or manufacture of a few extra bags, but the increase in the number of messages transmitted over the wires can only be provided for by propor-tionately increasing the number of circuits and operators re-quired for their transmission.

THE GOVERNMENT AND THE TELEGRAPH.

CORRESPONDENCE

BETWEEN

Hon. JOSEPH MEDILL

AND THE PRESIDENT OF

The Western Union Telegraph Company.

EXECUTIVE OFFICE,

𝖂𝖊𝖘𝖙𝖊𝖗𝖓 𝖀𝖓𝖎𝖔𝖓 𝕿𝖊𝖑𝖊𝖌𝖗𝖆𝖕𝖍 𝕮𝖔𝖒𝖕𝖆𝖓𝖞,

NEW YORK, *November* 6, 1872.

HON. JOSEPH MEDILL,
Chicago, Ill.

MY DEAR SIR—I found it impossible to keep the promise made you to call at your office before leaving, on account of the pressure of business which I could not postpone, and which occupied every moment of my time. My desire to have a further conference with you was increased by information received on the morning after our interview, to the effect that you favored the taking of the telegraph by the Government. I regret that any feeling of delicacy restrained you from the frank and full expression of your opinions last Wednesday evening. My opinions on this question have been formed after much study and as careful a consideration of all the elements involved as I am capable of giving. But I am always better pleased to listen to the opinions of others than to express my own, and I am quite sure that, with your ability, and your habit of reasoning your way to conclusions, I should have listened to your views with more than ordinary interest.

The progress of the American people is the wonder of the world. National prosperity is but the aggregate of individual success. The prosperity of the average citizen of the United States is not the result of any aid which the Government has contributed. Our Government does most and best for its citizens when it leaves them free to embark in lawful enterprises, whose success depends solely upon the zeal, energy and fidelity with which they are prosecuted. American genius, enterprise and capital will provide for all the wants of our people, and the question of cost loses its importance in the presence of the constantly increasing ability to pay.

It has not been considered heretofore one of the functions of our Government to make any necessary cheap. On the other hand, it has been the uniform policy for thirty years to make many products artificially dear. If it be right for the Government to require us to pay sixty per cent. more for telegraph wire than it would cost without Governmental interference, in order to insure a profit to American manufacturers of wire, is it fair to ask us to perform telegraphic service at the rates charged where wire and other material costs a third less, and labor less than half? If the policy of protecting the skilled labor employed in every department of manufactures from the competition of the cheaper labor of Europe be correct, what ground is there for complaint if telegraphic service, which requires special education and the greatest skill, costs more in this country than in England?

The capital invested in the telegraph business in the United States during the last ten years has paid less on the average than that invested either in railroads, in mining, or in almost any kind of manufactures. Yet its development has fairly kept pace with the growth of the country without having cost the Government a dollar, while in Europe, under Government control, the annual deficit, provided by taxation, has been from one to two millions.

I claim this proposition as fundamental : That whenever our Government undertakes to supply any public want, merely for the sake of making the cost less than the price charged by individuals and corporations, it should begin with what is most essential to the largest number. Is it just to impose taxes upon all the people in order to reduce the cost of messages to the few who have occasion to send them until after provision has been made for supplying food, and clothing, and fuel at the lowest possible rates?

Again, many more people travel on railways every year than send messages by telegraph. If, then, the Government should take the telegraph, why not the railways? And when it has taken these, why should it not embark in mining coal and metals and in manufactures? In short, when the door is once opened, and our Government, instead of being merely a protecting power, becomes an aggressive enterprise, at what point will it stop?

Personally, I have very little at stake. But I sincerely believe that it will be an unfortunate day for the country when our Government enters upon a competition with the enterprise of its citizens by embarking in any department of business. Patronage is always power, and in the judgment of many thoughtful men this source of power in our Government is already too great.

Have you reflected carefully upon the control which the Government would have over the press in the event of its taking the telegraph? The telegraph company seeks only to make money. The press are among its best customers. There is, therefore, small danger that it will pursue a policy which would dissatisfy these customers. The Government, on the other hand, takes no thought of profit. In an exciting political contest, like that through which we have been passing during the last four months, if the telegraph belonged to the Government would it not be used by the party in possession for its extension and the election of its friends? Would not that portion of the press which supports the party in power receive valuable favo:s at the expense of the portion opposed?

I submit these few suggestions for your consideration. They are but a small portion of the reasons which induce me to oppose the taking of the telegraph by the Government. I am not so unreasonable as to expect you to take time to discuss the subject with me, and I submit them only because of my respect for your opinions and my confidence in your judgment.

On the occasion of my next visit to your city I will endeavor to redeem the promise made at the last, and then, perhaps, we may resume the subject.

I am, yours very truly,

WILLIAM ORTON.

HON. WILLIAM ORTON,

New York.

MY DEAR SIR—Believe me that my long delay in answering your favor of the 6th ult. must not be ascribed to negligence or disrespect, but solely to want of time. I have been trying to spare enough to make such a reply as the importance of the subject and my high respect for yourself merits.

Whether what I have to say will be connected or disjointed will depend upon the "breaks" of the circuit of thought and interruptions during its composition. I have not the aid of a stenographer to rapidly jot down my views, but must slowly long-hand them between other engagements and duties. With this preface I proceed to reply to your very lucid and able letter arguing the negative of the proposition.

Your information that I favor the taking of the telegraph by Government is correct to this extent, that I deem it only a question of time when it must assume that control. "If the Government should take the telegraph why not the railways?" you ask. I reply, it will have to do that sooner or later. It may be a generation hence before it is done, but eventually the patience and endurance of the people with railway monopoly and extortion will wear out, and the Government will be ordered by them to regulate the charges of these corporations or to take possession of them and operate them. But as the capital invested in the railroads is 200 times greater than that invested in the telegraph, it will be proportionately more costly to purchase and difficult to manage them ; therefore, the public will submit to imposition and plunder a long time before venturing to purchase them and undertake their management; and it may not be done in your day or mine. But the assumption of the telegraph would be but a small matter in point of cost. A month or six weeks' surplus revenue, now devoted to the buying of bonds, would pay the expense of building as many miles of wire as now exists in the whole Union—so that the question of cost is not a very serious matter; and there are no legal obstructions in the way, as the Act of Congress passed in 1866 contemplating the acquisition of the telegraph by the Government, after a stated day, was accepted by your Company as well as others.

To my mind all the points you make against Goverment control of the telegraph apply with equal or greater force against

155

the Government control of the mails. If it is proper and expedient for the Government to manage the latter it is equally so to manage the former. Private enterprise has much more to complain of in the case of the mails than of the telegraph. The Express Companies can urge all your reasons, and many in addition, against the Government keeping the postal business out of their hands and depriving them of large profits. The enormous mail business, which now costs the people less than $28,000,000 per annum, if left to the uncontrolled discretion of the Express Companies, would be reduced three fourths in quantity by high charges, and the gross receipts therefor perhaps doubled. The smallest package, weighing less than a newspaper, sent by express, costs its sender fifty times as much as the Government charges for the same weight of newspaper, or other mailable matter, for the same distance. It would be a national calamity to let the postal service fall into the hands of " private enterprises," i. e., Express Companies, who would manage it with an eye single to stockholders' profit. We should then have as many rates of postage, and as exorbitant ones, as we now have on express packages. After their experience of the blessings of cheap and uniform Government postal service, the people would not tolerate the oppression of private monopoly for a single month. You refer to the comparatively few persons who use the wires as a reason against taxing the many in order to furnish cheap telegraphy to that few. But is it safe to assume that if the Government should greatly reduce existing tolls a serious deficiency would result, to be made good out of the National Treasury. I think not. The increase of business would keep pace with reduction of charges, until exceedingly low rates were reached. Where one man will pay a dollar for a ten word despatch, ten men would pay a cent a word for messages of all lengths, some of them containing perhaps a hundred words. Few persons now send despatches unless they have urgent business, on account of the high tariff imposed. But lower the price sufficiently, and the number of messages and words offered would be limited only by the capacity of the wires to transmit them. This is no random guess work or mere opinion of mine, but is proven by experience in Great Britain, where a moderate decrease of tolls caused an immense expansion of business. You and I remember when the Government charged twenty-five cents postage on a letter;. and we also remember how few were sent. When it was proposed to reduce the postage to ten cents there was a loud outcry against it. It was claimed that the reduction would enure only to the benefit of merchants, bankers and speculators, and cause a great deficiency of revenue to be made up by taxing the poor man's coffee and clothing. But the reduction actually increased the revenue and diminished the annual deficiency. Again and again Congress cut down the postal tariff until it was but three cents on a letter for any distance, one or two cents on a circular, and one fourth of a cent on a newspaper to a regular subscriber! and still the service is self-supporting; the reported deficiency being caused by the franked and free matter, and subsidies paid to ocean steamers. Like causes produce like effects, as the Government would seek no profit, but merely recompense; approximating to cost, it might safely raze existing tolls to rates as comparatively cheap as postage on letters, and thus popularize this lightning disseminator of thought and intelligence, and remove forever the sneer of thoughtless persons, that the telegraph is patronized only by bankers, brokers, produce dealers, stock gamblers, detectives and politicians. I claim, as a truth of political economy, that the consumption of whatever is desirable is always in proportion to its cost. Make a desirable thing cheap enough and there is no limit to the demand for it. Telegraphing would furnish no exception to the rule. What you state concerning the ill paying character of telegraph stock rather surprises me. I was laboring under the common impression that not 10 per cent. of the market price of the Western Union Telegraph stock was ever subscribed and paid in cash by the stockholders; but that 90 per cent. of its present stock and value are the product of undivided earnings, and issues of " watered " shares; that, as a matter of fact, the public have furnished nine tenths of the capital in addition to the cash dividends and cost of maitennance and operation. If I am mistaken in this opinion the whole public are also mistaken. But as the company has never published an official statement, setting forth the actual facts, the public will be apt to adhere to its present opinion until they do. You say " it has not been considered heretofore one of the functions of our Government to make any necessary cheap." I have just specified a most notable exception in the postal service. You also remark, " on the other hand, it has been the uniform policy " for thirty years, to make many products artificially dear." Is there not a slight inaccuracy in this statement? As I recollect, the policy of the Government, from 1846 to 1861, was just the reverse of that making products artificially dear; and the annual repeal of Federal taxes since 1867 convinces me that it is not the present policy of the Government to make products artificially dear by maintaining high taxes and imports. You lay down a proposition as fundamental, in regard to the duty of the Government, in leaving the supply of wants to private competition. I fully subscribe to the general principle; but I regard the telegraph system as an exception. You admit that " the telegraph company seeks only to make money," which is the sole object of all pecuniary corporations.

The present telegraph system is practically a monopoly. Com petition, such as will benefit the people, is out of the question. The Western Union has established itself beyond the reach of competition. It can crush out, absorb or control all rivals, and exact its own terms from the public; and this it does. The supposed competition of the other companies is little more than a myth, so far as cheapening tolls is concerned. A monopoly of a business is similar in effect to a "corner" on a stock or pro- duct, and places the public at the mercy of the corporation enjoying it. The rule of such a corporation is to perform the least service for the most money, because profit and not public good is the actuating motive of the share owners and managers. In the ordinary avocations of life competition regulates prices and reduces them to the proper relative level, and Government interference is not needed; but common carriers, millers bakers, market men and others have had to be regulated and controlled by the Government in order to protect the public against their rapacity and extortion. There should be allowed no monopoly or combinations of private parties to speculate on education or the diffusion of intelligence. Whatever makes education dear, or obstructs the spread of knowledge, promotes ignorance, and injures the moral and intellectual health of the body politic. Knowledge is power, and creates wealth. Ignorance is weakness, and its progeny are vice and poverty. The public schools are maintained at the expense of the tax-payers, whether they have children to send to school or not. Were education left to private enterprise the rich men's children would mono- polize it. So, if the diffusion of intelligence by mail was surrendered to the express companies, it would soon become a luxury of the rich and a burden even on the business classes, while the common people would be excluded from its enjoy- ment. The telegraph is a quicker method of sending the mails; a method which annihilates time and distance, and, with the coöperation of the press, "makes all men kin." It is the noblest of all human inventions, and, while it is a common carrier, it carries nothing more material than thought. The lightest of tolls should be charged for its labors, for it is one of the great educational instrumentalities of the nation and world. Its ser- vices should be as nearly free to the whole people as possible. The greatest of all Government blunders is a tax on information, which is like obstructing the vision and hearing of the natural body. How cheap the telegraph could be operated by the Government cannot be known until tried.

The new "duplex system" of transmission on a wire both ways at the same time, and other remarkable improvements, would enable the Government to transmit messages without loss, at rates which would surprise the country, and speedily multiply the business manifo.d. If I were fixing the tolls at the outset they would be put at one cent per word, for all distances in the United States, with a liberal discount for the press —so liberal that the daily papers could afford to take all the despatches their space would accommodate. By pursuing this policy benefits would be conferred on the whole people to an extent " not dreamt of in your philosophy."

From these observations you perceive that I hold the telegraph properly belongs to the educational and postal systems of the country, and that its mission and purpose are the diffusion of thoughts, ideas and information among the people instantaneously; hence, that a private corporation should not be permitted to monopolize it for the purpose of money making and stock gambling. Instead of being a corporate monopoly it should be owned by the whole people and managed for their greatest benefit, and its use made relatively as cheap as the postal service.

You speak of the possible abuses which the Government might practise to promote party ends. I have no fears of that. An administration which would make use of private information passing on the wires would quickly be removed from power. The people are in more danger now, in that regard, than they would be if the wires were an adjunct of the Post-office Department. I hear of no complaints against the British Government on this score.

You ask me if I have reflected carefully upon the control which our Government would have over the press in the event of its taking the telegraph. In my opinion it has nothing to apprehend. The press, of all agencies, is best able to take care of itself; any discrimination or favoritism would be sure to be seen, and a " howl " raised about it instanter. The opposition politicians would desire no better issue with which to go before the people. How long would a Postmaster General remain in office if found dealing harshly or unfairly with the press? Congressmen would enact the very cheapest possible rates to the press, in order to have the proceedings of Congress fully reported. The influence of the State Legislatures would be in the same direction, for the same reason.

You speak of the increase of patronage the telegraph would give the Government, which you deem dangerous. I do not partake of these fears. A service which you admit " requires special education and the greatest of skill " could hardly be connected with patronage. The present force of operators and experts would of necessity be taken into the postal telegraph service, with yourself, perhaps, as Director-in-Chief. Changes could only be made for cause, and appointments upon qualification. Party politics would cut but an insignificant figure in the matter. Novices could not be placed in charge of instruments or wires. What took place in England would happen here. The civil service system is bound to be established in this country. The popular demand is in that direction, and will never rest satisfied until merit and qualifications are the test of fitness for administrative office, and not partisan "bumming" and ballot box stuffing.

I have written thus freely upon your invitation, and it is the first time I have ventured to put any thoughts on the subject upon paper. It is not strange that we should come to a diametrically opposite conclusion, and yet each be perfectly sincere in his views, when our respective stand-points of observation are considered. You remember how the slaveholders and abolitionists differed in their estimate of the "peculiar institution," but you and I will avoid their mistake, and not quarrel over our difference of opinion. It would give me great pleasure to canvass the merits of the question at issue with you some evening over a fragrant Havana. I much prefer the dialogue style of argument, and it is quite possible that a free exchange of views would result in a radical change of my notions on the subject, and in a conversion to your views.

Very truly yours,

JOSEPH MEDILL.

𝔚estern 𝔘nion 𝔗elegraph 𝔠ompany,

NEW YORK, *Dec.* 30, 1872.

HON. JOSEPH MEDILL,

Chicago, Ill.

MY DEAR SIR—Your communication of December 17th, re-plying to mine of November 6th, reached me last week.

It is in the main one of the fairest, as it is the ablest of the statements made in favor of the assumption and operation of the telegraph by the Government that have come under my notice. A complete and fitting reply to all your points cannot be made within the limited time I am now able to devote to it, and I shall, therefore, content myself for the present with the consideration only of those which I deem most important.

The statement which I had the honor to make on this subject recently before the Committee on Appropriations of the House of Representatives, together with a more carefully prepared paper by Hon. David A. Wells, will be printed in a few days, when copies will be sent you. They will contain—and espe-cially the latter—so full and comprehensive a statement of facts concerning the operation of the telegraph in Europe and the United States, and of conclusions which the facts establish, that it seems unnecessary for me to go over in this letter the whole ground covered by them.

Your answer to my inquiry whether the Government should not take the railways as well as the telegraph—that "it will have to do that sooner or later"—is evidence that behind the question relating to the telegraph there is a fundamental differ-ence in our views concerning the objects for which our Govern-ment was established, and the best modes of accomplishing them. Those purposes are set forth in the preamble to the Constitu-tion of the United States—"to form a more perfect union, establish justice, insure domestic tranquility, provide for the common defence, promote the general welfare, and secure the blessings of liberty to ourselves and our posterity."

You seem to think that, in order to accomplish these, the Federal Government is to become a vast commercial enterprise; that one of its proper functions is to provide the people with whatever is deemed best for their welfare at the public expense, provided a larger supply can thus be furnished at a less cost *per capita* than would result if such supply depended upon private capital managed by private enterprise. Perhaps your view is the correct one, but it differs widely from

161

mine. I have supposed that the "blessings of liberty" were to
be secured, and the "general welfare promoted," in the first
instance, by the protection of every citizen in person and property
while in the pursuit of all lawful avocations. This protection
the people collectively have guaranteed to each individual.
Your scheme of government appears to be a grand Fourier
phalanx—a sort of Oneida community on an immense scale—
whose members are to receive—not the result of their separate
skill and labor—but are to be beneficiaries in a *pro rata* distribution of the net profits of the joint operations. It is not on this
plan that the successes of the American people have been thus far
achieved. While the paternal governments of the Old World
have been extending with one hand their illusive benefits, with
the other they have been heaping up burdens upon the people,
until debt and taxation are fast ripening into universal discon-
tent. Meanwhile, the people of the United States have abolished
"the peculiar institution" of which you speak, crushed the
rebellion which slavery invoked, and in their private capacity,
and almost wholly with private capital, have gridironed a continent with railways and carried the telegraph to the extremes
of civilization. Yet, in view of these important facts, you
appeal to the precedents established by European governments,
and appear to assume that they can be followed here without
being accompanied by the evils which have invariably attended
them elsewhere.

You would have the Government provide the telegraph before railways, apparently not because of any natural order of
precedence, but because it can get into the business at smaller
cost in the one case than in the other. You say: "The telegraph
properly belongs to the educational and postal systems of the
country, and that its mission and purposes are the diffusion of
thoughts, ideas and information among the people instantaneously."

I do not mean to deny that the instantaneous "diffusion of
thoughts, ideas and information among the people" is a result
greatly to be desired. It has not before occurred to me, however, that this is one of the functions of our Government. But
if it be, are there not other provisions to be made first?

The real basis on which rests the claim that the telegraph
should be put in charge of the Government, is, that it will
cheapen the cost. But before there can be much use for the
telegraph, people must be able to read and write; and you will
be surprised, I know, on referring to statistics, to find how many
persons of mature years there are, even in some of the older
States, who can do neither. What have these to do with the
telegraph as a means of "instantaneous diffusion of thought
and information?" Should not the powers of the Federal De-

11

partment of education be enlarged, so as to embrace the supervision of the educational systems of the several States before taking over the telegraph? Should not the Government printing office also undertake the manufacture of spelling books and New England primers, so as to insure the provision at the minimum of cost of those prime necessities for intellectual and moral culture.

Many more persons need school books than would use the telegraph at any price. Why should not the manufacture of them be undertaken by the Government, and the present monopoly of the Harpers and Appletons, aided and abetted by the laws conferring copyrights, be completely broken down. And when this has been done, why should not that other great feature of our educational system, that adjunct of the telegraph in the "diffusion of thoughts, ideas and information among the people"—the newspaper—also be furnished by the Government. Within the last ten years the extent of telegraph lines in the United States has been increased four-fold, and the average cost of messages reduced more than half, while the cost of school books and of newspapers has increased a hundred per cent.

If we admit that it is the duty of Governments to make provision for the education of the people, must we not admit also that there are other duties equally pressing which should be discharged first. Government charity naturally proceeds with: *first*, what is due to humanity; and *secondly*, what is due to the State. Should not provision be made for helpless infants, the indigent aged, the sick and destitute, the imbecile and infirm, before large expenditure is made of public money to cheapen so remote an incident of education as the telegraph.

You say, "How cheap the telegraph could be operated by the Government cannot be known until tried." And from this remark and others I infer that you consider it practicable to increase the volume of telegraphic business indefinitely, without materially increasing the cost. In fact, this appears to be the common belief.

In this connection let me remark that sixty per cent. of the expenses of the Western Union Company, during the last fiscal year, was paid for wages. Do you believe that the Government could have hired the persons who performed these services at lower wages, or that it would have got more work from them for the same cost? A lawful day's work by Government employés is limited to eight hours. Ten hours is the minimum in the telegraph service, and hundreds work an average of twelve. Surely it will not be expected that the Government will discriminate against so large and worthy a class as those engaged in maintaining and operating the telegraph. And yet, if it undertakes the business, it must either do this or diminish by twenty per cent. the present product of telegraph operatives without reducing the cost, or else increase the force and the cost twenty-five per cent. to maintain the present product.

Every telegraph message must be written out word by word by the hand of an operator. In its passage over the wire it occupies the circuit to the exclusion of everything else. One operator is engaged in sending, and another, at the same time, in receiving it. The average capacity of operators to send and receive can be readily ascertained. Whether it be 300, 400 or 500 messages in a day, when the limit of the capacity of one set is reached another set must be provided, whose capacity has the like limit. But as the volume of business increases something more is involved to take care of the increase than the mere provision of additional operators. The permanent addition of 400 messages a day to those now passing between Chicago and New York, requires the provision of an additional wire between those cities, and an additional operator at each. For every two additional wires between these places, at least one additional operator besides those at each end will be required at an intermediate station—say at Buffalo—to attend repeaters, and to assist in receiving and re-writing the messages when, as sometimes happens, the weather is so unfavorable that it is necessary to divide the through circuit into two shorter ones.

The stenographer who is taking this from my dictation can do a certain amount of work in a day. Would the product of his labor be any cheaper if he had twice as much to do as it is possible for him to perform ? In that case, however, the double work would involve hiring another, and would cost only double wages. But in respect to messages by telegraph, when the wires and operators are fully occupied, double work means—not only double cost for wages, but further investment of capital in the "plant," followed by an increase in the cost of delivery, stationery battery and repairs.

It does not matter whether the business is conducted by private parties or by the Government—a large increase of messages will always be followed by an almost proportional increase of operating expenses ; and as fast as the limit of the capacity of lines is reached a further permanent investment of capital must be made to enlarge their capacity. Whether it is better that the extensions of the telegraph shall continue to be paid for out of the profits accruing from the business or be added to the already large annual deficit of the postal service, and raised by taxation upon the people, it is for the people, through their representatives in Congress, to decide. But do not let the people be deceived by the fallacy that the copying of messages, word by word, by the fingers of telegraph operators, can be done at a nominal cost simply by increasing the work of those who have already about all they can do.

The duplex apparatus of which you speak we have now in successful operation; and perhaps some of the various devices for automatic transmission may ultimately be found practicable in this country. But the value of these appliances consists in increasing the capacity of wires, and thus lessening the amount of capital which would otherwise be required to provide them, and not in lessening the amount nor in reducing the cost of the labor required to handle messages.

I am somewhat disappointed that instead of meeting squarely some of the points presented in my letter, you seek to turn their flank by a comparison between the postal service and the business of the Express Companies, which you present with this general statement: " To my mind all the points you make against Government control of the telegraph apply with equal or greater force against the Government control of the mails." You say further: " The Express Companies can urge all your reasons, and many in addition, against the Government's keeping the postal business out of their hands and depriving them of large profits."

I know that you do not mean to ignore the fact that the postal service has always been managed by the Government, nor that the telegraph is the product of private enterprise. But you must have failed to remember that the growth of the immense and largely profitable business now conducted by the Express Companies has been greatly stimulated by the failure of the Post-office Department to transact a most important part of the business which naturally and properly belongs to it in a manner satisfactory to the public.

The expenses of the Post-office Department in excess of its revenues have been about $50,000,000 within the last 15 years. During this period a profit equal to at least half this sum has been gathered by the Express Companies, much of it derived from business which the Post-office has neglected to do at all, or has failed to do properly, or which the public is unwilling to trust to the risks of its mismanagement. Much of the Government's own business is not intrusted to its own mails, and between some of the principal cities of the country this singular spectacle may be witnessed almost every day in the year: On the same trains which carry the mails, packages of bonds, currency and other valuables passing between the Treasury and its branches are withheld from the officials in the postal cars and placed in charge of the agents of the Express Companies. Thus the instinct of security overcomes the temptations of the franking privilege, and the Government gives practical evidence of its confidence in the fidelity of " private enterprise."

In view of these facts, I submit that the Express Companies have no occasion to " urge reasons against the Government's keeping the postal business out of their hands, and depriving them of large profits." Perhaps the charges of the Express Companies are exorbitant, and their profits unreasonably large. But why is it, if " it costs the sender fifty times as much to send a small parcel by express as the Government charges for the same weight of mailable matter for the same distance "—why is it, I say, that the public continue to submit to such oppression at the hands of " private enterprises," while the Government is ready and willing, yea, anxious even, to perform the service for one fiftieth of the Express Companies' charge ? And why is it that in all sections of the country a considerable part of the correspondence, and especially letters covering remittances, contracts, and other valuable papers, after being placed in stamped envelopes, whereby full postage accrues to the Government, is then given to the Express Companies, and the charges of the latter paid thereon in addition ?

Your statement may be correct that " after their experience of the blessings of cheap and uniform Government Postal Service, the people would not tolerate the oppression of private monopoly for a single month." But it seems clear to me that a considerable portion of the public either do not coincide in your opinions concerning " the oppression of private monopoly," or else they—" rather bear those ills we have than fly to others that we know not of."

I do not think it probable that our people would consent to a transfer of the postal service to the Express Companies unless upon condition that the present rate of postage on letters and other mailable matter should not be increased, and that the facilities now provided should be in no wise diminished. But I apprehend if the offer were made to the Express Companies to take charge of the postal service, and to perform it in as efficient manner as it is now conducted for two thirds the present rates, that the offer would be accepted, and that, in view of saving the Treasury millions of annual deficit, and the public millions in postage, the latter would overcome any sentimental attachment for Government officials, and acquiesce in the change.

I do remember the time to which you refer, "when the Government charged twenty-five cents postage on a letter." I also remember that the Express Companies provided stamps and undertook the transmission of letters on the same routes at lower rates, including special delivery. The business grew so rapidly that it threatened to seriously diminish the revenues of the Post-office Department. Of course, the Government promptly interfered to check the growing evil. At the next session of Congress a bill was passed prohibiting, under stringent penalties, the carrying of mailable matter outside the mails, and at the same time, a reduction of postage was made to the uniform rate of ten cents, followed subsequently by further reductions, to the rates which now prevail. If I am correct in these statements, you will comprehend why it is I do not share your hostility to " private enterprises" in general, and to the Express Companies in particular.

So confident am I in the ability of private enterprise to compete successfully with official agencies in the performance of any service for the public requiring promptness, skill and fidelity, that in case the Government should take the telegraph, and should establish even so low a rate of charge as that suggested by you, namely, one cent a word for all distances, I would desire no surer mode of acquiring a fortune than the exclusive privilege to construct and operate private telegraph lines at such rates of charge as I should see fit to impose. And, in that event, I should confidently expect the Government would ultimately become one of my best customers.

I will admit the truth of your statement, " that the consumption of whatever is desirable is always in proportion to its cost. Make a desirable thing cheap enough and there is no limit to the demand for it." But with this proviso : *that in reducing the cost there is no deterioration of the quality.*

It is a peculiarity of Americans that they rarely grumble at the price of what is otherwise completely satisfactory. The competition of railroads has entirely broken up the business of carrying passengers on the canals, although the cost of traveling has been thereby largely increased. And in spite of what you deem the present exorbitant charges for railway travel, the Pullman palace cars are crowded everywhere with persons who cheerfully pay four dollars a day, in addition to regular fare, for the sake of the superior accommodations.

Your surprise at my statement "concerning the ill paying character of telegraph stock" is not greater than mine is at the low estimate you place upon the value of the Western Union Company's property, and your allusion to its " watered shares." Such phrases may tickle the ear and stimulate the prejudices of the ignorant, but they cannot, I am sure, affect the judgment of thoughtful men. The Western Union Company is not on trial for an alleged undue or improper expansion of capital ; and if it were, its stockholders are the only proper complainants. With such details the public at large have no concern. What is it to them whether a capital of forty millions represents that sum of cash paid in, or only four millions, and what difference does it make to the stockholders which sum is correct if they get no dividends at all?

During the seven years of my connection with the telegraph

business, the value of telegraph lines and property in the United States has been increased by the expenditure of at least twelve millions of dollars in cash. Is the capital so expended any the less entitled to be credited with the interest thereon annually because a portion of it accrued from the profits of companies which paid no dividends, or which divided only a portion of their earnings?

The telegraph system of the United States is larger in extent, and equal at least in efficiency, to that of any other country in the world; nor is it surpassed by any other in the amount of work which it performs. And considering the higher cost here of labor to construct, maintain and operate it, and of material and supplies of all kinds, and of the greater length of line required to reach the same number of people, the rates for messages in this country compare favorably with the average rates in Europe. In all other countries (except Canada) the telegraph is now owned and operated by the Government, and in most of them it has been built at the cost of the State. But in many European States the operation of the telegraph by the Government results in an annual deficit, which is raised by taxation. Even in England the question of profit is involved in doubt, from the fact that the capital account is added to largely every year. In the United States, however, its development has been the work of private individuals, who have received no assistance worth mentioning either from the Federal or State Governments. On the other hand it has paid in taxes, Federal, State and Municipal, in duties directly and indirectly, and in the value of free service for communities in times of peril and disaster, a sum greater than the "ten per centum of the market price of the Western Union Telegraph stock," which you appear to believe was the sum originally "paid in cash by the stockholders." But even if you were correct, how would the expediency of taking the telegraph, or the value of the property, or the rates to be charged for its use, be affected thereby? Suppose a farmer had planted twenty years ago a thousand fruit trees, at a cost of one dollar each, and had expended nothing on them since except to harvest the crop every year, would the fact of the small cost justify the demand of a purchaser that the trees should be sold at cost, or the fruit at a price which would be a fair interest on the cost of the trees?

The value of anything that is for sale is that sum which they will give for it who desire to buy. But in considering the expediency of having the telegraph in the United States operated by the Government, the question of the value of existing telegraph properties does not necessarily enter. We admit that the Government has the right to buy, and that the mode of ascertaining the price to be paid is fixed by law and agreement.

If it be true, as you state, that "the present telegraph system is practically a monopoly," does not this fact prove that your impressions concerning the profitableness of the business, and the trifling investment required to establish it, are erroneous? The stock and bonded capital of two railway companies, whose united roads connect New York and Chicago, is nearly two hundred millions. The mere statement of this fact shows the difficulty of opening a competing railway route between those cities. But whether the cost of all the telegraph property in the United States is "ten per centum of the market price of the Western Union Telegraph stock," or is ten or twenty times that sum, it would not be difficult to raise the capital requisite to duplicate every mile of telegraph wire now in operation, if it could be made to appear probable that the business would pay. The failure of competing telegraph companies to make profits during the last seven years is not a sentiment but a serious fact. Of this abundant evidence can be found among the stockholders of such companies in your own city.

We have absorbed rival lines many times, and, as like causes will continue to produce like results, it is highly probable we shall do so hereafter. With but few exceptions, however, this process of absorption has been simply the securing of property yielding no profit to its owners for a less sum than was expended to create it. In view of the facility with which telegraph lines can be constructed, is it not reasonable to suppose that, if we absorb them at a profit to their owners, they would be constructed for the express purpose of selling out to us until our capacity to buy was exhausted?

The secret of what you call the "monopoly" of the Western Union is an open one when you look at it from the stand-point of fact. It is not the exclusive possession of essential patents, nor the difficulty of raising the requisite capital, nor inability to procure the services of persons skilled in the scientific and practical departments of the business. The reasons are:

First. The Western Union Company has fairly met the wants of the public who have occasion to use the telegraph, and does its work better than its competitors.

Secondly. The expense of conducting the business is mainly for labor, and increases in a ratio nearly equal to the increase of the volume.

Thirdly. The annual deterioration of the plant by natural decay is equal to about eight per centum of the cost, and this must be earned in excess of expenses before dividends can be paid.

You ask—"How long would a Postmaster-General remain in office if found dealing harshly or unfairly with the press?" In reply, permit me to call attention to an incident in American history: On the 29th of July, 1835, at the City of Charleston, S. C., a number of persons made forcible entry into the post-office, and carried off packages of books and papers and burned them. Soon after, at a large public meeting of citizens, this flagrant violation of the laws and of the rights of individuals was distinctly sanctioned, and a committee of twenty-one was appointed *to take charge of the United States' Mails*, at the head of which was Ex-Senator Robert Y. Hayne. Amos Kendall was then Postmaster-General. Under date August 4, 1835, he addressed a letter to the Postmaster at Charleston, from which I quote the following: " We owe an obligation to the laws, but a higher one to the communities in which we live; and if the *former* be perverted to destroy the *latter*, it is patriotism to disregard them." On the 22nd of August he wrote to Samuel L. Gouverneur, Postmaster at New York, on the same subject. I quote the following from that letter: "I have no hesitation in saying that I am deterred from giving an order to exclude the whole series of abolition publications from the Southern mails only by a want of legal power, and that if I were situated as you are I would do as you have done."

How long after the perpetration of this outrage, thus publicly and officially approved, did Amos Kendall and his subordinates "remain in office?" And how long is it since another Postmaster General requested the opinion of the Attorney General of the United States as to the right of the former to break the seals upon matter passing through the mails, for the alleged purpose of ascertaining if the laws were being violated? Not many months since Sir Frank Scudamore was charged by the English press with suppressing a despatch giving an account of a strike among the telegraph operators on the Government lines. The charge was admitted, but the offense was sought to be justified, as I remember, by the plea that the despatch contained exaggerated statements, which it was not for the public interest to permit to be published.

In all the principal cities of the country the telegraph is available every hour of every day and night from the beginning to the end of the year; yet in the same cities, in the evenings, on Sundays and all legal holidays the post-offices are closed, except for an hour or two, and delivery by carriers suspended. How long would the public submit to such exclusion from the telegraph? You will say, perhaps, this would be changed if the Government had the telegraph connected with the postal service. To which I should answer: why does not the Post-office Department give evidence of an appreciation of the wants of the public, and of a disposition to make provision for supplying them *before* undertaking a new service, requiring far more vigilant attention than that which it now performs with only tolerable success?

I have thus, at much greater length than I expected at the

commencement of this communication, endeavored to reply to the principal points of yours. Your experience as a journalist, and the facility you have acquired by long practice in rapidly arranging your views in logical order, more than offset the convenience a stenographer affords to me, whose duties are mainly executive, and relate to almost every department of business in every state. If I have not succeeded in producing "a radical change" of your notions on the subject, I trust that the statements herein made will, at least, afford some justification for the tenacity with which I still hold to my own. Hoping that an opportunity for a further canvass of the question in the social manner you suggest may soon be presented,

I am, my dear sir,

Very truly yours,

WILLIAM ORTON.

www.ingramcontent.com/pod-product-compliance
Lightning Source LLC
Chambersburg PA
CBHW030554040726
47497CB00008B/2718